The Nibelungen Hoard

EDWIN M TODD

ISBN: 0692288562
ISBN 13: 9780692288566
Library of Congress Control Number: 2014916790
ET3 Publishing, Boulder, CO

Published by ET3 Publishing

For Berry

INTRODUCTION

The legend of the Nibelungen Hoard originated in a time when the ancient gods—Wotan, Frigga, Thor, and the others—still inhabited the great northern forests. There lived a king, Siegfried of the Netherlands. With little cause and manufactured lies, he attacked and conquered the land of the Nibelungs, who had always been friendly with the Netherlands before Siegfried's reign. These lands he occupied and ravaged, and he accumulated a fantastic treasure, which he took back to his home. He married Kreimhilde, daughter of Gunther, the king of Burgundy, and he gave her this treasure as a wedding present. However, the treasure was lost when Hagen, a mighty and awe-inspiring warrior and liege man of Gunther, treacherously stabbed Siegfried from behind while the two were hunting together. With Siegfried dead, Hagen deceitfully seized the treasure and secretly buried it beneath the Rhine, intending to recover it later. The hoard was forever lost when Kreimhilde avenged her husband and with her own hand cut off the heads of both Hagan and Gunther.

It is said whoever possesses the Nibelungen hoard shall be called the Nibelungers and that the cursed treasure waits patiently to reappear, even to this day.

PROLOGUE

Beelitz, East Germany
November 4, 1989

The old woman lay dying in a golden room.

The caregivers had pulled the yellow institutional curtains to keep out the low afternoon sun, but the material was flimsy and only succeeded in diffusing the fierce rays, creating a golden hue that filled the room and transformed the cream-colored walls into vibrant shades of shimmering richness. A slow-moving ceiling fan added to the illusion, causing the curtains to tremble as the wooden blades swept air down across the fabric.

Her sleep was always troubled with jagged dreams, her brain battered by two strokes. Awake, her soul was plagued with guilt from the burden of a secret she'd borne for decades, and from the fear that she might die and carry that weight into the next world. She knew no peace.

The glowing room, that other world, the real one, reached into her dream and dragged her reluctantly back into consciousness. For a while her eyes remained closed to the glare, but the gossamer skin of her aged eyelids was little protection against the light, and with a few involuntary flutters, they opened hesitantly. Confused, she struggled to reconcile conflicting realities, but her thoughts, strewn and stockpiled like pickup sticks, made this difficult. The harsh radiance of the room seeped into this disarray, and she panicked. She'd died, and it was too late; her last plan had failed.

Overwhelmed by this delusion, she wept.

She wasn't aware of the arrival of two men—one large and balding, wearing a white physician's coat, and the other a young man—so she didn't respond to the doctor's first greetings. He stroked her forehead and asked for a damp cloth, which he gently placed over her brow. He was patient. Eventually the deep, soft voice penetrated.

"Lena, are you awake? I have someone here to see you."

Prepared to be awed, she opened her eyes. A large dark figure, outlined by the shimmering light, stood over her, its face a shadowy suggestion. She was slow to recognize the speaker.

"Dr. Braun?" Her throat was dry, and it hurt as she strained to rasp out the words, which emerged formless.

"Yes, Lena. I'm glad you're awake. Here, let me give you a little water."

The younger man stood hidden behind the doctor, who carefully squeezed water from a plastic bottle. He watched in silence and waited.

"He's here, your grandson, Christoph. Your vigil is over."

Lena's response to the news was immediate. She closed her eyes and offered a silent prayer, Please, Johann, look down on me now. She steadied herself, controlling the excitement, conserving her energy, and focused on the looming task, which if successfully carried out would grant redemption and allow her that final peace. She opened her eyes. The afternoon's gold had hardened and was descending toward red.

Tentatively the American approached, studying the small ashen face that lay still upon the white pillow. She looked up at him, with baleful eyes, rimmed with yellow. Time hung suspended while the old women silently reached across two generations seeking to bridge the impossible chasm. They each knew little about the other, but during this brief moment something seemed to pass between them, and she was certain now that she could do what she must now attempt.

The last stroke had resulted in extensive paralysis over much of her body, including her facial muscles. When she tried to talk she could not form the words, and despite excruciating efforts, Lena could only utter approximate sounds, but now she must communicate. She had chosen the words and practiced them in her mind over and over again, and now the moment had come to try. She steeled herself for her last great effort.

He was saying something, but it was far away, as if in a memory. Lena's focus was on the words, and the force of her concentration lifted her consciousness and dimmed everything else around her. Willing with all the power she possessed for her lips to move, she uttered one word: "Bible."

The American stopped speaking as a look of confusion spread across his face.

She struggled to repeat, "Bible."

Lena had anticipated that she would have to say the first word at least twice, but no amount of forethought could have prepared her for the massive drain on her reserves that it caused. Oh God, have him pick up the Bible, she silently pleaded, as her breathing became labored, and small glistening beads of perspiration gathered on her forehead. Desperately, she moved her eyes toward the bedside table and then back to the boy. To her relief, his eyes followed hers; then he spoke.

"You want me to read to you?" He spoke English, and Lena didn't understand him, but that was not important. All that mattered was that he picked up the Bible.

The American continued. "If it's in German, I won't be able to read it. I never learned German." He shrugged apologetically. To Lena's joy he reached over and lifted the Bible off the table and casually thumbed through it.

"I thought so. I can't read this. But it's a beautiful Bible. May I?" He was just trying to be nice, but Lena was ecstatic.

She loved this old family Bible, beautifully bound in a black leather cover, the edges of the fine sheets gilded in gold, and containing many pages of colorful illustrations. It was the ideal place to keep the letter.

As he was examining this heirloom, it fell open somewhere in the middle, and she saw the old, yellowed envelope lying there, hidden between the pages.

The presence of some ancient keepsake didn't seem to surprise or interest him, and he started to turn the pages, eliciting a loud and urgent chesty grunt from her.

Dr. Braun, who had been quietly observing the unlikely exchange from the foot of the bed, moved closer, showing concern for his patient

"What's wrong, Lena?" he asked, as he maneuvered around her grandson. "You must be calm."

Lena ignored him and looked with steadfast intensity into the eyes of her bewildered grandchild. She forced out the next word: "Letter."

It was hardly more than a croak, but she could see that Christoph was locked in, fully aware that she was making an extraordinary effort to communicate something of tremendous importance.

Her heart thumped as the boy reached into the Bible and extracted the precious letter from its longtime resting place. Two words. That's all. He'll understand. Oh please, he must.

"Is this what you mean? This envelope?" Her eyes beamed out the affirmation. He returned the gaze and leaned closer. She could feel the blue veins that ran down her exposed temples throbbing; her breathing had become fast and shallow. Christoph reached out to gently stroke the tense and wrinkled forehead. In a whisper he urged his grandmother, "Say it. I'm listening. I'll get it."

The third word in German was expelled on a gust of breath forced between the woman's front teeth and lower lip.

"Finden."

"Find," he repeated. He understood.

For Lena there was little time. The room was growing dim as darkness ringed the periphery of her vision, slowly pushing toward the center. A constant roar was growing in her head and already drowning out all other sounds. As the great final blackness flooded upon her, the last word escaped to remain with the living. She uttered it in English, floating on her final breath: "Give."

1

March 1945

In the afternoon I drive out to Himmler to have a long talk with him. He is in Hohenlychen under medical care. He has had a bad attack of angina but is now on the mend. He gives me a slightly frail impression. Nevertheless, we were able to have a long talk about all outstanding questions. In general, Himmler's attitude is good. He is one of our strongest personalities. With Himmler the atmosphere is orderly, unpretentious, and 100 percent National-Socialist, which is most refreshing. One can only rejoice that, with Himmler, the old National-Socialist spirit still prevails.

During the drive home, I have an opportunity to think over all that we discussed. The drive through the darkening countryside in the dusk was impressive. Again and again we met columns of refugees on the move; they almost seem to symbolize this gigantic war.

Joseph Goebbels's diary

March 7, 1945

■ ■ ■

On the crest of a low, gently rising Pomeranian hillside, the school found-
ers erected their proud new edifice in the clearing of a small remnant
of the once endless primeval evergreen forest that blanketed the countryside along the Baltic coast of Eastern Europe. In 1870 they opened
its doors to the first students. The school was called Clarey Gymnasium
after the principal benefactor, Wilhelm Clarey, and for the next seventy-
two years provided boarding and education for the sons of Germany's
Prussian elite, including descendants of Wilhelm himself.

Lena Mueller recognized the potential of the building as a military
field hospital and convinced her superiors who, in return, delegated the
conversion to her.

It was a rectangular three-story structure, with small round towers
at each corner extending two levels higher, and a large central clock
tower that provided three more levels of private quarters, traditionally
occupied and highly prized by the most senior boys.

A wide pebbled driveway led up from the main gates directly to
the front entrance, which was dominated by two huge oak doors, simply carved by expert craftsmen and installed to form a great archway.
When both doors were opened, this entrance provided excellent clear-
ance for the flow of people and stretchers and bodies. Immediately
inside the entrance was an ample vestibule, and beyond that, through a
pair of glass doors, was the Main Hall, which opened to the ceiling of
the third floor.

From the center of the hall, a grand stairway rose to the second
floor. Its design was also well suited for its new use. The lower portion
was about twelve feet wide and terminated at a deep landing halfway
up to the second floor. Narrower flights of stairs continued up to the
next floor at each end of the landing and at right angles. For hospital
purposes, the right side was up and the left side was down.

The stairs were of oak, and were once covered with a plush carpet runner that swept down across the hall and through the vestibule to the front doors, but being unsuitable for hospital use, it was removed and stored away. A sturdy balustrade with solid oak handrails supported by ornate iron posts curved up to the second floor and continued around the entire opening. Designed for a school full of playful boys, the hand-rails had many small knobs attached to the top at regular intervals to eliminate what would otherwise be a perfect slide. These proved to be helpful to the medical staff as they struggled up and down with the wounded.

The wall at the top of the intermediate landing was covered with oak panels, into which had been carved a series of scenes depicting boys at work and play, but these were now hidden behind a large, bright-red banner with a swastika in the center, hung from the handrail above,

The Main Hall was little used during the building's days as a school. The boys used the spiral stairs that ascended from the back passage to the highest levels of the clock tower, and its stone treads had deep depressions worn in them from the millions of feet that had dashed up and down over the years. Because the front entrance was the quick-est and most direct means of ingress, with the wartime conversion, the once venerable hall now became the main emergency examination space through which passed the agony of Adolph Hitler's Russian adventure.

A war-worn, three-ton Opel "Blitz" transportation truck rumbled up the driveway, coughing and belching a steady cloud of gray smoke that seemed to hang in the frozen air like a long line of dreary washing out to dry. Slowly it circled to the front entrance, and with gears grind-ing it came to a jerky halt. Pulling on the handbrake, the driver kicked open his door and jumped to the soggy ground. In appearance he com-plemented the battered truck. His uniform, rumpled and dirty, hung loosely on his gaunt body, and he wore no hat. His face was unshaven. Bloodshot eyes set deep in his head complemented the sallow skin on his cheekbones. It was a time of shortages, and the effect showed clearly on this man.

Looking back over his shoulder into the truck, he shuffled up the few steps to the front doors and entered the vestibule, where he had to pick his way through the field cots that covered the floor. At that particular moment, business was slow and the cots were empty.

Lena Mueller, who was arranging the reception area for the next wave, approached and asked if he had another load of wounded.

"Just one, and I wish to hell you'd get him out of my truck. He's a madman, SS officer; you know what I mean? He hijacked my truck and ordered me, with a revolver aimed at my head, to bring him here. I've got a truckload of ammunition that I've got to get to Stettin. I've been separated from my ordnance group since nine o'clock this morning, and that asshole forces me to go fifty goddamn miles in the wrong direction, when there's plenty of hospitals around. They're trained idiots. They pick them for their stupidity. That son of a bitch could have died in the time it's taken me to get here."

A small group had begun to form around the irate soldier, and the growing audience seemed to inspire him. With increasing venom he retold the tale of how he'd been ambushed by this insane young SS officer, who'd barged into the cab of his truck while he was parked at the side of a street just outside Stettin. He was trying to read a map when the passenger door suddenly flew open, and this swine, covered with blood and waving a gun in his face, pulled himself up onto the seat.

"And like a stupid pig, I froze. I should've kicked him in the face before he even got in. I could see the devil's uniform, but his leg was injured pretty bad. There was a lot of blood, and the wound looked ugly. Got a bullet in the knee, and it couldn't have happened to a more deserving shithead. I thought I'd just take him to the nearest hospital. Then the bastard tells me to drive south. South! Shit, I'm in trouble already, and the bastard wants to take me to the front. They're all mad."

A few of his listeners muttered in agreement, evidence that the black uniforms of the Schutzstaffel no longer held the forced respect of the German populace, who believed much of their present condition was the direct outcome of the excesses by the various arms of this organization. Lena had heard rumors of executions and hangings in the streets of German cities performed by the SS, which was fanatically fighting both the Russians and its own countrymen in a final doomed undertaking. The truck driver's story seemed like one more example of its unbalanced conduct.

As he was speaking, Lena flagged two orderlies, and with one of them carrying a stretcher, they went outside and returned some minutes later carrying a young man in a torn, bloodstained uniform. He was in obvious pain.

As the orderlies maneuvered into one of the examination bays, Lena stopped to address the driver. As she approached, he eyed her with suspicion. Lena had an air of authority and was always recognized as the one in charge. To set him at ease, she spoke softly as a teacher would to young children. "Please, before you go, we must get some information from you," she said as she motioned to the back of the hall where a heavy oak desk was located beneath the huge swastika. She led him to it, sat down, and attempted to conduct a brief interview, but the soldier was in no mood to cooperate. The exchange quickly deteriorated from unfriendly to openly hostile.

"Name, please."

"Conrad, Willie Conrad."

"You're a corporal, I see. What's your division?"

"Sister, I'm hours overdue, and your lousy patient has got my ass hanging out with a great bull's-eye painted on it. I don't need to be screwing around here, waiting for the Russians to blow it apart, unless I can escort them directly to that bastard. I hope they tear his eyelids off, and—"

"Shut up, Corporal," snapped Lena with a tone of steel. "You will confine your comments to direct answers and refrain from further editorial outbursts."

Conrad laughed. "Like I said, I'm already swimming in a lake of shit because I'm late without explanation, and my superiors won't take kindly to the idea that I stayed around to swap war stories with a matronly nurse with large medals." He paused, no doubt to let the abuse sink in, and was a little taken aback when Lena showed no sign of having had her sensibilities assaulted. Expressionless, she returned his stare, and for a moment a silent duel waged. Then, with a loud angry growl, he turned away from the table, heaved his shoulders once, and stomped out through the vestibule into the dying afternoon. As he passed through the outer doors, he turned briefly and flicked a jaunty salute back into the hall, and then he was gone.

Lena sighed. She had no contempt for the belligerent soldier. The war was shit. It had always been shit. She added a few sentences describing the manner in which the wounded man had arrived and her initial observations of his condition, got up, and went over to join the doctor, who was working rapidly on the young man. The right leg of his blood-smeared trousers had already been ripped away revealing what remained of the knee. The entire kneecap was gone, and in its place was a gaping hole in which she could see the splintered ends of bone and frayed cartilage, but mostly blood and dirt. The whole area was red and swollen, but most ominous was the ring of black, spongy, dead flesh. She looked up at a second doctor who arrived at that moment and, with one look declared, "Prepare to amputate."

■ ■ ■

Outside, as he climbed into his truck, Willie Conrad was smiling. It had felt good to shower abuse on the SS and that stupid nurse. He was glad that one of those bloodthirsty buggers was finally getting his due, but as he steered the battered truck back down the driveway, the smile left his face, replaced by a look of strained concentration. He had something to ponder, a little puzzle. He found it no easy task. He was a clever man who sensed a great opportunity but hadn't had enough time to organize his thoughts.

The SS lieutenant hadn't kept his wits together for the whole ride. There had been periods when he slipped into states of mild hysteria with incoherent babbling, but there had been words and phrases repeated often enough for the listener to attach importance to them. Conrad now struggled to put meaning to them, for he was certain that in these utterances lay clues that explained the significance of the key his passenger had clutched tightly for most of the ride—the same key he now examined as it swung gently to and fro at the end of a string attached to the rearview mirror of his truck.

2

At the same moment Conrad drove away, the telephone rang in the private office of the commanding officer of the Army Group Vistula, Heinrich Himmler.

"Herr Brandt, what is it?"

"Sorry to bother you, Reichsführer. It's Count Bernadotte on the phone. I thought it might be important."

"Yes, please put him through."

"Also, Reichsführer"—Brandt's voice was hesitant and nervous— "General Guderian has just arrived. He demands to see you. Apparently he's been to Penzlau already, and General Lammerding informed him you were here."

Brandt heard an irritated mutter followed by a brief pause. Herr Himmler was a bothered man these days.

"I can't see him immediately. He'll have to wait."

"As you wish."

A muted curse escaped the lips of Heinrich Himmler. His stomach tightened. Guderian could not have timed his sudden, uninvited arrival worse. It had been a day and a half since the disappearance of Lieutenant von Ritter, along with his car and driver. When he first heard the news, he'd immediately placed a call to Count Folke Bernadotte in Sweden and had been waiting for a call back. He'd become immobilized with anxiety, hoping that the drop-off had been made. Only the count could have that answer.

Himmler both disliked and feared Heinz Guderian. The Generaloberst, the "father" of the Blitzkrieg, didn't fit into a convenient stereotype. The strong-willed and hardheaded man had once declared, "It's sometimes tougher to fight my superiors than the French." He had lost favor and was dismissed when, in disregard of Berlin's directives, he'd ordered a strategic retreat in the severe winter of 1943 from the very gates of Moscow; but in the aftermath of the failed July 20 attempt to assassinate Hitler, he was recalled and charged with cleaning up the ranks of the army, a task he pursued with the same energy and diligence that he had as a commander in the field, thus rehabilitating his career. Hitler made him chief of army staff, which at that time was considered a puppet position because Hitler called the shots. Guderian didn't see it that way. Himmler had witnessed many heated exchanges between the general and his Führer that no other subordinate would have dared to enter. From Himmler's perspective, Guderian was a dangerous man.

Finally the phone rang. When the call was over, Heinrich Himmler was a badly shaken man, and no amount of medication would ease the tension that gripped his abdomen. For a long time he sat motionless beneath the massive portrait of Adolph Hitler, staring at the wall in front of him and tapping his upper teeth with the tips of his fingers. When his telephone rang again, he slowly picked up the receiver.

"Yes."

"Reichsführer, the general says he won't be kept waiting any longer. What shall I do?"

Himmler's small, slanting eyes blinked a couple of times behind his round wire-rimmed glasses. "Show him in."

He might as well get this over with. He knew the purpose of Guderian's visit. Himmler had received his first true military command just one month before, over the strenuous objections of Hitler's Wehrmacht generals, led by Guderian, and he knew Guderian was fighting to convince Hitler to replace him. He'd heard of the fiery exchanges between the determined general and the Führer, who defended the choice of his loyal servant, *der treue Heinrich*. Just a couple days ago, Guderian had to be dragged out of the meeting room, and the Führer had fallen into such a rage that he could only stammer and froth at his greatest general.

As Himmler now sat absently stroking his small moustache, trimmed in the Führer's style, his thoughts were not on the Russian advance. Instead, he was considering how quickly he might complete the transition of command, thereby enabling the concentration of his efforts where they were most needed—namely, the saving of his own life. Perhaps it was just as well that Guderian had arrived at this moment.

A few moments later, a man of medium height with broad shoulders and a stern bearing entered the room. Guderian looked older than his fifty-six years, though he still possessed clear, glaring eyes that warned of a firm determination and a short temper. He was one of the great military minds of the war, responsible for creating the armored techniques that brought about the fall of France in less than a month. As chief of the Army High Command (OKH), but for the incredibly insane misdirection from higher places, he might have also changed the situation in which Germany now found itself in the east. He smiled thinly and extended his hand as he approached Himmler, who was perfectly aware that the general despised him. Guderian proceeded directly to the purpose of his visit.

At four o'clock, hardly forty-five minutes after his arrival at Hohenlychen, Guderian emerged from his meeting with Himmler. Amazingly both men had achieved their objective: an agreement that

Guderian would approach the Führer and again request the replacement of Himmler as commander of the Army Group Vistula, and the latter would not object.

The general smiled as he descended the stone steps at the front entrance of the sanatorium's main building and entered his car. As he leaned back in his seat, Guderian let out a long sigh and closed his eyes. His heart was troubling him again, and he needed rest, but there was so much to do.

"To the bunker," he said. "And let us hope that Hitler is as easy a conquest, just this once."

For Himmler, the outcome of the meeting provided a soothing satisfaction. It was as if some god had heard his prayer and sent to him the only man brave or fool enough to challenge the Führer and extricate him from the loathsome distraction that his military command had become. Now he could put all his energies where they were most needed.

He slumped in his chair, his glasses propped up on his forehead, his Asian eyes closed. The acute stomach cramps had again become unbearable. He picked up his telephone and rang through to Brandt.

"Rudolf, arrange for Ernst Kepler to be here first thing in the morning. I'll meet with him at nine o'clock. I'll need von Ritter's full dossier. And have Dr. Kersten fetched, immediately."

About one hour later, Ernst Kepler walked out of his office, located in another bunker deep beneath the badly damaged streets of Berlin. In his hand he held the orders and travel authorization permitting him to proceed immediately to Hohenlychen, one hundred kilometers to the north. He was smiling. The Reichsführer had another job for him, and it couldn't have come at a better time.

3

The surgeons wasted no time, slapping a chloroform mask over the young man's face, and in less than thirty seconds they began the operation. Quickly and efficiently, with a skill honed by considerable practice, they prepared and removed the shattered leg above the knee, tied off arteries and veins, sewed up and bandaged the swollen stump, injected a rather small dose of morphine, and sent their patient unceremoniously off to one of the many dorm rooms that filled the upper floors of the old school building. The attendants who carried him up laid him on the first available bed. One of them marked its number on the outside of a folder and placed it on the table at the front of the room along with others already there. The young lieutenant was now on his own, his future securely in the hands of fate.

He dreamed.

■ ■ ■

He was in woods, surrounded by a thick fog, and struggling through deep powdery snow. Nervously, he clenched his automatic weapon.

He was afraid, and he waited. He didn't know why. He was walking and came across a black shape. It seemed to move, and gradually he realized that he was looking at the top of a beret. He backed up to get a better view and saw that the beret rested on top of a head that was bowed down. Ever so slowly the head rose, and he found himself looking into the eyes of a young boy. Large and saucer like, they reminded him of the eyes of the great dogs in the Hans Christian Anderson story, and as he watched they seemed to grow in brightness and size, and he was filled with terror. The boy's expression never changed. It was emotionless, except for the eyes. Silently they pleaded. There was a gun and he wanted to run, but his legs seemed to have simply faded away. He couldn't feel them, and they didn't respond to his desperate need for action. All he had to do was take one quick step forward and grab the gun, but he couldn't move. He saw the grip tighten on the trigger, and a red flash lit up the darkness. Searing pain shot through his knee, and he fell.

He was on his back looking up. All he could see was the boy's face. The same pleading look stared back at him. His leg ached, the pain growing steadily.

■ ■ ■

Lieutenant Johann von Ritter awoke with a start. His body cried out in pain. There was a cramp in his foot, and the blanket must have fallen off because his entire leg was freezing cold. His head ached. He tried to sit up, and it was then he realized something was different; his body wasn't functioning. The entire machine was out of synchronism. He couldn't move, and soon the leg was burning from his thigh to his toes. The drug had worn off, and as he lay there, a low moan began in his chest and rumbled up through his throat as he opened his eyes and tried to understand, to remember.

The dream had been long and disconnected, and he only vaguely remembered fragments, but one image remained vividly rooted: the uplifted face with large pleading eyes. Even the mounting pain failed to dispel this recurring demon, which had dominated his dreams for months, making sleep something to be feared. This subconscious visitation, which had been haunting his life, now seemed to have passed through the veil of slumber, and as he lay awake, the burning image of those eyes lingered.

He understood. It was the face of the Dead reaching across the great void to grimly display the fruits of his appalling crime. A terrible judgment had been passed, and von Ritter's sentence was already begun. He'd seen it happen to others. He'd seen the war at its bloodiest without turning away. He knew men who had fought and killed without remorse. He'd known men he thought could always be relied upon suddenly collapse, unable to continue. He'd once thought it was cowardice, but he was wrong. It was obvious now. They'd finally been struck down by the uselessness of it all. They, too, had been visited in one way or another.

Mercifully, the throbbing from his leg came to dominate the torment of his dream, at least temporarily. Flushed with agony, he was barely able to raise his head. He looked down the large open room over scattered beds filled with the wounded, to where the attending nurse's table was located. There under a single bulb that hung naked at the end of a long cord, tied to the exposed rafters above, he saw what he was looking for. Somewhat out of focus, and through the hazy film of pain and sleep, he could discern in the dim distance the shape of a nurse. His weak condition made shouting impossible, so he reached over to the plain wooden chair that separated his cot from his neighbor's and found, under his folded uniform, the P-38 he'd refused to relinquish even in the delirium. He began to rap it against the metal bed frame.

■ ■ ■

Lena Mueller sat at the table processing a small pile of folders, the meager case histories of a constantly fluctuating body of patients, little more than the sporadic reminders to an overwhelmed staff that a hospital only functions adhering to strict procedures. Methodically she transferred each completed file from one side of the table to the other—an act of rigid discipline, which she deemed all the more necessary due to the gradual decay around her of structure and systems. The refusal to discard such clerical responsibilities was a vital personal measure to help fend off the ubiquitous descent toward chaos.

At the sound of the urgent summons coming from von Ritter, she looked up from her papers and peered into the darkness. She entered a few final notes into the open file before her, and after placing it on the correct stack, she removed her glasses, folded them purposefully, and put them in her apron pocket. Pushing back her chair, she opened the shallow drawer in the table and took out a candle and a box of wooden matches. Her progress down through the room was slow due to the erratic maze of beds.

At the foot of his bed she stopped to light the candle. Carefully she rounded the bed and moved up to where she could better see the patient. As the yellow glow of the candlelight flickered across von Ritter's face, her chest muscles tightened, causing her to emit a small gasp, as if she'd seen a ghost.

At that moment the now familiar thunder of the large guns rolling in from the front seeped in and seemed to break her reverie. The war had awakened for another day, and from the sound of it, much closer than before. It had finally come to this. There had been rumors that the Russians were close to capturing Danzig and soon would turn westward again in full force. It was also said that the enemy had already driven to the Oder and that the escape corridor to Stettin was all but closed.

Von Ritter, through his pain, heard the guns too. His eyes met Lena's. He attempted to rise, only to stop short with a clenching grimace as pain shot through the residual of his leg. When it passed, his eyes reopened, and though he remained silent, they pleaded for relief.

Lena, who seemed to have collected herself after the startled reaction to her initial glimpse of von Ritter, quickly turned and reached down for the blankets. Carefully, she pulled them back, exposing his wound.

"I have to examine your leg." He looked away to hide the pain in his face. She worked gently to remove the protective wrappings, which were damp and stained from the oozing flesh. The stench was bad. As she lifted off the last layer of bandage, a large piece of rotten skin pulled up with it, and fell onto the bed. The stump was ugly and black, and when she touched the blistered flesh, it sagged like soggy toilet paper.

"Narkose, Schwester, bitte."

He uttered the words quietly, and it seemed she hardly understood what he said. Through half-opened eyes he saw her staring down at what was left of his leg. He followed her eyes, and a look of bewilderment and shock descended on his face. This was the first time he had seen the damage, and until that moment he had no idea that the leg had been removed.

Calmly she unfastened her apron and carefully laid it over the grisly sight.

"It's necessary to keep the cold night air off," she lied. "I'm going to fetch the doctor to have your wound checked, and I'll bring back the painkiller and some clean bandages as soon as I've found him. Hold still and keep the wound covered."

"Bitte, Schwester. No doctor. It's not necessary. I've seen it too many times. My leg, what's left of it, is rotting away, and the disease will spread until it strikes my heart. Please, just get the painkiller. And let me die peacefully."

Two pale eyes searched her face with icy intensity, looking for a sign in her expression, but when none appeared, he continued.

"The doctor will tell us nothing that we don't already know. He'll weigh in his mind whether or not my chances are good enough to use up more drugs to keep me alive. And we know what his decision will be, don't we?"

She turned to go, but again he interposed, "Please. Stop." There was urgency in his voice.

"Hear that?" he said, gesturing with his head. "It's the Russians and they're close. They're racing to get to me before the infection does. Either way I lose. Actually, I don't care who wins, except that the Russians won't be gentle."

For a moment they both listened to the approaching battle, staring at the blackout curtains as though seeing beyond them to the dark horizon, where lurked an even darker future. It was von Ritter who broke the silence.

"Do you know what regiment I'm in?"

"Yes, I know your uniform. You're a member of the Leibstandarte Adolf Hitler," she said. "I've seen the silver and black cuff title on the sleeve of your black dress jacket. I'm curious about the uniform. Combat troops wear field gray, and lately the SS have taken to keeping their affiliation hidden from the revengeful enemy."

"Excellent!" he whispered. "And do you know anything about our record in this war?"

Her eyes drifted back to the blackout curtain. She shook her head. "I only see Germans, wounded and broken."

"It's said we're the supreme fighting regiment in the Reich, the elite. The enemy fears us and hates us." He paused, but when Lena displayed indifference to his boast, he continued. "Did you know that the Waffen-SS no longer leaves its wounded men to become prisoners on the eastern front? True, we've shot our own men rather than letting them fall into their savage hands. I can tell you what they do to an SS soldier when they catch him alive."

There was great sadness tinged with hatred in his voice.

"Once, after we had retaken a city—it was Kharkov, two years ago—we found the remains of some of our men. It was horrible, inhuman. I was sick. That's when I learned to hate. I lived to hate. For two years that's all I've done. But now it's over. What I hate is this war, this useless, fucking war and the idiots who created it and run it."

He paused and closed his eyes. "I won't be taken alive. You know what I mean? I want to die easily."

A cold chill passed between them. She, too, feared the Russians; terrible stories had been circulating. During the last few weeks, the once small stream of refugees had been transformed into a swollen river of desperation flooding through the town. They brought with them tales of Russian savagery, of villages plundered and razed, town leaders rounded up and summarily executed, and the brutal rapes. No one was spared, and as the evil got closer, the depravity seemed to grow as if fattened by the fulfillment of previous deeds. There was the story of a hospital that despite the absence of any resistance was invaded and gutted by hoards of drunken soldiers. It was rumored that they even bludgeoned their way into operating rooms with surgery in progress to drag the assisting nurses away for their sordid pleasure.

They both knew the rules of war allowed the basest of human traits to run free. Revenge, hatred, and cruelty were the right of the victor. The once feared and always despised SS would be a particularly good catch. In the dim candlelit globe, they both understood that his death at the hands of the Russians was possible and would be both horrible and degrading.

"We've already begun the evacuation," she offered. "Soon transports will start taking the wounded to Stettin. I'll arrange for you to be among the first to go. Your special circumstance will support my decision, and—"

"No." He looked away and was silent. The pain spreading from the infected stump, like the war itself, was consuming him. He needed to think, but his mind was unable to function.

"I'm dying. Let me. I won't spend my last hours on a jolting truck ride, the end of which I'll probably never see. You'd be wasting the space on me."

A low chuckle came from the next bed, followed by a voice that sounded like a dried riverbed.

"Very heroic, asshole," it rasped. "Good thing for you, even assholes can be heroes; real assholes, I mean." The source of this peculiar idea rolled onto his side, his back to von Ritter, and continued to laugh, apparently enjoying the joke.

Lena tensed, but von Ritter reacted with only a faint smile, the corners of his jaws bulging slightly as he clenched his teeth. It was the pain swirling around the stump that hurt, not the soldier's comment.

She left the bedside abruptly and began negotiating her way back down the ward. Behind her the soldier's laughing continued, then trailed off. To von Ritter it seemed full of sorrow and despair, almost like crying. He watched the nurse fade into the gloom, thinking the easy acceptance of his death had disturbed her. It occurred to him she must have seen men die in many ways; she had to be an expert on the subject, yet she seemed affected by his quiet, passive acceptance of the inevitable. Everyone has a breaking point, and he suspected hers was close.

■ ■ ■

Von Ritter shut his eyes, and to deal with his pain, he concentrated on the sounds of the room. There was a stillness that muffled the constant, low-level murmur of heavy breathing, soft moans, and occasional throat-clearing coughs rising from the crowded occupants, as they suffered through their wounds. He slipped into a shallow unconsciousness.

4

He reminded her of those naive boys who many years ago had proudly marched off to war. They didn't exist anymore. They were either dead or changed, and those who had died were the lucky ones. The survivors, she did her best to fix them and make them as comfortable as possible. If they chose to die, well, that was their business, but this one was different. He had touched her, brought forward the past. She wanted him to live.

Absorbed by these thoughts, she entered the long, narrow corridor outside the wardroom and nearly collided with one of the doctors, who was about to enter the room she had just left. Nimbly he sidestepped the oncoming nurse, greeted her with a curt good morning, and brushed past into the room.

"Doctor," she said, turning to follow, "may I have a word with you? It's about one of the men in here, von Ritter. I'm afraid the gangrene has spread despite the operation, and I think you ought to see him immediately. He just woke up and needs morphine. The smell is bad, and I was on my way to make arrangements for his transfer up to one of the isolation rooms."

Dr. Paul Reisen turned and looked down at her. He was tall, well over six feet, and carried himself in true Prussian style, erect with trained precision. He carried a clipboard in one hand, tucked behind the elbow as though it were a baton. The close cut of his fair-colored hair failed to disguise the fact that he was already going bald though only in his midtwenties. By nature he was condescending and haughty.

"How's he dealing with the pain?"

"Right now he's quiet, but the pain must be severe. Obviously his threshold is high."

"Good. Then we'll keep the dosage low for as long as possible. Is he lucid?"

"Yes, but weak. He understands the nature of the infection and talks like he wants to die. Do you know he's SS?"

"Yes, I was downstairs when he arrived. There's something strange about him. He received a gunshot wound but not at the war front. In fact, the man who brought him in said that he was lying by the road at Stettin, and that's a hundred kilometers to the north of here. If I had to guess, I'd say someone finally had enough of his kind and simply let him have it. The bullet entered from the back, you know."

The idea sickened her. Even during these desperate times, the old loyalty to traditional patriotic values kept her from sympathizing with such treachery, even when it involved the SS. It was all the more repugnant in this case because she was convinced von Ritter was not of the sinister breed that filled the ranks of the Gestapo, or Death's Head regiments, whose reign of terror had charred the name of Germany, perhaps forever. He didn't fit the mold.

They were standing by the table where the patients' files lay, and while the doctor was talking, she searched for and picked up von Ritter's.

"The thing that bothers me, Doctor, is the observation noted here that the wound appeared to be quite old, over forty-eight hours, when he arrived. Isn't it possible that someone who couldn't find a hospital facility, refugees perhaps transported him back from the battlefront? And rather than wandering about looking for one while the Russians were advancing, they kept heading north, hoping to find something along their direct route. A lot of casualties are finding their own way to the hospitals these days, what with the general breakdown of order. You know the field units are not able to handle the volume anymore."

Reisen couldn't suppress a sneer, which told Lena that he considered this to be completely stupid.

"Why was he abandoned, especially after traveling so far?" he replied with cold civility. "Surely he would have been left much sooner if he was a burden, or at a less remote and inhospitable location. And what compelled him to hijack a transport at gunpoint and demand that he be brought here, closer to the front and certain death? No, there's something extremely queer about that man. He has something to hide, and he's desperate. You're aware he still has his handgun."

"Yes, and I find it strange that it was returned to him after the operation."

The doctor's eyes narrowed, and leaning over so his thin lips nearly touched her hair, he lowered his voice.

"The weapon wasn't returned. It was never taken from him. Throughout the entire operation, even anesthetized for hours, he held on to the gun like rigor mortis. I've never seen such a thing. We couldn't pry his fingers away from the handle. I'm glad he's awake; I've wanted to talk with him. I'm curious to find out what's driving him. Go on now and fetch the morphine. I'll take a look at his leg."

It took her ten minutes to find the night matron who kept the key to the dispensary. The woman had wandered off looking for coffee or whatever pretended to be coffee. With the drug finally in her hand, she instructed the matron to have one of the tower rooms prepared for von Ritter and to send an orderly to assist with moving him up there.

At least twenty-five minutes had passed before she arrived back at von Ritter's bedside, and she was a little surprised to find the doctor still there.

"Ah, here she comes," she heard him say. "It will only take a few moments for the morphine to take effect, and then we'll have you moved up to a private room. You'll be much more comfortable there, and I'll make sure that paper and something to write with are brought up to you as soon as possible. Thank you, Nurse Mueller."

He took the syringe, drew in the morphine solution, and quickly administered it to von Ritter. Immediately a change came over the man's face as the tension eased, and he was finally able to relax. To Lena it seemed like three or four years of aging suddenly faded from his features, and suddenly he looked even more like the memory of Ralf. Ralf, the first and only person she'd ever come close to loving. The war had made sure of that.

When she'd first rounded the end of his bed, when the yellow glow of the candlelight flickered across the man's face, a strange, unnerving sensation had flooded her body and touched places long forgotten. At first she mistrusted her memory, but she couldn't take her eyes off the face. A shattered youth, with a face prematurely aged, too taut, and somewhat hollow—a curious contradiction so common now in this war—appeared before her in the dancing candlelight. It was a face that resurrected the forgotten image of a boy long dead. The image was a little older and considerably harder, but otherwise she saw the long-departed Ralf, a victim of this war and the only person to have touched her heart. It seemed so long ago.

For the briefest of moments, a crack opened in the wall around that heart, just a sliver, and a ray of sadness escaped before her other self, Chief Nurse Mueller, could close it again. Ralf had been disposed off, buried, cast out from the protective fortress she had erected around herself, exiled to a place where he couldn't hurt her. Now this lieutenant revived the memory of the one who was her once and only—beautiful, blond, and joyful. This very presence now touched a chord and administered the fatal blow to her counterfeit self.

She entered nursing intent on disappearing into the regiment, and for four long years, she had kept the sadness locked away. Thoughts of Ralf were never permitted to enter her disciplined mind. She used the war to keep these memories away, attending to her real life duties and filling her waking hours with a fanatical commitment to her patients, but von Ritter had breached the fortress. Lena was shaken, but her discipline held firm. She had duties to fulfill.

When they reached the worktable, the doctor stopped and said to her, "You will supervise the transfer?"

"Yes, Doctor. I've already instructed my staff to make the necessary arrangements. An orderly will be here momentarily. I'll personally take responsibility for his care."

"Good. He wishes to write a letter. Can you set him up with everything he needs? I believe there's a courier scheduled to leave for Berlin this evening, and he seems anxious to have it done by then."

Lena was a little surprised by the personalized treatment Reisen was giving this patient. It was unusual for him. She doubted the patient's ability to write anything.

"I'll have it taken care of, though he's in no condition to write."

"Nurse Mueller, the man is about to die. He knows it, and it's natural that he should want to communicate one last time."

Lena knew he was right. With stark, dispassionate accuracy, Reisen had cut to the truth of their position. A man whose life might easily be saved under different conditions had just been abandoned under the expediencies of the present. It was a reality she had dealt with often enough before, but now her heart was torn with rebellion. In her mind she'd already taken the first step along a new, unknown path.

"You're right, Doctor. Do you know where he wants it to go?"

"Yes, to his sister. He thinks she's at their family's country house in Uberlingen, on the shore of the Bodensee." He seemed to drift into some thoughts of his own. His voice softened. "Its very pretty there, and it's been such a long time."

For a few moments he stood, looking at nothing. And then he left.

The soldier in the cot next to von Ritter was in the same position as when Lena last saw him. He seemed to be asleep. Lena, out of curiosity, stopped at the desk and checked his file. He was identified as Sergeant Kurt Webber.

5

At Hohenlychen, a beleaguered Heinrich Himmler paced nervously about his office. His gray SS field uniform seemed ill fitting and lumpy on his awkward body. He stopped behind his desk to look out the large picture window and gaze over the rolling grounds of the sanitarium to the placid water of the Zenssee, one of the seven lakes of Lychen. On this particular morning, even the serenity and quietude of this beautiful place failed to sooth the boiling tension that continued to churn in his stomach. Unlike the other villains who had reached the highest echelons of the Third Reich, through some bizarre mutation of civilized society, Himmler always suffered. He was the victim of his own internal struggle between a Catholic morality he couldn't eradicate and a deep fear of his leader to whom he had long ago committed his future, relinquishing his individual conscience as he submitted opportunistically to Hitler's domination and intimidation. He did his master's bidding.

Times had changed. His stomach cramps were deeper and more frequent, and there were pressing, forceful reasons for a reevaluation of his loyalty to the Führer; but, as had always been the case, rather than coming to terms with the significance of the present, Himmler was caught in a downward spiral of trying to rewrite the past. It was Hitler, he reasoned, who had created the Nazi policies. Himmler's job had been to implement them, and while it was possible, if one stepped out of context to condemn the men who had been chosen to carry out the Führer's plans, to do so would be to ignore two vital facts. First, the Führer reflected the will of the German people as a whole. They elected him, and enthusiastically supported the many achievements and changes brought about by his National Socialist Party. What had been accomplished was done solely for the good of the nation. Secondly, everything had been done according to the laws of the state. With this contorted argument, Himmler had set aside any moral aversion that might have interfered with his work.

These and similar thoughts preoccupied his mind with growing urgency as he struggled to devise a trick of logic, some slight of reasoning, to establish an island of redemption and save himself from the rising sea of pending defeat and inevitable retribution. He would show them that he wasn't a monster and took no sadistic pleasure from the horrible activities he'd been directed to control. After all, he'd experienced outright physical revulsion to acts of violence and had on occasion become quite sick when forced to witness executions, those distasteful events required by duty and the rule of law. He let his mind wander.

He'd gone to Minsk to observe a problem firsthand. Upon his arrival a mass execution was hurriedly organized, and a hundred Jews were viciously herded naked to the edge of a deep pit where they were forced to kneel. As they made their final communications with their God, reluctant soldiers shot them through the head from behind. The effect had been shattering. Himmler, as well as many of the soldiers, was physically sick. Some time later, once he'd regained his composure, the sympathetic Reichsführer announced that a more humane method must be found. Yes, he thought, I am a humanitarian.

Even as defeat and chaos surrounded him, it was impossible for Himmler to confront reality. While the other Nazi leaders prepared themselves for the approaching end—some by readying their escape routes, others with cyanide capsules—he seemed frozen with inaction. It was Felix Kersten, his Finnish masseur, who reasoned that, because of the Bolshevik threat, the western allies would seize upon any mitigating evidence to keep the strongest organization in Germany operating. They didn't want to punish Himmler; they wanted to use him. Felix had always been able to see the sympathetic side of things.

His whole world had turned upside-down. The apparent defeat of Germany, which was looming ever closer, was driving him inexorably toward actions he wouldn't have thought possible just a few months before. Heinrich Himmler, the most loyal of Hitler's minions, was in the process of betraying his leader, and it was tearing him apart, particularly since things didn't seem to be going well. He knew what awaited him should things continue badly. He was like an exhausted fox that, having run out of tricks, had gone to ground.

Since the phone call from Count Bernadotte on the previous evening, Himmler had been in a state of extreme agitation. Guderian's appearance and the fortunate turn of events that appeared to be forthcoming did little to quell his agony. Only the miraculous hands of the good doctor, Felix Kersten, afforded him any comfort. Even this relief came with a price tag, although by now Himmler considered these payments as an investment. Last night's session had been the most extraordinary, but he still felt uncertain about the document he'd signed and delivered to Kersten.

He set up two appointments that morning, neither of them with persons of rank, but each one vitally important for his own peace of mind, if not his future. The first meeting was with Ernst Kepler, a Gestapo agent with unique qualifications. Kepler was an excellent detective with an unmatched record of success. Like Himmler, he was quite ordinary in appearance and manner, extremely quiet and reserved, and completely emotionless, to the point that his presence often seemed to disturb others by its very nothingness. It was his lack of ambition that attracted him to Himmler. It wasn't often that a man with his talent could be so completely trusted. As a result, the Reichsführer had come to employ the unostentatious agent frequently on matters of an important nature that affected him personally. Today he was going to dispatch this paramount servant on a mission of unparalleled consequence. At nine o'clock sharp there was a bold rap on his door.

"Herein."

The door opened abruptly, and a man of average height and build, with dark brown hair combed straight back, entered the room and stopped respectfully in front of the Reichsführer. He was dressed in civilian clothes—a brown suit, white shirt, and brown tie. He carried a black leather coat, neatly folded over his left arm.

"Heil Hitler." He spoke softly, extending his right arm in the familiar Nazi salute.

"Heil Hitler," reciprocated Himmler with even less enthusiasm. "Please close the door, Ernst, and come and sit down."

Patiently Kepler waited for his boss to speak.

Himmler sat back in his chair, took off his wire-rimmed glasses, and started to clean them with a white handkerchief he'd taken from one of his breast pockets. His small, delicate, almost feminine hands nervously polished the thick round lenses. Finally he cleared his throat and spoke.

"Ernst, you've been an excellent agent. The Reich is proud of you. In fact, I've personally commended you to the Führer."

"Thank you, Herr Himmler. I am honored."

"I haven't told you this before, but he wanted to honor you with an award, and so he shall, but it was decided that anonymity was more valuable to you, at least for the present. I'm sure you agree."

Kepler nodded his approval. There was no doubt that he enjoyed his lack of notoriety.

"I've known you since we dealt with those stupid students and their treasonous leaflets back in Munich, the 'White Rose' affair, yes? Since then your record has been astounding, and I've come to rely upon your particular skills a number of times. You've performed superbly, and with discipline and discretion. As a result, I've come to trust you more than any other agent." Himmler paused to put the glasses back on and, for the first time, looked directly at Kepler. "What I request of you today is of such importance. It involves information of such extreme delicacy for both me and the Reich that I demand you make a special oath before God and the Führer, and upon your life. You have to swear that nothing I tell you in this room today, or that you discover in the course of your investigations, will be revealed to anyone but me ever! If you are not willing to make this oath, I must ask you to leave immediately."

Less than half an hour had passed when the door of Himmler's office opened again, and Ernst Kepler walked out past the Reichsführer's personal secretary, Rudolf Brandt, who had responded to the silent summons sent from the button under his boss's desk. As he entered the hallway, he heard Himmler's voice, now a high painful whine. "Send for Felix. Quickly. I can hardly breathe."

6

Without hesitation, Kepler walked briskly down the hallway. He carried a large paper envelope that bulged from its contents. A couple minutes later he was sitting at a small writing desk in his own room, the door locked and the blinds closed. Slowly he opened the envelope that Himmler had given him and extracted its contents. For the next two hours he remained at the desk, reading and rereading every document. As he labored through the dossier, he made notes in a small leatherbound notebook. Finally, he slipped the papers back into the envelope. He wouldn't need them again. All the relevant information he would need was now consolidated in his notebook. He pushed back his chair, stretched his legs out under the desk, and read through his notes one last time.

He closed the notebook, got up, and walked over to his bed. He removed his shoes, lit a cigarette, and lay down. He had a lot of planning to do, but try as he might, he couldn't expel the tiny worm of a thought that was squirming around in his head, tickling and distracting, and he kept recalling the last directive from Himmler.

"You've made the oath. No one must know of your mission," he was warned. "Regardless of what happens to the Reich, you must press on toward your objective until it's been achieved. Remember, you've sworn obedience until death. Only then will you be relieved from these orders."

It wasn't the oath that bothered him. Himmler's bizarre world of secrecy, treachery, and false loyalties was rife with empty oaths that formed its fraudulent core. These were as meaningful as the Lord's Prayer, thought Kepler, who knew of Himmler's schizophrenic struggle with the religion of his childhood, and he chuckled aloud at the obvious connection.

It was the sight of the man who'd sat behind the huge desk that bothered Kepler. Dressed as usual in the uniform of the Waffen-SS without any decorations, Himmler looked as insignificant as any petty official. Kepler, who excelled at judging the character of an individual from appearance, had often thought if he met the Reichsführer on the street, he would have taken him as an unimportant clerk and paid him little attention. This morning his face was colorless and puffy; large shadows sagged below his strange eyes, eyes that had a slightly haunted look and darted about nervously, like a wild animal trapped in a corner. The war had taken its toll.

What disturbed Kepler more was the obvious fact that Himmler had withheld information during the briefing, something very unchar-acteristic of the man. He knew Himmler had always been acutely aware that his exalted position was earned and sustained by successfully ac-complishing the tasks assigned him. This in turn was due to the efforts of others, and while he always made sure that the rewards were his, he was also wise enough to ensure that his people had every necessary advantage. He was a thorough man, and Kepler wasn't used to behavior that could jeopardize the outcome of a mission. Even by Himmler's standards the secrecy here was disturbing, and he couldn't help wondering what he was really about to investigate.

It made no sense that the package of information that had been assembled and turned over to him was typical of the detail and preparation normally committed to a mission by Himmler, yet the true objective was embarrassingly withheld. To aid in the quest, Himmler had compiled a more extensive file on his nominal quarry, von Ritter, than Kepler had expected, and he had also been provided with two complete sets of identification papers: one showing him, Kepler, to be an officer in the Waffen-SS, and the other, a civilian employed by the SS-run Deutsche Erd und Steinwerke. It was an ingenious choice because one of DEST's main activities was the construction of roads. It was a perfect cover for someone who might need to travel anywhere. He was to use these identities at his own discretion.

Kepler also had his own papers identifying him as an officer in the Sicherheitspolizei, for he was a member of the Geheime Staatpolizei, the dreaded Gestapo, and possessed special talents that had many times in the past proved useful to the Reichsführer.

Ja, Herr Himmler, he thought as he inhaled deeply on his cigarette, I'll look for your little lost sheep and perhaps will also find the mysterious cargo. It could take a long time. So what? That's the least I owe you for these papers, my ticket to freedom. And who knows, the trove may also be rewarding.

There was an hour left until lunch. The day had turned mild, and Kepler listened to the emerging sounds of spring. Gradually the cheerful songs of the courting birds that filled the sanitarium grounds, ignorant of the embattled humans around them, lulled Kepler to sleep.

7

The Gestapo hadn't been Ernst Kepler's choice. It was his father's idea, and as was the case throughout his life, the younger Kepler simply followed orders.

He was Austrian, born in Graz. His family claimed as one of its ancestors the great mathematician, Johannes Kepler. Recent generations, however, had developed a firm tradition in the legal profession, and so it was to be with Ernst. His domineering father declared his son's profession on the day of his birth, and for the next two decades, the issue was never open to discussion. Gustavus Kepler, a stern and forceful patriarch, didn't believe in democracy, particularly when it came to his family. Ernst, for his part, grew up passively accepting his unquestioned subservient position.

While this prescriptive domestic structure may have led to marked social introversion, it also provided a secure climate in which his intellectual growth flourished. He had a brilliant, inquisitive mind and as a schoolboy exhibited some of his famous forefather's aptitude for the science of numbers, while also excelling equally in all subjects. His intellectual development also benefited from extensive travels, which his wealthy father arranged for him. His son's enhancement wasn't the father's principal objective. The elder Kepler was primarily interested in avoiding being a father to his maturing son, a task he found both tedious and discomforting. By the time Ernst entered the University of Vienna in 1935, he had become completely detached from the rest of his family. He'd become a subtle complexity of shy worldliness, complicated by the possession of a logical, absorbing mind that now included a proficiency in English and French. He was content to quietly enjoy his intellectual pursuits alone.

Kepler wasn't particularly reclusive, but he never developed friendships of any depth, as this required social wises that he'd never learned and didn't understand; nor was he politically attentive. He managed somehow to remain mostly indifferent to the whirlwind events whipping through central Europe, where the dark cloud of Nazism cast its shadow. As he studied, the people of Austria—many who had marched to the idealistic beat of Germanic unification—became increasingly engaged in a suicidal debate. *Anschluss* was the question, the evolution of the two racially and historically bound nations into one great Germanic state. It was an argument battled over at the highest levels in an environment of treachery and deceit.

At university Kepler did well. He proved to be extremely adept at both research and investigative work. He devised techniques and cross-referencing systems that combined his grasp of mathematical applications with an intuitive flair that bordered on a sixth sense. His academic reputation grew, and it wasn't long before he came to the attention of the secretary of state, Dr. Michael Skubl, who also happened to be the police president of Vienna. Skubl was charged with creating a cadre of detectives, in reality spies, to counter those working for Hitler inside Austria.

Ideally, these detectives would provide the chancellor with some inside information, and as a bonus, it was hoped that some might even infiltrate the appropriate organizations, discover the channels of communications, and take measures to disrupt the flow by means of harassment, direct interference, or dissemination of misinformation.

Skubl recruited and trained a number of secret agents, the best being Ernst Kepler.

It was Kepler's neutrality of opinion that attracted Skubl's people. They knew his family's right-wing associations would enhance his ability to infiltrate the party, for which he showed no affection. The conjecture proved accurate, and in February 1938, just days before Austria's fateful appeasement meeting with Hitler at Berchestgaden, Kepler, attracted more by the idea of mystery and intrigue than by any political feelings, was easily recruited. With no further training or preparation, he was directed to return to Graz, convince his father that he'd finally seen the light, and use the situation to establish his new life as a mole within the pro-Nazi factions of that city.

Eager to get started, Kepler quickly set about the business of terminating all his commitments in Vienna. His father, he said, wanted him to return to Graz. He did nothing to counter the quiet rumors that he'd opportunistically cast his lot with the Nazis, a likely story. He arrived home in Graz the day the Anschluss was declared

It's curious how one remembers little insignificant things from the past: a smell, a piece of clothing, something served at a dinner, a song. Kepler awoke from his nap in his room at the sanitarium in the late afternoon, that long-forgotten moment in his life in the front of his mind. He remembered that Mozart's *Eine Kleine Nachtmusique* was the tune he'd been whistling as he climbed the front steps of his father's house seven years before.

All that seemed so far away from his little room at Himmler's headquarters. He yawned, stretched, rubbed his eyes, and began to hum the eternal classic once again.

Dusk had descended muting what little color was left. Somewhere, seemingly far away, a telephone began to ring, and the noise slowly pulled him out of his peaceful state. Looking about, Kepler noticed how late it was. He fumbled for his watch, his father's watch, with the chain of small lead tabs, each inscribed to read, *Gold fur Wehr, Eisen fur Ehr* (gold for defense, iron for honor). His father had "loaned" the gold chain, which had once complemented the watch, to the Kaiser's government to help finance the first war. The lead chain was the promissory note to be redeemed when the war was won, paid for by the reparations imposed upon the vanquished French and British. His father had refused to replace the substitute chain, even when he could have easily done so, because it reminded him that governments left to their own devices were capable of the foulest treacheries. The watch and chain had passed to Kepler after his father died in jail, ironically the victim of a local purge within the Nazi party. Kepler tried to read the dial, but it was too dark, and he realized that he must have been sleeping for hours.

Before he could gather himself, the telephone stopped ringing, leaving an oppressive silence in the cold, dark room. Kepler thought he could hear the enemy's guns in the distance and felt the cold anxiety of the future.

Things had been pretty bad lately. What inner peace he'd once enjoyed was eroding, like sand castles before the inevitable tide. From his privileged position inside the security center of the Reich, he had the opportunity to follow the true progress of the war. He was well informed. Unlike Hitler's propaganda, unadulterated statistics told no lies. He knew the armies were dwindling, lines of defense were grossly overextended, production was grinding to a halt, the distribution network was virtually shut down, and the little that was leaving the factories was more than could be transported to the fronts. Germany was like an orange in a vice, its life juices slowly draining away and about to burst apart in one final catastrophic explosion. There were no miracle weapons ready to spring forth from the research and development centers, and he didn't believe, as did the Nazi leadership, that the Allies would suddenly have a change of heart and enlist the remnants of the nation in a new war against the Communists. Kepler had never been a dreamer. He was a cold realist.

The war was lost. It should have ended long ago. Wise leaders would have negotiated while there was something to discuss, but with "total war," as Goebbels called it, one thing was assured: total defeat.

Kepler knew all this, and the one fact that burned deepest in his mind was that retribution would follow, and he would be on the list, although certainly not one of the big fish. He had the advantage of his special relationship with Himmler that made his role within the dark world of the Gestapo a secret. His name was conspicuously lacking in documentation because anonymity enhanced his effectiveness, but his successes in tracking down and capturing the enemies of the Reich, as they were conveniently labeled, guaranteed that he would in turn be sought and subjected to the victors' justice.

For months the problem had gnawed at him, and he had considered numerous possibilities.

He stretched out his legs, yawned again, rose out of the chair, and started toward the bathroom. His mind was still groggy, and he wanted to freshen up before talking to Berlin. It was nearly five o'clock so he would have to hurry. There was little time to connect with his office, especially since he hadn't obtained the necessary authorizations for a priority call. Filling out request forms left tracks. He picked up the telephone and began the aggravating process that would eventually link him with his office. A few moments later, after leaving his instructions with the sanatorium's switchboard operator, he replaced the handset on the receiver and headed for the bathroom. He knew that while the various operators struggled to link his call, he would have plenty of time to clean up and shave. Before he reached his destination, he was diverted by a knock at his door.

"Who is it?" Kepler didn't expect any visitors.

A soft muffled voice replied, "Kersten."

Kepler's mind jumped alert. Felix Kersten was one person from whom he least expected a visit. Himmler's prized masseur, Kersten was a Finn who through some magical method had the capability of relieving his master from the tortures that visited his stomach with growing frequency.

As Kepler opened the door, he was confronted by a tall, fat man, notorious for his lust for food and ability to get it even during these lean times. Kersten used his special status with Himmler to good advantage. It was generally known that he exercised more influence over the Reichsführer than anyone but Hitler himself. Kepler, like most men who came into contact with Kersten, considered him extremely dangerous but had the good sense to keep this opinion to himself. Those who dealt in rumor and innuendo often spread insulting and derogatory lies about the man, including the possibility that he was something less than just that, with sexual preferences that were, to put it nicely, nonconforming. With fat rolling down his body, which swayed and bobbed in response to his clumsy gait, and his perfectly bald head glistening from the effort, Kersten could easily be imagined at home in some Persian harem, protecting the purity of his master's stable.

"Good day, Herr Kepler," said Kersten through full, sensual lips as he entered the room. "I hope I haven't chosen an inappropriate time to descend upon you, but I feel it is important that we talk. You spoke with the Reichsführer this morning?"

Kepler nodded. "Yes. He doesn't seem very well. I've never seen him so nervous." He had wanted to say "terrified," but his ingrained caution led him to use a less derogatory description, knowing that his every word could be communicated to Himmler.

"It's quite a difficult time for him. He has been rather distracted, and as you know, he does suffer. I'm sure that in a little while when I've given him his treatment, the Reichsführer will be much more like himself. His situation is impossible, you know. The Führer continues to heap more and more responsibility on him while others are failing at this time of crisis. But such is the lot of great men, yes?"

Again Kepler nodded, though not agreeing in the least with this sentiment. He suspected that Kersten's true opinion was also quite different. He detected an edge of cynicism in the big man's tone. Just the same, in the surreal world of the secret police, it was wise to keep one's thoughts to oneself. Reports that had unofficially circulated throughout Berlin indicated that Himmler's short tenure as commander of the eastern army had been a disaster, and his meeting just concluded had convinced him that the man was near the end. He had no doubt that Himmler was suffering, and the more the Reichsführer suffered, the greater the power Felix Kersten held over him.

Most people hated this Finn. It was a well-known secret that he had extracted many favors for the services he performed on the Reichsführer's stomach. Enemies were everywhere, and it wasn't wise to socialize with one so detested. Kepler's instinct told him that the masseur must know something about the strange assignment he'd just received so he intended to make full use of this visit. Kersten had something to tell him.

"It's obvious that he has a great burden and it weighs heavily on him. Again, I'm honored to be of assistance to him," said Kepler, "but I must tell you, Dr. Kersten, it's an unusual task he's given me this time."

"It's an unusual time," said Kersten, slightly raising his eyebrows. As always, the fat man looked relaxed, the pudgy fingers of his large hands folded together and resting on top of his extended stomach.

"Of course, but he's set so many restrictions and kept information from me, which is unlike him, especially when the outcome seems so important. It makes my chances of success that much less."

"He has his reasons, Herr Kepler."

"I wonder if you'd let me ask you a few questions. You needn't answer; I'll defer to your judgment on that, but you may well be able to provide me with important information. You do know something about this von Ritter affair?"

"Yes. It's been a disappointment to the Reichsführer and most distressing that the young officer, a magnificent soldier I must add, has apparently failed in his mission and quite disappeared. He came highly recommended, and we had such confidence in him. He was Waffen-SS, you know."

"Yes, Herr Himmler told me. I'm curious, do you know how this young officer came to be assigned the position of the Reichsführer's adjutant?"

"Certainly. He was recommended by his commanding officer. You probably know him, Colonel Joachim Peiper."

Of course Kepler knew of Joachim Peiper, commanding officer of the First Panzer Division of the Leibstandarte Adolf Hitler, the hero of Kharkov, and bearer of the Knight's Cross. The Nazi propaganda machine had made him famous throughout Germany for his exploits. His swashbuckling image wasn't unlike that of the famous American actor Errol Flynn, but that aside, he was also a brilliant leader. Kepler was aware that recently he had led the ill-fated thrust in the Ardennes, Hitler's last-ditch attempt to reverse the Allied offensive in the west, although the failure of this operation was known to few outside the military.

Despite all this, it seemed a bit unusual to Kepler that an officer with the rank of colonel could exert sufficient influence to place one of his men so close to the Reichsführer. He probed on.

"Everyone has heard of Colonel Peiper, a splendid soldier, I am told. The Reichsführer must hold him in the highest regard."

"Absolutely," swooned the masseur. "He's known Peiper for many years, since he was a young lieutenant and held the same adjutant position.

That was back in the thirties. He was such a dashing young man, I'm told. Himmler was so pleased to have such a gentleman by his side. And Peiper has never let him down. So when he came to Himmler and requested that von Ritter, who apparently needed a recuperation period away from the front, be assigned a less stressful position, the Reichsführer suggested that the lieutenant become his personal adjutant. I do so hope it wasn't a mistake."

That answered the first question, how Peiper had access to Himmler. Kepler was a little annoyed with himself for not knowing of this connection. It was the kind of information he absorbed in volumes, but somehow this had evaded him. In the back of Kepler's mind, Kersten's concern about von Ritter's mission registered as significant. He wondered what Kersten's involvement was with this mission.

There also was the question of the Peiper-von Ritter connection. Why did the colonel go directly to the second-highest office in the Reich on behalf of this junior officer? Kepler knew nothing about First Lieutenant Johann von Ritter, although the dossier from Himmler had given him a little background on the man. Anything more he would have to uncover himself. Again he addressed the Finnish masseur.

"When did the lieutenant first report?"

"I would say a little over a month ago."

"Do you remember where?"

"Vistula Group Headquarters at Prenzlau."

"Am I correct to assume you were with the Reichsführer at the time?"

Kersten laughed. "Come now, Inspector, I am always with him. His magic, herbs, and other mystical cures are useless against the clenched fist he carries in his stomach. I alone can release the tension and soothe his troubled abdomen. He takes me everywhere. He must. I have no existence except that which he grants me."

"But you're rewarded for what you do," said Kepler.

Kersten smiled. "I eat well."

"And you enjoy the Reichsführer's confidence."

"We talk."

"What was Himmler's opinion of Lieutenant von Ritter?"

"He was impressed by the lieutenant, who seemed to live up to his reputation. Is that his file? I'm sure it presents the picture of an intelligent, dutiful, and dedicated officer of the highest breeding. But, you know, the war does things to men. I think he was cracking. I thought so the first time I saw him, and I told Himmler, but he was too preoccupied to listen, and he didn't pay much attention to his new adjutant. He should never have sent him off."

"I understand he was entrusted with a cargo of some sort, with orders to convey it to Stettin where it was to be unloaded and left. Do you know anything about this?"

"Apparently the cargo never arrived," confirmed the fat man, rocking his head side to side as he wiped off perspiration with a small white towel.

"What was the cargo, Herr Kersten?"

"I'm sorry, my friend, but I can't tell you. That must come from Himmler in person."

"But you do know what it was?"

"What the cargo *is*," said Kersten with emphasis on the present tense. "I doubt it's been lost. I have an idea what it is, but it's not important for you to know."

Kepler's hope that Kersten came to share this information was slipping away. He tried one more time.

"Every piece of information is important. Knowing the nature of the missing cargo can substantially reduce the reasons for its disappearance and provide avenues of investigation. What was to happen to it once it was left in Stettin?"

Again Kersten shook his head. "No, you must proceed with what you have. I can only say that it's extremely important to the Reichsführer that the trunk be found and returned to him." The fat masseur paused. An expression of indecision crossed his face and as quickly was gone, but Kepler saw it and knew the man was wrestling over some critical piece of information.

"What is it?" Kepler spoke softly.

Kersten's usually placid face suddenly hardened, and he looked straight into Kepler's eyes as he replied, "Its value is priceless. But I feel I should warn you that if you find it and for some reason are unable to return it to the Reichsführer, it would be wise to dispose of it and tell no one that you've even seen it. And now I must go. He's waiting for me."

After Kersten left the room, Kepler looked at his watch, wondering what had become of his call to Berlin. A check with the switchboard confirmed that the connection had not yet been completed, and yes, they would ring him when the link was made, so he returned to the bathroom.

As he shaved, he focused his thoughts on his quarry, reiterating the facts that he had memorized so he would need to carry few notes. He went over the background facts. On March 10, von Ritter left Hohentychen at approximately ten o'clock in the morning. He was traveling in an SS staff car, one of Himmler's personal fleet—no plate number, no insignia. It was a Mercedes, one of the supercharged, armored prototypes. It was in excellent condition and should be quite easy to get a trace on. People would remember seeing it. He was traveling with a driver, a corporal from the Deutschland regiment named Emil Bachmeier. Von Ritter was wearing his black Panzer uniform, not the most common choice these days. Bachmeier had on an old gray field tunic, the kind with the dark green collar and scalloped pocket flaps. He must have had that one saved up somewhere. They had travel passes personally issued by Himmler, and the destination was Stettin. There was also a preplanned route, so it should be easy to narrow down the geographical location of the car by contacting all the SS checkpoints along that route.

The phone rang, and wiping the last spots of shaving lather off his face, he hurried out into the bedroom and picked up the telephone. It was Fraulein Belcher, his secretary and the only person at Gestapo headquarters with whom he communicated. He had handpicked and trained her to be his assistant, and for the last three years, she alone knew his system of information storage, and handled his secret files, which were kept locked in a large safe in her office. When papers had to been signed, it was her name that was used. There was a clear understanding between them that one of her primary functions was to protect the illusive nature of his identity, and she had never veered from this duty.

The conversation was characteristically brief. Kepler provided the minimum facts necessary before issuing precise instructions. He would call again at eight o'clock the following morning.

Confident that at the designated hour Fraulein Belcher would have the backgrounds on Bachmeier and von Ritter, as well as a few other more specific pieces of information that he'd requested, Kepler dressed leisurely, slipped his notebook into his jacket pocket, and went out of his room, locking the door carefully. He was quite hungry, and a tasty dinner in the kitchen with the domestic staff promised the probability of satisfying more than one need.

8

The short trip up to the small, secluded room in the rounded tower had been arduous for von Ritter. Due to the narrowness of the spiral staircase, Lena had him strapped to the back of one of the orderlies and carried up like a knapsack. Three or four times his inflamed stump hit against the handrail, exploding pain through the thin shroud of morphine. His groans echoed through the stone tower and were heard as far away as the kitchen deep in the bowels of the building. He would have been content to remain in the crowded, smelly room below, but the nurse who berated her helpers for their clumsiness ignored his pleas. He was exhausted and sweating profusely when they finally got him onto the bed and covered, and when the nurse came and gave him another injection, he remembered feeling grateful and relieved as he sank back into a mist of numbness, and then to sleep.

His sleep was again troubled. A cacophony of images rioted at will as he traveled through a surreal landscape composed of people and places he vaguely recognized, but couldn't always identify. It all took place with a backdrop of explosions, muffled at first but growing in intensity until the thunderous noise blocked out all else.

He awoke to find that the explosions were real. He heard the deep whine of low-flying aircraft traveling at high speed and the percussions of their fire. Less clear were the sounds of returning ground fire, mostly the pitiful crackle of hand weapons, which were of little use against the screaming fighters.

He tried to see out the window, but his view was in the wrong direction, so he had to content himself by following the action with his ears only. He could tell that there were just two planes. Yaks, he judged from the sound. They were making a series of passes at some target close by; then abruptly it ended, and the planes droned off into the distance.

It was quiet in his room now. He lay motionless, feeling hollow. The war didn't exist for him anymore, and he was left with the conviction that it had all been a waste of time. He had no attachments; there hadn't been time to make friends, only comrades in arms, and they always seemed to die anyway.

He rolled his head to look out the small, narrow window and could see the tops of the trees that bordered the old school's grounds. There was a gentle breeze, and on the tips of the thin uppermost branches of the naked beech trees, he thought he could see the little points of green that heralded the onset of spring weaving their own exotic dance of rebirth. The sky was cloudless and blue.

He remembered another time—how old was he, fifteen, sixteen?—back when the entire world was wonderful and immortality surged through his veins. There was a girl. Her name was Katarina. Hardened as he was now, he doubted that he ever loved her, but the lightness of their being now flooded upon him. He tried desperately to hold it, but the feeling faded, and a heavy longing filled his heart.

Throughout the war, surrounded by death, destruction, and defeat, he had clung to the belief that there was a noble purpose, and someday when it was all over, the happiness would return. But the war had crushed his spirit, just as it had devastated the landscape.

It was the lie that had finally devastated him. Everything had been done for counterfeit leaders with selfish goals, and now that all was lost, the great betrayal had begun. The small room, high up in the place that had once represented much of what was good, now resounded with the wailings of a broken man.

The tipping point was that frozen December day when his Kampfgruppe had swept into a small Belgium village on its disastrous attempt to break through the advancing Allied armies to the Meuse. Stavelot! There, he could even recall its name.

They dragged them from the cellars and bomb shelters, mostly old men, women, and children. There were angry questions: Where are you hiding the Americans? How many were there? Did they leave any weapons behind? Tell us! The panic-stricken Belgians only cringed and pleaded for mercy. They knew nothing, and this made it all the worse. He didn't know how it started, but suddenly, in an orgy of misguided frustration, he and his men engaged in a bloodbath.

At one point a woman was dragged past him. She was crying out for mercy; her poor children would have no mother. He forced himself to remember. It was necessary. He had to face it. Someone had walked up behind her. The barrel of a rifle was placed against the back of her neck. With a loud explosion, the woman's body flew forward, facedown in the snow. She fell at his feet, and his boots were covered with her blood. Moments later three children were thrown on top of her. The image was so vivid. Slowly, one of them raised his head and looked at him. There was no fear in the boy's face, but the eyes were big, round, and pleading. Aiming his handgun between those eyes, he pulled the trigger. The boy's head jerked back and then fell forward. The demon in his dreams lay in the mud at his feet.

There in the darkness of the small turret room the accusing eyes burned bright in his mind. Fever swept through his body. Mercifully, he passed into the peace of unconsciousness.

The delirium would last two days.

9

The next day, all morning long, a cruel wind roared off of the Baltic with malicious intensity, battering the defenseless plain, breaking apart the frozen crust of snow, and whipping up hard crystalline particles into blinding sheets of abrasive fury. It was the kind of wind that penetrates, stings, and numbs. People did not normally venture out into such weather, at least not by choice, and during saner times the road would certainly have been deserted. On this day, however, when the beasts of northern Germany were in their lairs, burrows, nests, and barnyards waiting out the storm, man was on the move.

In a great shuffling, huddled mass, worn out and worn down, the fleeing refugees clogged the roads, each individual pushed on by the one behind. They had had no choice but to suffer in the biting wind because behind the last German of this gigantic serpent came the Russian juggernaut, an army of a million men whose fellow countrymen had died at the hands of the German aggressors in extraordinary numbers, and in whose memory they now drove onward in search of retribution and revenge. When collective human passion reaches such monstrous propositions, even the harshest dictates of nature pale in comparison.

They had come from the east, the lucky ones who had survived so far. By ship, boat, and submarine they had escaped from the now encircled cities of Danzig and Konigsberg in East Prussia, enduring horrendous journeys across the Baltic in winter. By foot they had fled Pomerania and Poland, taking advantage of the escape corridor created by Himmler's militarily unsound east-west defensive deployment of the Army Group Vistula. They carried, pulled, and dragged whatever belongings they could, all piled high on bicycles, carts, wagons, and sleds, and as the distance and duration of their journey increased, even these treasured items became fewer and fewer, most discarded along the way. By now most carried only what they wore as they plodded silently across Germany.

So many had already died. Eight thousand alone perished when the ocean liner, *Wilhelm Gustloff*, was torpedoed just outside the Gulf of Danzig. Others simply froze by the side of the road and were left behind unceremoniously by family and friends, to be swept into the ditches and gutters and forgotten along with the other abandoned belongings of the miserable refugees. It wasn't unusual for those who brought up the rear of this desperate march to meet their end under the tracks of the massive Russian tanks.

Like a great river, little tributaries of human misery trickled onto the main roadways to combine and form larger flowing masses, all heading for the same destination. Funneled by the dynamics of the war, they headed toward and then through the only passage to the west, a bottleneck at the only remaining bridgehead over the Oder at the city of Stettin.

Ernst Kepler drove against the flow like a salmon desperate to spawn, east into the city. The closer he got, the more he struggled against this march of humanity. His normally cool temperament was ready to blow. The time he'd anticipated it would take to cover the distance to Stettin turned out to be optimistic by over three hours. Twenty kilometers outside the city he had joined a traffic jam of monumental proportion, which reduced his progress to a painstaking crawl, as hundreds of vehicles destined for the front with needed supplies and reinforcements joined in the chaotic struggle.

He'd been through this before and had learned to deal with it patiently. There was no choice; it was a fact of war. But this day was different, and the fact that he'd failed to even anticipate this kind of delay made his frustration worse. What little sympathy he might have once felt for the wretched flotsam of the war evaporated in the rising heat of his anger.

Sinking into a more relaxed slouch, and filling the car with the blue-gray smoke of the British cigarettes he chain-smoked at a frightening rate, he now reconsidered this plan. The one element, which he was determined to maintain, was the departure time. He wouldn't jeopardize his life by staying in Stettin any longer than one night, and if it meant abandoning his objective, so be it. If the search took him past dusk, he would at that time determine whether to continue in the dark or quit and return. At least he would have the multiple identities provided by Himmler. With this all settled in his mind and his patience restored, Kepler relaxed, content to let time take care of itself, as he crept northward to Stettin. In the late afternoon, he arrived in the embattled city and headed to the warehouse where von Ritter was to deliver his cargo.

Dusk deepened toward night, and the storm suddenly broke, its fury spent, and a great calm settled upon the beleaguered port of Stettin. The abrupt change in the weather created an illusion of almost balmy warmth, even though the temperature remained well below freezing. The Russians also seemed worn down by the mad dash across Eastern Europe that had seen them drive back the German army nearly five hundred kilometers in two months. Their guns were also silent this night.

It was in this rare stillness, where small sounds rang out with a hollow clarity, that Kepler picked his way in the growing darkness along a debris-strewn pier in search of the padlock that would turn to the key Himmler provided. His leather-soled shoes clapped the pavement and noisily crunched the shattered glass and broken concrete that lay everywhere. He moved swiftly, with little attempt to be quiet or furtive, because his blood, aroused by the sudden unmistakable scent of his quarry, was surging through his veins and pounding at his temples, and the adrenalin it released drowned all caution in a rising tide of excitement.

Located at the bottom of a high, slanted embankment of wet and slippery stone, the three piers jutted out like long elegant fingers into the harbor at an angle to match the ramp connecting the waterfront with the main transit road above. Each pier was about one hundred feet wide with a brick warehouse constructed the full length covering all but the quay area where capstans, cranes and other equipment for offloading cargo stood idle. Along each quay a lonely rail spur extended down the middle. A tall chain-link fence had been erected across the entrance to the piers with a large double gate secured by a heavy chain and lock. Unlike the rest of the port city that overflowed with transient humanity, behind this fence it was dark and menacingly deserted, but it was the sign that had raised his heartbeat. Attached to one of the gates, its message was direct. Beneath a black swastika set in a white circle, its warning was posted for all to read and obey:

Warning!
This Is a Restricted Area
Entry Is Strictly Forbidden without Proper Authorization
By Order of Sicherheitspolizei-Stettin
Reichssicherheitshauptamt
Schutzstaffel

As he approached the gate, he saw the padlock hanging open on the hasp—the first sign that either something was wrong or he was on the right track. Either way he would have to proceed with extreme caution.

As he picked his way along the pier in the inky darkness, Kepler felt a strong and ominous feeling that he was not alone. He paused to listen. He heard only the hollow noises of water slapping against the pilings and the distant cries of gulls that hung in the air. Whether it was from this foreboding feeling or the nervous excitement that had steadily increased from the first sight of this quiet pier, he felt a chill rising up against his skin. He tried to pretend it was only caused by the cold of the approaching night. But as he shivered inside his old overcoat, he knew the source of his discomfort came from within. Yet irresistibly he was drawn on.

Entry to the warehouse was accessed through sliding doors of heavy-gauge steel that rolled on tracks embedded in reinforced concrete-grade beams along the face of the building. A large padlock like the one at the gate typically secured these doors, but as Kepler approached the first of the three large gray doors evenly spaced on that side of the building, his excitement became acute, for in the dim light he could see the lock; it, too, hung open. For a moment he stood there, as though not quite believing what he was seeing. Then he quickly slid the lock out of the staple of the hasp and, placing his shoulder against the edge of the door, pushed gently to open it enough to let himself in. The door was in good shape, and to his relief, slid open with little noise.

Inside it was completely dark, but Kepler resisted using the flashlight that remained in his coat pocket. Instead, he stood just inside the door and listened. He waited without moving for a few minutes, the stillness of the huge structure oppressive and menacing around him. Gradually his eyes adjusted a bit, and as far as he could tell, the space appeared to be mostly empty. He turned on the flashlight, holding the beam end in the palm of his hand to limit its illumination of the area around him. Like a cold in summer, he couldn't shake the feeling that he had company. Here and there a barrel or crate lay scattered about, along with brooms, shovels, a ladder, and a few bundles of rope and cable— nothing of obvious significance. Unperturbed he set immediately to the task of patiently conducting a thorough search, starting at the end closest to the doorway he had just entered.

Inch by inch he covered the warehouse. Every crate, box, or other container was carefully examined inside and out as he slowly worked his way down the long building. Nothing was overlooked. But after ten minutes, when he had covered more than half the area, there was nothing to indicate that his quest would have a triumphant end. A little eye weary, he stopped next to a stack of crates to rub and close his eyes and give them a brief rest. At that moment he heard the warehouse door moving. He froze, held his breath, and snapped off the flashlight. The world went black. Looking over his shoulder, he saw the dancing beam of another flashlight, and his heart began to pound. Who sneaks around a secured warehouse in the night? Slowly he maneuvered behind the crates and squatted. He could hear the footsteps of the other intruder shuffling in his direction, and then they passed and continued toward the far end of the warehouse.

Cautiously he straightened and peered over the crates. There, at the far end of the restricted warehouse, gleaming in the beam of the other's flashlight, he could see the front end of an automobile, its two headlamps reflecting the light like two harvest moons. He was able to distinguish the little flags that hung limply above and slightly to the outside of each of these orbs. The twin lightning bolts told him here was his objective.

He heard the car door open and could see the light searching the interior. Kepler wondered who else would be interested in the car, von Ritter? He decided it was time to act. Quietly he crept toward the car

"Don't move." Kepler's voice was soft and low. "Very slowly place your hands on the dashboard and keep your eyes straight ahead." A slight nudge to the side of the head with the barrel of his 9 mm Walther provided a clear, strong emphasis to the order. He complied.

"Good. Now I suggest you remain perfectly still while I ask a few questions. You'll answer each one completely and truthfully. First of all, who are you?"

"Conrad, Wilhelm, corporal, Thirty-Second Ordnance Transport Division, Vistula Army Group."

"All right, Corporal, tell me what you are doing here in this restricted area."

"Why don't you tell me who you are and on what authority you're here," said Conrad.

"This"—another nudge—"is all the authority you need to know; however, if it'll make our discussion proceed more smoothly," said Kepler, "it should be sufficient to inform you that I'm here as part of an ongoing investigation by the Sicherheitspolizei. Now you'll just answer my questions, yes?" Kepler knew a mention of the Gestapo would produce a willing collaboration. He could already see beads of sweat gathered across the corporal's forehead. It was some time before he could answer.

"I was sent here by my sergeant to check this place out."

"Why?"

"We're getting clogged up. The ordnance we're bringing into Stettin isn't getting out fast enough, and we don't have anywhere to put it. Someone knew about this warehouse, and my sergeant sent me out to see if it was available."

"A restricted SS facility?" Kepler said incredulously.

"Why not?"

Kepler ignored the retort and asked another question. "What's the name of this resourceful sergeant of yours, the one who should know better than to disregard such a clear and sensitive restriction?"

"Gross, Fritz Gross."

"Did your sergeant know this was a secured facility, and if so, did he give you a key?"

The trap was set. If he had a key, it could only have come from von Ritter; this warehouse was a highly restricted location, and sergeants in the transport divisions didn't have access. He could see the reference to the key took Conrad by surprise and struck a sensitive nerve. It opened an avenue of discussion he was no doubt loath to follow. The vice was closing.

"Yes, sure."

"Where is this key?"

"In my coat pocket."

"Exactly which pocket?" Kepler's voice had developed an unpleasant edge.

"The right, I think."

"Would you please reach with your left hand and produce this key?"

Conrad started to take his left hand off the steering wheel, paused, slowly replaced it, and looked up at Kepler.

"Actually, I lied about the key. I didn't get it from Sergeant Gross. I got it from another source, and if you'll take that gun away from my head, I think we can come to some kind of mutually advantageous agreement."

Kepler didn't reply immediately; then he laughed, a smooth quiet laugh. "I hardly think you're in much of a position to bargain, but it might amuse me to hear your offer."

Conrad seemed to struggle to collect his thoughts, so Kepler gave one more little prod.

"Go ahead," he said, "I'm not a patient man. Perhaps you could start by telling me where you got the key."

"Yes," said Conrad dreamily. "The key. I got the key from an SS officer. He was hurt, and I took him to a hospital. He left it in my truck."

"Describe this officer," snapped Kepler.

"He was a lieutenant, tall, blond, wounded in the right knee, and the injury was bad. He was dressed in the SS black, and the cuff label indicated that he was a member of the Liebstandarte Adolf Hitler, but the uniform was muddy, torn, and disheveled, almost as if it had been worn into battle, and he had no hat."

"Where did you find this officer?"

"Here, in Stettin."

"Where, exactly?" There was a cold edge on the question.

"I was on my way to the depot. I was taking a shortcut from the ring road and going through an alley just on the other side of the frontage road that follows the river, not far from here. He fell out of a doorway right in front of my truck. He was lucky I stopped in time."

"When did this happen?"

"Day before yesterday."

"That would be Monday. At what time?"

"In the afternoon, maybe one o'clock. I was already late for reporting in with my load. I was due by noon. I should have run him over."

"But you didn't. You said you took him to a hospital?"

"Wasn't my idea. I was just going to drag him out of the way so I could get on my way, but he had a gun."

"And the lieutenant had no intention of being left to die in the alley. Strange, isn't it that a badly wounded man should be waiting in an out-of-the way place like your little alley. It would make more sense for him to get out on the main road where he would be more readily seen and helped. Correct me if I'm wrong, but it almost sounds like he ambushed you."

"I couldn't say," Conrad replied to the faceless comment.

The next question shot out of the dark as if drawn by his very thoughts. "Where did you take him? Which hospital?"

"If you don't already know, you won't learn from me. At least not without us coming to some kind of understanding."

"So that's the deal," said Kepler with a chuckle. "Well, Corporal Conrad, I regret to inform you that the Gestapo doesn't make this kind of deal. You've already provided me with some excellent information, and the few facts you're withholding will only cause me a minor inconvenience. You've narrowed the scope of my search more than you'll ever understand. There will be no bargaining. I have no further use for you, although a complete divulgence would make my job easier for me, and your death considerably easier for you. You understand that you must die."

Conrad blurted out a last desperate message. "No. The lieutenant is probably dead by now. He had gangrene. Listen. Do you think I'm that stupid? If I die, you'll never know what he told me."

Conrad squeezed his eyes shut, and his whole body trembled as he waited for the blast he would never hear.

■ ■ ■

Far in the distance a Russian officer delivered the order to fire. Simultaneously, six large field guns exploded with mighty roars, sending their fused shells hurling through space in a giant arc. The calculations had been good, and as velocity declined, the shells began their descents toward the designated targets, screaming out their eminent arrival in a piercing whistle.

Down on the ground, inside the dark warehouse, the two men heard the warning of the incoming shells, but there was nothing they could do about it. Seconds later the building was rocked by a massive explosion as the two-hundred-pound shell detonated, sending fire and molten destruction throughout the interior.

10

Lieutenant Johann von Ritter slipped into his fever-racked coma three days after he went rogue, hijacked Himmler's Mercedes, and along with his driver, crashed into a muddy, frozen ditch. For the next forty-eight hours, he struggled through a nightmarish labyrinth of distorted and disconnected images. Fugitives from deep within his memory were assembled as if someone had filmed his entire life, then hacked up the cellulose, and spliced it all back together randomly for this special showing. And while he lingered enticingly close to death throughout this unconscious performance, the eyes of Stavelot didn't return.

In the delirium, people from his childhood were transported into unreal scenes and places. School friends playing soldiers were suddenly confronted by real tanks rolling through their fantasy game, leaving everything charred and flat. When the boys cried out "water"—water meaning the "dead" playmates were now allowed to rejoin the game—the bodies didn't spring up as they were supposed to. Next, he was in a field by a stonewall, or it might have been a long mound of rubble in a bombed-out city. There was a girl. They were laughing and kissing, but when he looked into her face it was blank, except for a thin-lipped frowning mouth, like an unfinished angry marionette. She laughed at him. He grabbed her by the throat and shook as hard as he could. Enough. No more senselessness. She only laughed louder until he could stand it no longer, and he ran away, calling for his mother, longing to rest his head upon her breast and feel her protective arms encircle him. Briefly he seemed to be there. He couldn't see her, but he felt her soft hair brushing lightly against his face, and he recognized the warmth and comfort. Too soon that dissolved into nothing.

The dreams went on and on. Now and then he was vaguely aware of the presence of others, but they were translucent and dark. They, too, faded in and out of the rambling confusion that composed the landscape he now inhabited.

One of these equivocal shadows was Lena, who hovered like an anxious mother bird, tending and nursing him through the life and death ordeal. She did so secretly, without proper authority, and in disregard of the personal consequences. She suffered in many ways and headed perilously toward collapse because she wouldn't let this clandestine activity interfere with the performance of her regular duties, and these she did at her usual level of thoroughness. As the hours slipped past, exhaustion descended like a great suffocating cloud, yet she continued. His survival became her salvation.

It was Lena's face that von Ritter vaguely perceived on the few brief occasions that he returned to the edge of his prolonged nightmare, and when he lapsed back into the depths of unconsciousness, he carried with him that image—a face with calm and clear blue eyes. Tranquility slowly spread and made his dreams softer, and the specters of fear, doubt, and disillusionment faded. Finally the ordeal ended, and von Ritter sank into deep, restful sleep. Lena's efforts were rewarded when the fever broke shortly before sunrise on the second day. It was Thursday, March 15, 1945.

Von Ritter awoke to find himself alone. The return to consciousness had been slow and reluctant. He lay motionless, wrapped in a new calmness; his spirit had climbed out of the deep chasm of despair away from the ghosts that had haunted his dreams since Stavelot.

With clarity he knew his purpose. There was one final task. How many days had he been in the hospital? Three? Four? Maybe more. It had been impossible for him to keep track of things—the drugs, the fever, the operation—and now time was running out. Act he must, or the fateful course of action he'd undertaken; the direct breach of orders; the deceit; the death of the driver, Bachmeier; and even his own loss would be wasted.

His eyes drifted down to the writing paper and fountain pen lying on the bedside table. Painfully, he raised himself until he could lean back against the wall in a sitting position. The effort drained him, and for many minutes he remained still, feeling his weakness. Then he reached over, picked up the implements, and began to write.

It was late in the morning when he paused from the letter he was writing.

His isolation for whatever reason was a blessing, but whenever he tried to figure it out, the dreams and realities of the last few days only coalesced into a confusion of images. Vaguely he remembered the painful journey up the spiral staircase and before that another room, one with cots and patients. There was a doctor and a nurse. He recalled the nurse; she'd commanded the ascent of the stairs. Her image, unlike everything else, stood clear in his mind and lingered there. He couldn't remember what they'd said, but he was certain that he'd embarrassed himself and exposed weakness. This momentary masculine hang-up quickly faded and was replaced by a more primal response, a stirring in his groin, a feeling he hadn't had for a long time. This surprised and pleased him. His recollection was of stern but not unpleasant features and a shapely body, and as he dwelt on these thoughts, he hardened.

He smiled and once again turned his attention with renewed energy to the letter, and the simple ingenious plan he'd devised to ensure his secret reached the only persons who would understand the significance of what he had done, and why. This letter, the first of two, to his sister would hold half the clues. There would be a second written to his friend and commander, Jochen Peiper. Only with both letters together could the strongbox be located. This way, if either letter fell into the wrong hands, his secret would at least die with him.

It took him another few minutes to complete the first letter. He read it again.

March 1945

Loco Imperatoris, Tiergarten, 37.2°

Dearest Hilde,

By the time you get this letter, if indeed you do, you will know that I am dead. I write to you badly wounded in field hospital near the eastern front, expecting the Russians to arrive soon. When they do, I will die.

Some days ago, I was entrusted with orders from none other than HH (I will not honor him with any of his official titles) to deliver a small strongbox to a warehouse in Stettin. But he is a rat fleeing a sinking ship, and for the first time in my military life, I disobeyed an order. HH will not find his filthy contraband waiting for him. It has been diverted, and only I know where it is.

I want the truth to be known and the rat to receive his due. You must help. But I fear for your safety, as this is a dangerous course I have taken. My initial thought was to tell you the hiding place in this letter, but I realize that such knowledge could put you or anyone who has it in harm's way. Should this letter fall into the wrong hands, what I have done and risked could be for nothing. So I have tried to be clever, I hope not too clever.

I have written already to an old friend, and if he gets that letter, you may expect him to contact you. Together, you may be able to locate the hoard.

I am unhappy to be putting this burden on you, but I have no better idea.

Please think well of me, and do not grieve.

> HIER RUHT IN GOTT
> UNSER LIEBER SOHN

Your loving brother,
Johann

With these mysterious instructions written, he finished off the letter wishing her well, and asking her not to grieve.

As he wrote, a small dark cloud hung over his thoughts, casting a meandering shadow across the landscape of an otherwise perfect day. Something was stirring in his head, a memory, a warning. His mood wavered. His brow creased as he tried to make out the source of his concern. Putting the letter aside, he slid down off the pillows. This careless movement sent bolts of fire up through the stump, and he cursed himself. The morphine was wearing off.

He knew the nature of that dark cloud. No matter what he did now, the great betrayal had left a gaping hole that no amount of revenge could ever fill. Somewhere he had made a wrong turn and chosen a dead end. He was lost. For Johann von Ritter, there could be no absolution; his downfall was in his breeding.

He was only three when his father drowned in a boating accident. His yacht was struck by lightning off the coast of Schleswig-Holstein and had sunk, taking Friedrich von Ritter and his Italian mistress with it. The year was 1923.

Only three years old, Johann naturally didn't understand death; all he knew was that his grandfather, Mathias, made a decision that would affect both their lives. The old man took Johann into his home and raised him. It was from Mathias that he heard all those wondrous tales that had been passed from generation to generation. For him, these weren't legends and myths; they were truths. Grandpapa had told him again and again that the gods exist in the trees and stones and waters that cover the land. They watch and wait. "And you, Johann, have been chosen to learn and carry these truths into the future," and he'd believed it.

Even as a boy, he'd committed himself, body and soul, to live the life of a warrior, dedicated to the cause of the great German leader, who'd dared to resurrect the essence of the gods of old—the heroic Teutonic gods—who for so long had patiently hidden deep within the universal German soul. Like those ancestors of the mysterious forests, he now resolved to follow as best he could the truly heroic path, but this war had crushed the myth.

Death to the warrior was heroic, but modern war wasn't. A dead hero was not supposed to be thrown into a pit and quickly covered over. He was buried next to his comrades, who sent him off with solemn ritual. A hero wasn't torn apart grotesquely, raw flesh exposed, screaming like a tortured animal. No, a hero was supposed to die quickly, uttering some last noble, patriotic phrase. A dead hero wasn't left lying upon the boiling Russian steppes, bloated and black, dried into lime-covered mummies, hissing and sputtering like hideous ghosts in the night as the foul gases escaped from the open wounds. Heroes weren't meant to be a home for thousands of worms that oozed from their corpses. Heroes never suffered the horror of Stavelot and the confusion and disorientation. There were no heroes in real war, this he now knew, only *Zerrissenheit*, disillusion, contradiction, inner strife, and a painful sense of dissonance. The ancestors had been betrayed. He'd been betrayed, and it was up to him to do what was necessary to regain and avenge the warrior within.

Anger filled his heart, and from it came a strengthened resolve. Destiny, he realized, wasn't necessarily the same road as salvation, and he was perfectly aware that the future wasn't completely out of his hands.

The choice was his, and he had no doubt that the most important thing was to fulfill his oath and finish his life, a warrior to the end. The ordeal of the last few months had been a test, but he had come through. He wouldn't lose his honor.

His mind was alive. Never would he have believed that the fate of Heinrich Himmler, one of the most powerful men in the world, would rest so certainly in his hands. How did he come to this point? What was he to do?

He was vaguely aware of distant footsteps coming up the stairs, but their presence hardly registered because a vision had taken possession of his mind. He saw himself as the mighty Hagan. His ordeal matched that of this legendary Teutonic warrior. It was incredible, dazzling. The Nibelungen Hoard had passed into his hands. He had betrayed the trust of its villainous master, stabbing him in the back as in the past, and now, like Hagan, the secret of its resting place was his alone. He saw all this in one fleeting explosive moment, and it filled him with a resolve and a surging sensation of power. He shot forward off the wall, erect from the waist up. Unlike the mythical warrior, von Ritter still had the opportunity to ensure its hiding place remained alive.

In the clutches of his revelation, he didn't hear the door open nor see the white-clad figure enter his room. When he did look up, he recognized Dr. Paul Reisen.

At the same time that von Ritter began to write, battered transports with rough red crosses painted on the tops of faded canvas covers waited in the dim grayness of the early morning in a long line at the west anchorage of a narrow triple-arch bridge. The graceful architecture and fine stone craftsmanship of this old structure went unnoticed by the captain in charge, who sat nervously in his lead vehicle, a war-worn half-track, waiting for the men ahead to complete the task of clearing off the remaining refugees. He was anxious to begin the mad dash to the southeast. All night the Russians had mercilessly bombarded the port city, a sure indication that there was worse to come. This old bridge of stone was the only bridgehead on the east bank of the Oder, and there was no doubt as to what the enemy's main objective would be. The worried officer had no desire to find himself trapped should they take the bridge before he completed his mission. The damned hospital better have everything ready to go, he thought.

Finally, through the mixed haze of smoke, morning mist, and pulverized dust, he detected a dim silhouette loping along the side of the bridge in his direction. As he watched, the shape grew and slowly transformed into the distinguishable figure of an infantryman. In a few moments, the soldier finally halted at the side of his vehicle.

"All clear, Captain." There was no salute, nor did the man wait for a response. He immediately turned and headed off back across the bridge and disappeared into the gloom. The captain stood, made a large sweeping gesture with his arm, and sat down again. "Okay, Max," he quietly said to his driver, "let's go."

With a loud backfire, the half-track lurched forward. The bridge would be in Russian hands by the end of that day, but the captain couldn't have known this.

11

It was sunny that morning, but Paul Reisen hardly noticed nature's rare benevolence. It was possible the change in the weather did intrude momentarily upon his concentration, perhaps when a few drops of perspiration eluded the careful attention of the assisting nurse and ran behind his glasses into his eye. He had been that way for a long time, oblivious. Somewhere in his mind it might have registered that it was warmer than usual. Looking up, he saw the door had been propped open to allow the pungent smells of blood and death to exhaust to the outside, but these thoughts were fleeting. He continued, otherwise unaffected, probing for another piece of black, jagged shrapnel in the mangled confusion of what was once a young stomach, and after stitching together the great gaping wound with less precision than a peasant mending old clothes, he moved on to the next one. He had no time for more skillful closings, let alone allowing himself to enjoy the sensual pleasures that a fresh spring morning offers. One or two more patients, he decided, were all he would treat before he would have to abandon the operating area, leaving the rest of the exhausted staff even more shorthanded.

The nurse by his side, the one who had failed to intercept his sweat, uttered a matter-of-fact exclamation. "No pulse."

Automatically, Reisen applied the stethoscope and listened for a heartbeat. There was none. Lifting the patient's eyelids, he confirmed the obvious. Two other pairs of eyes looked over surgical masks at his, knowing already what his decision would be. He nodded and, with a slight sideways gesture of his head, indicated they would leave this one for the orderlies and moved down to the next table where another man laid waiting. High-output surgery. Reichsminister Speer, the maestro of armaments and war production, would be proud of this production line, he thought humorlessly.

They moved slowly, carrying their instruments with them. The nurse produced a reasonably clean towel and used it to wipe them off, and with a little more preparation, the next procedure was underway, this one another shattered leg. Pre-op had consisted of cutting away the man's pant leg and a hasty sponging of the area to remove the worst of the matted blood and dirt. Reisen took a couple of seconds to assess the wound and, drawing a line with his finger, informed his assistants with a tired voice that they would remove the leg, close up the main arteries, and bandage it tightly. Fortunately the man was already unconscious, and they didn't have to use any of the precious chloroform.

It took all of fifteen minutes, and when he was done, Reisen removed his mask and handed it to the nurse.

"I have to go now. Captain Elser is waiting. Do what you can."

For once, the stream of patients had an end. Captain Elser had agreed to close the gates and post guards to direct incoming traffic away from the hospital. Reisen had told him that this would be the only way to gain sufficient time to prepare for the evacuation, but even with this measure in place, the staff had found it necessary to work through the night in a desperate attempt to stabilize as many of the wounded as possible. Damned little else had been done to otherwise get ready for the evacuation.

As he headed toward Elser's office, the full weight of his fatigue hit home. Physically, he was a wreck. His eyes burned. His back ached, and it seemed as if every joint in his body was stiff. Every step was an effort, and he could expect no relief for quite sometime. Even during the long winter in Russia he'd not been so extended.

Paul Reisen was a tall, slender man with a sharp aquiline nose, high forehead, and an arrogant bearing that emitted a perpetual air of condescension even when none was intended. He strode about his duties with the firm resolve of one who believed completely in his superiority and the correctness of his beliefs. All of his life there had never been reason to doubt this truth.

His father was a fervent Nazi, his party number low enough to both highlight the rarity of his membership in a predominately working-class organization and to substantiate the claim that he was among the marchers on November 9, 1923, when Hitler attempted the infamous Putsch. Paul, like his father, was extraordinarily proud of these facts. It wasn't unexpected, therefore, when he followed his father's example, joining the Nazi party at the age of ten by entering the Jungvolk, the "cub" organization of the Hitler Jungend, whose doctrines he consumed eagerly.

In 1939 he entered the venerable University of Munich to study medicine, a decision that surprised many of his friends who had logically expected him to enter a military academy. As he immersed himself in his studies, he knew only that the Germany for which he felt such pride and love had become strong and directed. Its people were better off than they had ever been. It was a light to hold up before the entire world, and it was all because of the Führer and the party.

Even after war arrived to darken the landscape, he remained convinced that his beliefs were right. He did not waver, not even in the horrible winter of 1943, where deep in the ice-bound steppes of Russia the soul of the German army was torn out and devoured before his eyes; nor during the yearlong retreat, when hundreds of thousands of deaths screamed before his heart; nor after the loss of his mother and father to the invisible whistling British bombs. None of these could change his faith. None of this could open his eyes, because he willed it that way and had developed a shield that seemed impenetrable.

At some point a seed of doubt germinated and grew in Paul Reisen's mind. Imperceptible at first, but feeding on a rich and increasing diet of stark and brutal images, it sprouted and spread its tendrils like ivy on a wall until it choked and killed the lie. When it finally arrived, Reisen's crash was harder than most, because he had believed fiercely and practiced accordingly and waged the longest battle.

It happened that fine morning somewhere between the makeshift operating area in the old school's front hall and Elsner's office. He couldn't see Elsner right then or throw himself into the task of organizing the evacuation. He was on a quickly sinking ship.

He wandered the building mindlessly, searching for an anchor, a home port, a place to come in for a landing, a quiet place to think. He found himself drawn away from the frequented areas to the quiet clock tower, to the door of von Ritter's room. He turned the handle and entered, closing the door quickly behind him. At first he didn't realize he was not alone.

Neither man had expected the sudden intrusion, and for some time they each paused, suspended in time, confused, hoping the other would go away. It was von Ritter who finally spoke. His voice, though strained from exhaustion, had an edge of excitement to it.

"You've come, Herr Doctor. I thought you'd forgotten me."

In his malaise Reisen had forgotten the gangrenous lieutenant or their brief exchange two days before. Von Ritter was nothing but an unwanted occupant of this sanctuary, and Reisen fought to contain his resentment as he reached for the doorknob, intending to leave.

"I'm sorry; I'm in the wrong place. Excuse me but I must go. The nurse will be along soon."

If Reisen's reaction to this chance reunion was completely lacking in recognition, von Ritter's, on the other hand, was one of surprise and expectation. Reisen's appearance took on deep meaning. Von Ritter knew it was fate, work of the gods. Fragments of their previous encounter were rushing back. This was the doctor who got him the writing materials, and here he was again.

"Stop." He snapped out the command with authority, abruptly halting Reisen's departure. "Doctor, your arrival here was no mistake. Forces far beyond our ability to comprehend destined it. You must believe me. You were sent to me. This I know."

Slowly Reisen shut the door and turned toward von Ritter.

"Please explain," he said softly.

Ten minutes later Reisen left von Ritter for the last time. A change had taken place. Calmness had replaced confusion and doubt. It wasn't important whether or not he believed the fantastic story told by the strange officer. All that mattered was he'd been given a new opportunity, a small one to be sure, but one that fit his need at that desperate moment in his life.

As he descended the spiral staircase, he placed his right hand in the pocket of his blood-spattered overcoat and cupped it under the letter he'd promised to deliver, comforted by its presence. He allowed his thoughts to turn to the immediate task of managing the looming evacuation, which was the first step in keeping that promise.

The evacuation was on, and he immediately became fully occupied with the effort to the exclusion of all else. His first stop had been Elsner's office where he found the weary captain standing over a signalman, who was repeatedly trying to contact someone, anyone, in Stettin.

"Have they left yet?" he barked.

"I don't know," Elsner replied. "We haven't been able to contact them. The city is under heavy attack, but we must assume they left at the designated time."

"Which was?"

"Eight hundred hours."

"My God," bellowed Reisen, "they could arrive at any moment."

He didn't wait for any reply from the captain. Charging out of the office, he spent the next ten minutes rounding up every doctor, nurse, orderly, and soldier he could find and, with a manic urgency, began the process of preparing the hospital for the arrival of the transports. He made the simple decision to take all the medicine and supplies they could load in two trucks and then separate the wounded into two categories, those who could walk and those who couldn't. The ambulatory patients would be directed to the back door of the building, and those who had to be carried were to be taken to the front hall and the corridors that led to it. He sent a couple of men to the gates with instructions to direct the incoming vehicles to the front of the building. They would load everyone they could.

Having set this plan into action, he returned to Captain Elsner's office. He didn't know how big a convoy was heading their way. It was more than likely that the number of vehicles would be woefully few, and if there was insufficient transportation for all personnel, they had better have a priority list worked out. Who would be ordered to stay behind and tend to the patients unfortunate enough to be able to walk? The obvious decision was to have the women, nurses, and others go with the first wave. More difficult was the assignment of the male staff, including himself. He entered Elsner's office hoping it was not a decision that would have to be made.

12

As Reisen circled down the dimly lit stairwell and faded out of sight, Lena, who'd been standing in the hallway a few feet back from the second-floor opening, darted unseen in behind and scurried anxiously up the stairs in the opposite direction. Her concern was not that her extraordinary secret had been discovered. If anything, she felt relieved that it was over and that she had luckily avoided a confrontation with her superior. That would come later, when she was better prepared to defend herself without guilt or fear.

It had been more than six hours since she last visited von Ritter, an unforgivable span of time—far too long for a patient in his condition—for which she angrily blamed herself. The burden of the last few days, the flood of wounded driven by the Russian storm, had drained the hospital staff to the point of total collapse, and Lena had worked harder than anyone, carrying out all of her regular duties as well as making the frequent trips up to the clock tower. Finally, her reserves consumed, she'd involuntarily succumbed and slept.

Now, grim faced with unfocused eyes, she continued to the tiny landing, her emotions in a jumble. This was weakness, she thought, allowing these feelings to impinge upon her performance. It was a new experience for her, and she had no idea why. She'd been rousted out of her mental redoubt and freed of its inhibiting constraints. Driven by the exhilaration of being so exposed, she was drawn to the young lieutenant by unfamiliar urges; time was so precariously short.

She was at his door. Her hand reached to open it, then abruptly fell to her side. She stood upright and rigid, her face inches from the age-darkened wood grain, as she struggled to compose herself before entering. Then, with a deep sigh, she entered the room.

To her surprise, the resplendent light that filled the small chamber greeted her. During his coma she had kept the heavy wooden shutters closed and the room dark. This unexpected change caused her to pause just long enough for von Ritter to speak first.

"Dr. Reisen said you were an excellent nurse, but I hardly expected such a lightning response. Needless to say, I am impressed and pleased."

He smiled, but with these words what little strength he had left was spent. He'd pushed himself as upright as he could when she entered the door, but now he collapsed back, unable to move.

His brief smile had grabbed at her heart. He was alive and conscious. The fever had dissipated and the gangrene had arrested, but a muffled groan told her the morphine had worn off and a new dose was needed. She worked rapidly, breathing heavily, her jaw clamped tight as adrenalin surged through her body. She didn't care about Dr. Reisen's opinion.

The lieutenant now lay peacefully asleep, his face relaxed, almost smiling, and despite the matted, tousled hair and week-old beard, his beauty struck her more than ever. Reaching out, she brushed the blond locks off his forehead, then leaned down and gently kissed his smooth skin, as a mother would when saying goodnight to her sleeping child. She, too, was smiling, and while she changed the soiled bandage on his leg, she absently hummed a long-forgotten lullaby.

From far in the distance, a faint whine entered the room, growing steadily louder as it vibrated in her ear. Moments later it had grown into a violent, window-shaking roar as a group of low-flying aircraft thundered across the treetops past the old school. As she sat hunched over the lieutenant grittily attending to the task at hand, wave after wave followed, all heading west, shattering the magical interlude with their presence. By the time the sound of the last plane had faded and merged with the general rumble of the war, she had completed her dressing. She pulled up the blanket and left the room in search of Dr. Reisen.

She had expected a difficult confrontation, but it never happened. In fact, except for one brief glimpse of him later that morning as he passed through one of the many corridors, she didn't see Paul Reisen again. In the half hour she'd spent in von Ritter's room, Reisen had charged forward upon the enormous task of preparing for the last-minute evacuation with frenzy.

He was still with Elsner when Lena descended from von Ritter's room. The suddenness of the evacuation's implementation caught her by surprise, and despite the urgency of her quest for Reisen, she couldn't avoid being drawn into the operation. Those who now toiled in disarray expected her leadership, and soon she found herself supervising and coordinating their efforts.

This time she was determined not to forget her lieutenant, and while she darted about the corridors, organizing and encouraging her nurses with all the cool efficiency they had come to expect from their senior nurse, she also quietly and discreetly made her own secret preparations. Before an hour had passed, she filled a pillowcase with a few carefully selected supplies and hid it in the nurses' room located near the back stairs on the second floor.

She guessed some kind of transportation was coming, but knowing the way things were, she had little expectation of a massive, orderly operation. Immediately after she tucked the bulging pillowcase into a corner, behind a worn and faded overstuffed armchair, she went in search of an orderly to help her bring down the lieutenant.

It was at that moment that the first bomb landed just outside the building. With one great rumbling blast, it destroyed forever the large statue of Chancellor Bismarck mounted on an equally massive charger. This colossal though grotesque tribute to the heroic man was all muscles and sinew, no doubt inspired by the work of Josef Thorak, though it lacked even a small spark of the creativity and form of that Hitler favorite. It had been erected in the late fall of 1933, the year the Nazis came to power, and had dominated the long driveway ever since. The explosion also shattered numerous windows adjacent to the point of impact and threw the hospital into further panic and chaos.

Lena had just stepped off the back stairwell onto the ground floor and was heading toward the main hall went the bomb hit. She didn't hear the dreadful warning whistle, and its sudden violent impact caught her completely unprepared. The explosion shook the building, and Lena crumbled to her knees and cascaded forward, hitting her forehead on the stone floor. There was blackness with little streaks of light shooting in all directions. This light show gradually diminished, and her vision returned. It wasn't the first time she'd been stunned like this. Quickly she regained her senses, but the pain remained, throbbing as if a gigantic motor had been turned on in her head.

She heard screams and shouting coming from the direction of the main hall and knew what the situation must be; the large vestibule had been crowded with the most critical patients waiting for the convoy. She struggled to her feet and ran awkwardly through the dust-filled corridor toward the front of the building.

High above her, resting in a morphine-induced sleep, von Ritter lay for the moment forgotten.

As she entered the hall, she punctured a gray haze of pulverized dust, which filled the space and obliterated the vestibule beyond. She paused, peering into this choking cloud just as a terrifying shape staggered out of its opaqueness, clutching at the air with outstretched arms and groaning; then it collapsed. A feeling of complete despair broke over Lena as she knelt beside the prone body, whom she recognized as another nurse. Fighting back the urge to scream, she gently rolled her cohort onto her back and pulled the nurse's bloody hand away from the wound. It was impossible to see the extent of the damage.

"Water, we need some water over here," she called out. But when she looked about to see if anyone had heard her, she knew she was wasting her time.

Confusion was everywhere, and she realized she would have to fetch what she needed herself. Her knees throbbed as she pushed herself up onto her feet. A wave of dizziness hit her, and she had to grab the side of a nearby operating table to steady herself before cautiously negotiating her way to a sink that had been added to the main hall when it was converted three years ago. She filled a bowl with water and returned to where she'd left the wounded nurse.

She wiped away the dust and blood and could now see that one eye was lost. She needed bandages. Lena painfully got to her feet and looked around her.

The dust had settled and the confusion had evolved into a hectic, fast-paced process of damage assessment and treatment. Chaos had been contained. She looked toward the vestibule and out through the gaping entry to where the mangled remains of the Iron Chancellor now stood like a hellish silhouette against the dull afternoon sky. Her eyes were attracted by movement far in the distance at the bottom of the driveway.

As she watched, the object came into focus, and she realized it was the lead vehicle of the evacuation force, which had just turned in through the gate and was approaching the building at great speed. My God, she thought. Johann!

Lena Mueller froze with indecision, her jaw muscles clenched tight and a grim mouth darkening her pale face. The evacuation convoy was hurtling up the driveway, and the lead vehicle had already swerved around the ruined memorial and was screeching to a halt outside the fractured entry. At her feet lay the nurse, half blinded and bleeding.

In a person's life there can be many paths to the future. Sometimes they're wide boulevards presenting an easy choice; other times they're nearly invisible, momentary fissures through which an unsuspecting traveler will fall, often without ever knowing of the change. One such crack had at that very moment opened in front of Lena Mueller. Had she answered her heart's pounding summons and fled the raging hall she may well have passed through, but the brief hesitation was all the time it took for the passage to close with sudden finality.

"Nurse Mueller." The far-off voice burst the bubble around her thoughts and pushed her irretrievably into the journey that was to be her fate. The voice came from a distance, sharp and loud. She turned toward the grand stairway, but with all the chaos around her, she couldn't make out its source.

"Nurse Mueller, up here."

Looking up at the landing of the second floor, she saw two figures standing at the railing directly over the swastika flag. It was Reisen and Elsner.

"She's in the way. You have to move her. Quickly, there's no time to waste." It was Reisen, and to reinforce the message, a new voice from behind her shouted back to him.

"I've got a half-track and three Sankas," the speaker shouted, using the short name for the Sanitatskraftwagen, the small, white buses made by Opel for the specific purpose of carting the wounded to and from the fronts. Lena turned to see a dust-covered soldier looking up at the doctor and captain as he shouted.

"There are four more trucks somewhere, but we lost contact with them ten kilometers back. God knows if they'll ever get here. The air is thick with Yaks, and Russian pilots don't respect a red cross. I intend to pull out of here in twenty minutes, and any of your wounded not loaded at that time will be left. I mean it."

This outburst of edgy tension was followed by a brief pause as the excited officer calmed, and with a small, apologetic smile, he waved his arm and added, "So, Captain, tell me what I can do to help."

Lena saw in this man's haggard face a fierce tautness that added keenness to his words. There was no mistaking that he intended to do exactly what he said. Automatically she went into action, her mind clear for the moment.

"Then help me move this one," she ordered. "We'll put her on that table where she can have the head wound dressed."

Together they raised her from the floor and carried her the short distance to the vacant table. The officer held the nurse with one arm under her back, her head carefully nestled against his chest, and used his other arm to sweep the dust and debris that had showered down after the explosion from the top of the table. Then they carefully laid her down.

Reisen and Elsner had descended into the hall. The two Wehrmacht officers saluted, shook hands, exchanged names—the newly arrived man's being Schleckter—and then turned and strode away toward the front entry. Reisen stopped briefly to look at the injured nurse.

"Don't spend a lot of time," he said softly. "Clean the wound, get it covered, and have her put in one of the Sankas. If we make it out of here, I'll make sure she gets immediate attention there. We've got a lot of patients to move, and I need you to direct traffic in the vestibule." Then he was gone.

Lena looked at the nurse.

As she stood over her wounded cohort, she realized she could no longer be the somnambulist, sleepwalking through the suffering, alone in her manufactured fortress, blind to the misery and insanity that had taken her family and now perhaps this nurse, a comrade and friend. The whole revolting, senseless carnage that this war had brought upon her world could no longer be endured. There, in the savaged school, the discipline of a trained and hardened professional, behind which she had hidden for so long, was undone. It fell away at that moment, and her heart opened.

One by one, long-submerged emotions flowed through in quick succession. First was anger, at herself and at those around her who went on grimly fighting, loyally bleeding and dying, believing in victory or, even worse, in the righteousness of it all. They had only to open their eyes and receive the truth. Nothing, her mind screamed, justified the slaughterhouse that her country had become.

Longing followed anger, and she realized she wanted out and how impossible that was. Death, she thought, offered salvation, but she despised death as much as the war; they were one and the same. That was the epiphany: she could not give in to the war and its leaders, those ridiculous and sinister little men who had forced it upon them, or to the base and inhumane emotions that it dredged up from a dark, savage past.

Her reverie dissolved at the sound of the death scream of a wounded aircraft as it hurled toward the earth, forcing those who heard it to pause, hardly breathing, eyes tracking the agonized cry as it crossed the sky, anticipating the final confirming explosion. Lena heard the fiery descent of the wounded Yak, its pilot already a bloody corpse, as it traced a line directly over the top of the school, barely missing the clock tower, and ended with a huge explosion fifty yards from the driveway in the trees. Moments later, a streak of silver flashed by the upper windows of the building, and as the American fighter lifted over the trees, it wiggled its wings, turned sharply to the west, and disappeared. Lena returned her attention to the nurse.

She was dead. She had died without saying good-bye. All around her there were people—good people, soldiers, doctors, nurses, hospital staff—but no one had time to care. She was just another corpse occupying a space better used by someone still alive. A soldier and an orderly stopped at the table. Without a word they lifted the body and carried it off to the back corner of the hall. The orderly covered it with a sheet, then left. Lena watched, knowing there was nothing more to do but wanting to, so she stood by the table where her friend had died, determined not to return to the war business as usual, yet undecided as to what else she should do.

The sound of the motors sputtering to life drew her attention to the front entrance. Centered in the massive oak frame, the two Wehrmacht officers and Reisen were grouped in animated conversation. The smoke from Bismarck's statue whisked about behind them. Suddenly the small conference broke up, and Reisen with Elsner disappeared down the stairs. That was the last time Lena ever saw Paul Reisen.

Moments later the half-tracks and ambulances moved forward, circled the smoldering monument, and headed down the drive.

Lena stood numbly looking out the front entrance of Clarey Gymnasium. The last truck of the convoy faded out of sight into the chilling gray haze of the sinking afternoon light, and her gaze drifted aimlessly to the wreckage of Bismarck's statue. She had no perception of time. It might have been seconds or hours. Eventually a bitter breeze arose. She shuddered and emerged from her trance. Slowly she turned and, ignoring the other abandoned men and women—the flotsam at the edge of the evaporating Reich—who wandered aimlessly about her, she picked her way though the vestibule across the main hall and began to climb the stairs. With each step her pace quickened until she was running by the time she reached the second floor. With tears nearly blinding her vision, Lena ran to the back stairs. Scrambling, tripping, and crawling, oblivious to any physical pain, she staggered on to reach the singular haven upon which her mind was now locked. Upward she climbed, without shame or restraint, driven by a compelling desperation.

The door seemed to burst open before her, and she heard a voice, her voice, call out his name. She saw him; he seemed so far away, as if viewed backward through a telescope. He slept. She was lying beside him, holding the unconscious body in her arms, trying to find a place of peace. Warmth and softness flowed into her, comforting and sedating. She closed her eyes, and with a sense of falling, a wonderful lightness filled her, and she, too, slept.

13

The afternoon wore on and night began to fall, which was just fine with Corporal Jamie Turnbull. It meant the cold, depressing search would soon be over, and they would be marching him back to the compound and dinner. Not that dinner was anything to get excited about—lukewarm, watery potato soup and perhaps a piece of hard black bread—but it was better than nothing, which was all he got during the day while he and the other handful of "French" prisoners in his work gang scoured the wreckage for corpses. For that last few weeks, this was all they did. Each morning they were taken out to the place where the bombs had done their destructive duty the night before, and there they moved rubble under the lackadaisical supervision of the Feuerschutzpolizei, fire protection police, usually old men these days, but also a few of their younger countrymen who had been so severely wounded they could no longer be sent to the front to die. His life had become an endless routine of lifting and tossing, creating long rows of mounded bricks and stones where once there had been sidewalks as they reclaimed streets that had been filled with shattered building blocks. It reminded him of ants.

Each passing day brought the jaws of the vice a little closer, and as the taste of freedom became stronger, so did the fear of death. He worked hard to rid his mind of these fears. Each night he dragged himself back to the camp more exhausted than before. His back had become permanently bowed, his hands were callused and raw, and he ached in every joint, but it made him sleep, and after four years as a prisoner of war, his threshold had increased greatly, so he kept on; there was nothing else to do.

He was just about done for this day. They had been searching through the rubble around the waterfront where a heavy bombardment the night before had leveled a number of warehouses. He noticed the absence of civilians and an unusual number of SS guards who had been particularly attentive to the labors of the prisoners, but he was too tired to think much about it. One didn't think too deeply when the SS was involved. It was better to keep your wits and be ready to react.

For the past half hour he'd been working on a rather large pile where the walls had collapsed in after the roof had fallen down. It had been a large, long building, and so far it appeared to have been mostly empty. As he painfully pulled a jagged chunk of concrete off the pile, he thought he heard a low, almost inaudible groan from inside the mass of debris. He stopped and listened, but heard nothing, and fearful of displeasing the SS guards this late in the day, returned to the task at hand. He heard it again, this time unmistakable. There was a living person under there.

"*Kommen sie hier,*" he shouted to the nearest guards. "Goddamn it, you bloody Krauts, there's a live one in here."

14

It was night when she awoke. The sanctuary of sleep was replaced by
strange sensations, the perception of something surrounding her, something rhythmic, pleasant. It felt like the ending of a warm and happy
dream, and she resisted letting it go, content to linger and enjoy the
sensory experience. She yawned and tried to snuggle closer, smiling, and
then, with a sudden start, she remembered. In an explosion of panic,
she opened her eyes, saw nothing but darkness, tensed, and tried to rise
only to find herself imprisoned, gently yet firmly, within the arms of the
lieutenant.

"Don't move. Not yet."

She felt his arms squeeze a little, then relax. His voice was soft, a
whisper, yet urgent and pleading. The effect was soothing. Unable to see
in the darkness, she closed her eyes and allowed the tension to escape
from her body. She lay on her side, her face resting on his chest close
enough to his heart to hear and feel its strong, steady beating. As she
listened, her head rose and fell slowly in time with his breathing, and the
apprehension that had momentarily flooded her mind vanished, leaving
a peacefulness she'd never felt before. She thought she could stay this

way forever. Even the rumble of the Russian guns had contributed to the moment by its absence. The whole world seemed to be at rest, leaving them alone.

Minutes, perhaps hours, passed, during which she may have slept or drifted into waking dreams, until at some point she became aware of movement. The arm that had encircled her lifted, and his hand slowly glided upward toward her shoulder, then across to the nape of her neck. His fingers slid up under the tightly rolled bun, exploring, seeking the solution to the puzzle that would release her long tresses. Patiently, gently, he worked until at last she could feel the loosening that preceded the eventual release, and her thick, soft hair cascaded over his hand and down upon the bed.

Their lovemaking was difficult, but the challenge his condition imposed on their passion worked to extend the buildup, during which they discovered a shared awareness that became stronger as they moved with growing intensity toward the final climatic release. Afterward, as they lay spent and satisfied, both knew that something indefinable had passed between them, something that would fuse their souls together—a bond that time would never sever.

As they rested happy and exhausted, a silent change was taking place. In the quiet darkness, the Russian army came up and engulfed the ancient school building, and the last acts of the war began the fuzzy transition into the first of the peace.

15

The toughness of Lena's character was a thin shell, a charade, behind which its structure was ready to crumble under the weight of relentless war. The young woman inside who had never flourished, who had been suppressed so long, burst open. That it was lust or infatuation, or even love, wasn't important, but it released like a coiled spring, and she flew willingly from her arid, emotionless imprisonment. It was wonderful. She soared like a phoenix to happiness unlike any experienced before. For a few brief hours, she was young again, floating. She basked in the glow, and the thought came to her that she could die, and she would go in peace. Later, as she lay exhausted, warm, and deeply contented, another new feeling was born: hope. Until von Ritter there was nothing but dull, grim survival. Now there was a desire for it all to come to an end—the war, the horrors, the charade. For the first time since Hans and Ralf marched into Belgium, she dared to think of the future.

As she lay with him, his hands gently stroking her long blond hair, she thought longingly of the hours, days, and weeks to come, and for the moment the war and all its death and terror was far away. She was happy in her fragile utopia, but von Ritter was still far from recovery and she was still his nurse and life-giver, so it was time to leave him.

She slid out of the bed, put on her clothes, kissed him one more time, left the room, and returned to the real world, which, unknown to the lovers, had changed.

The Russians had arrived, and most of the organization of the hospital had collapsed. The few doctors and nurses still there had either given up or pressed on with the care of the remaining patients as best they could. Each worked alone or with one or two associates. It would take a long time before any central administration would be restored—if ever. Entering this atmosphere of despair, she hardly knew where to start, and she wandered about the building, taking note of the few Russian soldiers, who seemed strategically placed and disinterested. Finding herself in the corridor on the second floor by no particular design, she entered the nearest wardroom and let her professional training take it from there. She had no idea what she would find, and the complete calm in which she found the room surprised her. Many of the beds were still occupied, and every patient turned to see who was entering the room, and they now looked expectantly at her. For a moment a heavy silence hung over the room before voices called out with symphonic anxiety.

"What's happening out there, nurse?"

"Are they taking prisoners?"

"How many of them are there?"

Lena waved her hands in the air and pleaded for quiet. Gradually the men settled down and listened. Lena, standing erect, spoke to the patients.

"There are just a few Russians inside the building. They seem reasonable. No one has been hurt or taken away. As far as the hospital staff is concerned, until ordered otherwise, we'll continue with our responsibilities to the best of our abilities. Now I'm going to do my usual rounds. There's nothing else to tell you."

With that, she proceeded to the first bed where a young man lay, his head wrapped in a stained and soiled bandage. She routinely opened her notebook and began to take notes.

At the far end of the old dormitory, she noticed Sergeant Kurt Webber, who sat on the same cot he'd occupied when he mocked von Ritter just a few days before. He was smoking a cigarette butt, which he held pinched tightly between the ragged nails of his thumb and index finger. He smoked slowly and clearly in no hurry. He seemed deep in thought.

Remembering his cynical attitude and mocking comments toward von Ritter, Lena looked for and found his file, still in the pile on the desk where it had remained since that exchange. She read through the contents. His wounds were received when a shell exploded close by, causing a broken collarbone, a number of broken bones in his left foot, and shrapnel gashes across his torso and legs. She knew he'd healed and his strength had returned to the point where he was capable of getting up and about, and she wondered why he'd not gone with the convoy.

She peered again in his direction. He sat in the growing dusk, a specter dissolving gradually in the shadows of the distant corner, a strange enigma behind the glowing red dot from the last drag on the cigarette. She felt unnerved by his presence and abruptly left the room.

She stood in the corridor outside the door, disturbed by her reaction to the sinister sergeant and not sure what to do next, when a sound came floating up the long pebbled driveway and in through the windows of the building—a sound that forebode the crisis soon to crash upon the hapless staff and patients of Clarey Gymnasium.

16

It was the sound of a small vehicle, probably a jeep, thought Webber. Its motor labored noisily as it approached at high speed. As it came closer, he could distinguish voices, roaring with laughter, loud enough to be heard over the throaty clatter of the vehicle. Even before the vehicle began a series of screeching turns, no doubt racing around old Bismarck, Webber knew what had arrived. Anxiety surged through his mind, and he quickened his dressing.

He was once again ready to take responsibility for his own survival; that was the objective. It had been the only objective for him since the summer of 1942 when the last semblance of the German offensive withered in the vastness of Russia. He'd killed Russians to survive. There had been occasions when he'd acted heroically, placing his life in extreme danger, but those who applauded his actions never understood the real underlying motivation: to live.

His mind drifted back to another time, the dark, frozen winter of 1942–43. He was among the two hundred thousand men of the Sixth Army who, having fought the long and vicious battle for Stalingrad, suddenly found they were surrounded and cut off. As the enemy drove far to the west, on both the north and south flanks Webber had felt the noose tightening. It was an eerie sensation. The city was won, and the sounds of battle were far away. It was a time for celebration, but for the exhausted infantrymen there was only dread. There was no food, and supplies were running out, so he leaped at the opportunity to lead a small patrol that would gather surveillance and other tactical information for the commanding officer, General von Manstein, to support the critical counterattack, and if authorized, provide a route for retreat.

When they set out down the snow-covered valley, he and his men didn't know that the encirclement was complete. The nearest German division was over fifty miles away in retreat, and the Russians had already turned and were heading right at them. To make matters worse, a winter storm came rolling out of the north across the steppes, bringing with it freezing temperatures and icy rain that lashed the land as only it can do in Russia.

Two and a half weeks later, suffering from frostbite on the small finger on his left hand, he alone staggered into the city of Kotelnikovski, a hundred miles from Stalingrad. The memory of those eighteen days and the scars they had left would never go away, but he'd survived.

When he emerged from the Russian plains, the sentries who were the first to see his struggling figure didn't notice when, as he approached their outpost, he discarded the tattered map satchel, leaving it lying on the ground behind him. No one ever knew of its grisly contents and the vital contribution they had made to his survival. Few questions were asked about his ordeal. He was the only survivor of his patrol, and he never revealed the full account of his escape. It was something that he'd have to live with the rest of his life.

Two months after he'd emerged from the frozen wilderness, the commanding officer of the Sixth Army, Field Marshal Freidrich von Paulus, surrendered the city of Stalingrad. He was the first field marshal ever to be captured since the unification of Germany. Ninety-one thousand soldiers were led into captivity, and almost none of them returned to Germany. Karl Webber received the Knight's Cross, which he never wore.

Now he was faced with another such journey, and by the dim light of his last cigarette, he pondered the future. Tonight he would have to make his escape. He may have already left it too late. The suddenness of the Russians' arrival had caught everyone, including him, by surprise.

The more he thought about it, the stronger became his resolve, but he was also aware of the dangers. In his present condition, and lacking any local knowledge, he knew it would take at least two days to get to Stettin, if everything went well. He couldn't move on roads or open terrain in daylight, so it was possible, depending on the geography, that it could take even longer. His chances would be better if he had a guide, someone who knew the land well enough to help him plot a course that would provide the most direct route possible while reducing the risk of discovery.

It was at this point in his deliberations when Lena had entered the dormitory.

Except for the general clamor from the rest of the patients, he probably wouldn't have even noticed her arrival. For a while he paid her little attention and was unaffected by her presence, but then as he absently watched her, he saw the answer to his problem. His cigarette went out, and his attention focused squarely on the nurse.

He recognized in her strength and a rigid will, the kind that kept a person going when the body was ready to quit, and there was no doubt about her physical condition. He'd seen her move men in and out of bed unassisted. He was certain, with his help, that she could endure the trek. While she might not be familiar with the entire stretch of land from the hospital to the sea, she would at least know the immediate vicinity, and that was a start.

She was also a nurse who could look after his injuries, which, though improved, were not ready to withstand much of a test. She would know where the medicine stores were and might even have access to them. These were invaluable survival resources.

He saw her suddenly turn and leave the room, and in that instant he made his decision. Swinging his legs off the bed, he sat up and dressed, taking his clothes from the small wooden chair where they had lain for the last two weeks. It was getting late, and he had no other options except to rely on fate, but fate was a fickle ally, and it was time to act. Moments later, he limped between the beds and out the door. He entered the corridor quickly and almost bumped into Lena. It was then that he, too, heard the laughter outside.

"You hear that?" he said. "I can't lie around here in my underwear waiting any longer for the damned Russians to come and get me." He lowered his voice and beckoned for her to come close. "I'm getting outta here tonight, and if you were smart, you'd come with me."

Lena drew away, startled by this stark statement. The idea of escape apparently hadn't entered her mind, nor had the concept of captivity and all its associated horrors, Webber reckoned.

"You can't do that," she went on. "We have orders, all staff and patients, to remain in the building until further notice, and they've posted guards."

"Where?" Webber shot back. "Where are they posted? At all the doors?"

"I-I think so. I'm not sure. There were two at the main doors, and I assumed—"

Again Webber interrupted. The glimmer of a plan had formed in his head, a way to draw her into his escape without putting her in the position of making an immediate decision.

"Listen, you don't know these people. The things they're capable of doing make the Gestapo look like children. I'm going to get out of here tonight and take my chances. Will you help me? You don't have to do much. I need to know where all the guards are posted. Can you find out?"

Webber could see her mind was speeding and could only wonder what her thoughts were. The idea of escape must have come out of the blue, and she was trying desperately to assimilate its implications.

"I can try," she replied.

"Good," said Webber. "Then you should go quickly. When you come back, I will have more questions for you. I'll need a coat too. Now go, and thank you."

He went back into the dorm room and crossed his fingers as he sat down on the canvas cot.

17

Due to the combined effect of her night with von Ritter and the jumbled emotions that had preoccupied her for days, she'd not thought much about the reality of her circumstances. Was escape possible? Could she get von Ritter away? She heard the Russians, their crude voices echoing through the building, as she set off on her mission. She had no notion of the evil about to descend upon her world.

It took about five minutes to check all the possible exits, but when she was done, a new sense of excitement had taken hold of her. The service entrance, which was easily reached via the backstairs, had no guard, and a quick conversation with one of the scullery maids confirmed that none had been placed there all day. Lena's hope was growing. If she could enlist the help of the sergeant, Johann could be secreted away, and once they got to the back courtyard, it was only a hundred yards or so to the gardener's shed where she knew a flatbed pull cart was kept. It would be perfect for transporting her wounded lover. With this impossible plan in mind, she headed back to the dormitory. She had to talk to Webber.

She'd forgotten about the noise, but as she hurried along the second-floor corridor, nearing the dormitory door, she heard loud angry shouts and a chilling scream that seemed to come from below. Without sensing the danger that lurked ahead, Lena slowed her paced and cautiously walked on to the wide landing and up to the railing from where she could observe the main hall below. There she stood, sickened by the horror of the spectacle unfolding below, her knuckles white as she unconsciously gripped the handrail in terror.

As she watched transfixed, she was vaguely aware of the medical staff huddled in the far corner next to the vestibule doors, herded there by two Russian soldiers who were alternately screaming threats at them in their loathsome guttural language and watching with lustful expressions the gruesome scene unfolding across the room.

There were five Russians in the hall, and three of them had dragged a nurse onto an operating table, where they held her spread-eagled while one was upon her—still wearing his heavy brown winter coat, his trousers at his ankles—in the final throes of the sordid act. The combined sounds of cackling Russians and agonized moans from the set-upon woman seared Lena's mind, and a wave of nausea welled within her. Her stomach began to heave, sending the bitter taste of bile into her mouth.

Slowly, so as not to draw attention, and holding her breath, she began to back away from the railing, her eyes riveted on the enemy below. Four or five steps and the floor of the upper corridor, which spanned between the stairs and the old library, would intersect their line of vision. By crawling, she could escape into one of the wings of the building, undetected. Cautiously, she took one step and then a second, the brink of the opening to the hall rising with each, cutting the sickening drama from her view. Two more steps and she would reach a position of relative safety.

She started the third step when, suddenly, behind her was a loud crash, and she spun around to see a half-dressed German, wearing only a pair of gray battle trousers, burst through the glass door of what had been the school library. His head was wrapped in a white bandage. In one hand he held a small wooden chair, and his eyes blazed with hatred. He shouted as he charged past her toward the top of the stairs.

"Bastards. Filthy Russian pigs. I'll kill you, God help me."

Through the rails she could see all eyes look up, including those of the engaged Russian, who interrupted his rhythmic quest just a moment and then, burying his dirty unshaven face against the neck of his victim, resumed his sexual attack, seemingly secure in the knowledge that his comrades could deal with the distraction.

For his lack of concern, he was soon to pay.

The outraged German, driven by his hatred, leaped over the railing and bounded down the central stairs in total disregard for his own safety, straight at one of the Russians who had started to intercept him. As the German streaked toward him, however, the drunk Russian stumbled on his face with a loud grunt and lay groaning as the German passed him, arriving at the bottom with such speed that he was upon the rapist before any of his countrymen could react. Twice the chair smashed down upon the Russian's head and shoulders with awesome force. The second blow landed the edge of the solid seat squarely upon the base of the man's skull, filling the hall with the sound of a loud, ominous crack and rendering him immediately motionless on top of the nurse.

With the heroic German towering triumphantly over the unconscious Russian, briefly savoring his victory, time seemed to hang suspended. The onlookers in the hall, a tableau, were frozen by the sudden outburst of energy, overwhelmed by the startling change of events, and unable to absorb the meaning of what had just occurred. Only the piercing screams of the nurse provided evidence that the scene was other than some monstrous theatrical performance.

This pause was the avenger's downfall, because when he swung round to face the next enemy, it was already too late. Across the hall, well out of his reach, one of the Russians had recovered his senses, and as the German raised the chair, intent on duplicating his previous success, a thunderous explosion echoed through the room. A single bullet smashed into the man's bandaged head, shattering his skull as it exited, and spewing blood and other particles against the white wall behind the operating table. The soldier flew backward under the impact and came to rest arched over the dead Russian and flailing nurse, a large pool of blood rapidly expanding on the floor as it flowed freely from the gaping wound.

Lena heard the scream before she knew it was hers.

Again all eyes rose in unison.

The fallen Russian soldier at the bottom of the stairs, now on his knees, grunted again when he saw Lena, looked back toward the hall, and without waiting for any encouragement, started crawling upward like a ravenous carnivore, leaving no doubt in Lena's mind as to his objective.

Like a fox before the hounds, she sought a place to go to ground, and desperately tried to think of a hiding place. She didn't realize the uselessness of her flight. There was no escape. Every room on the second floor was a dead end, and there were only two ways to get off the floor: down the main stairs from which she now was fleeing or down the back stairs. It was to this spiral stairway of worn granite and wrought iron that she was inexorably drawn. It was the same stairway that von Ritter had painfully traveled a few days before.

Faced with the option of going up or down, she headed for higher ground. From every angle the choice was wrong, but even as she hauled herself hand over hand along the bannister, up and around, closer and closer to the ultimate dead end that lay ahead, she failed to see her mistake. The shouts and grunts from the bloodthirsty Russians as they pounded in their heavy boots through the corridor, filled her with a revulsion and fear; there were at least two behind her now.

Faster, faster. Must keep going. Where can I hide? Oh God!

Suddenly she stopped. The realization of where her panicked flight had taken her struck like a vicious slap in the face. She stood heaving and flushed outside his little room, facing the door, shocked by her senselessness. And then she heard his voice.

"Lena? Is that you? What's going on?"

As later years dragged by, Lena would trace the agony of her survival back to this exact moment. On that late March afternoon, the young nurse, terrified and exhausted, heard the clatter of her attackers on the stairs below her and took the next step in the unfathomable plan of destiny that had started perhaps at the small Belgian village of Stavelot, perhaps many years before that, and entered the room where her wounded lover lay.

All that day, the first day of defeat and occupation, the sky had been a blanket of low gray clouds, nature's contribution to the gloom that pervaded the hospital, but with the day finally approaching its end, the setting sun had suddenly emerged beneath the thick concealing layer. While Lena and her pursuers were locked in the grim chase through the dark corridors of the old stone building, a bloody sunset started to blaze across the land. Von Ritter's room on the west side of the building received the full impact of this fiery display, and the old plaster walls were aglow when Lena burst through the door, slammed it shut behind her, and leaned back against it, breathing heavily, staring about wildly, trying to assimilate the surreal effect of the radiant glow. Things were happening too fast.

Physically exhausted and reeling mentally, she felt the ground slipping away from her, the objects and shapes about the room softening and going out of focus. She closed her eyes and started to slide her back down the door. It's no good, she thought, might as well just sit down and wait. Then the sharp voice coming from the bed a few feet in front of her sliced through and grabbed her mind.

"Lena. Lena, what's happening out there? Lena, Do you hear me?"

Drawn like a stormbound ship to the beam of a lighthouse, Lena crossed the room and fell on her knees at the head of the bed in which von Ritter sat, upright and alert, and as she thrust her head into his lap and wrapped her arms around his waist, she felt the calmness of finally having reached a safe harbor. At the same moment, she began to cry as her anguish sought to find release through the tears. She wanted only to close her eyes, feel his warmth, and sleep; then awake and find herself, once again, alone with this man.

Strong hands grasped her shoulders, and she felt herself being pulled gently upward. Opening her teary eyes, she found herself looking into von Ritter's face. He was saying something, and though she could see his lips moving, the sounds weren't penetrating. A confused expression descended across her face. He was shaking her, and with great difficulty she tried to focus on the lips. What was he saying? Why couldn't she hear him?

She caught a blurred movement out of the corner of her eye, followed instantly by a stinging jolt on the side of her head, and then his voice, strong and urgent, commanded.

"Lena, pull yourself together. Look at me, Lena. Look at me."

The slap had done its job, and as von Ritter let go of her shoulders so he could cup his hands around her reddened cheeks, she regained a measure of control. Through the heaving of her breath she gasped with punctuated phases.

"Russians. Oh, Johann, it's horrible. Johann, don't let them. Oh God…" She broke off and wept.

"Quiet," said von Ritter as he pulled her forcibly to his chest, smothering her face between his arm and breast. Outside the door the Russians could be heard, their heavy, hard boots lumbering up the stairs. It was apparent that their energy had somewhat diminished from the chase, or maybe they knew their quarry was cornered for there was no hurry in the footsteps

"How many?" whispered von Ritter, releasing the pressure from the back of her head enough to let her speak. It took a moment for her to get control and, with a deep sigh, manage a reply.

"I don't know, two, maybe more. There were five, I think, in the hall. Oh, Johann, they're animals."

"Shhh." He gently laid a finger across her lips, kissed her softly on the forehead, and wrapped his arms around her again, this time allowing her head to rest lightly on his chest. She could hear his heart and was surprised that it beat so fast. He seemed so calm and still.

The heartbeat was the truer indication of his disposition, for he knew well that a mortal confrontation was only moments away. As he listened intently, trying to determine the exact number and location of the enemy, his mind worked furiously. He had surprise on his side, surprise and the Walther under his pillow. Slowly, so as not frighten Lena—it was vital that she remained composed and controlled—he withdrew his right arm from around her and reached behind him, twisting his body as little as possible, until he could slide his hand under the pillow. The feel of the familiar contours in the palm of his hand had an immediate effect, and an idea began to take shape, a risky plan that relied a lot on Lena and a snap assessment of the Russians but with enough logic to make it worth trying. It was better, he concluded, confined as he was, than waiting for the door to open and taking his chances on a quick shoot-out where the odds on eliminating all the enemy soldiers weren't in his favor—the first one, yes; the second one, maybe, if he was in the right location and his reactions were good. If there were a third, never.

If he failed to get all of them, he and Lena would certainly die, and—his eyes drifted over to the table—the letter would never leave that room.

Outside, the sound of the footsteps had changed. They were closer but no longer the slow heavy thumps of men climbing stairs. Instead they were shuffling and hesitant. More noticeable were their voices. Von Ritter thought he heard just two but couldn't be certain because the foreign utterances seemed so similar, and distinguishing one from the other was virtually impossible. What he could discern was they were on the narrow landing that cantilevered over the central opening of the clock tower, through which the spiral staircase wound on its way up to the small chamber two levels higher, where the mechanism of the clock was housed.

"How many rooms are on this level?" he asked.

"Four."

Four rooms, von Ritter's being the one opposite the top to the stairs. He hoped they would work together, searching each room one by one, starting with the one closest and then proceeding around the landing, making his room the second or third one on their route. This would give him enough time to set his trap. To his relief he heard the first door open. Now it was time to act.

"Lena, listen to me carefully."

He spoke softly, yet with a firm urgency as he held her away and looked deep into her eyes, willing her to find the strength to carry out the simple instructions he was about to give.

"I have a plan that will rid us of these pigs, but you must do exactly as I say. You must be brave. Do you understand?"

She rose to her feet and, brushing away the loose hairs that were matted to her dampened cheek, held herself erect and nodded.

"Good. Quickly now, you must go over there and stand by the window."

He pointed to the dormer window built into the sloping wall of the clock tower. It was located about five feet to his left. Lena hesitated, reluctant to leave him. Out on the landing, a door slammed and angry Russian voices grew closer.

"Go." The command was only a whisper, but he delivered it with such vehemence that Lena nearly tripped over her own feet as she spun away from the bed and moved to the small alcove. The second door opened, and they could hear the muffled voices through the adjacent wall. There was little time left.

"When they open the door, do nothing. Stand and face them. Do not move. Do not look at me or say anything. Let them come at you. When they're all in the room and you know how many there are, without moving or looking at me, shout that number. One word. No more. Do you understand?"

Lena's eyes were fixed on the door. Again von Ritter asked for confirmation.

"Lena, do you understand? Answer me."

Jerking her head to look at him, she nodded and then returned her attention to the door. At the same moment, the second door slammed and the footsteps approached their door. Out of the corner of her eye, she saw von Ritter wiggle down into the prone position and was astonished to see him pull the sheet up over his head. There was just enough time for the fact to register in her mind that he now posed as a corpse before the door was thrown open, and she found herself staring into the half-open, bloodshot eyes of a short, powerfully built Russian soldier, a Mongol.

For a moment he stood motionless, breathing hard through a toothy smile, his wide frame filling the lower portion of the door opening. That the winter war had been hard on him was evident from the condition of his clothing. The bulky overcoat was muddy and ragged, held together by the single remaining button just below the collar. One pocket had been ripped off, and the other was on its way. Exposed below the coat, his thick legs were made to look even larger by the extra flannel material that had been wrapped around them, mummy style, for added protection. The boots, however, looked like new. They were German made. He wore no headgear, and his hair was long, unruly, and greasy.

Slowly he brought a hand to his mouth to wipe away the heavy saliva that had collected on his thick lower lip and rolled his tongue across, licking as a man might do when observing a feast being placed before him. Finally, after what seemed like an eternity to Lena, another voice out on the landing said something, and, as his smile twisted into a sneer, he nodded, grunted in the affirmative, and started forward toward Lena.

He'd taken a couple of steps before he noticed von Ritter, but the sudden awareness of the presence of a corpse only caused him to hesitate for an instant. Apparently the thought of sharing the bed with a dead man was of little concern. A quick shove would clear off the unwanted third party once he got the woman there, so he ignored this minor obstacle and, unbuttoning his coat, continued his advance.

He was a couple steps from her and she could already smell the foul, musty odor of his body when the second Russian entered the room. He was considerably taller, and Lena could see his face over the nearer man's shoulder. The sight made her gasp. He had only one eye. Where the second would have been, there was an ugly red socket. He looked at her by turning his head a little to one side, providing the one eye with a clear view, and spoke the only German he probably knew.

"Fraulein." It was to be the last word he would ever speak.

The first Russian had now reached Lena and was in the process of untying the rope that held up his trousers, as his eyes roved up and down her body. She could hold herself no longer, and with one deep breath, she released the explosive tension that had been building inside with a violent, terrified scream.

"Two."

The suddenness of her cry momentarily caused both Russians to check their movements, a hesitation that led to their imminent demise as it set them up perfectly for what was to come next. In that moment before either attacker fully recovered, the corpse began to move. Mesmerized by the astonishing sight, they could only watch dumbfounded as the upper half of the dead man rose inch by inch to vertical. They continued to stare in stunned disbelief as the sheet that covered this apparition slowly slid off its head and down across its body to reveal a German SS officer clad in full parade attire, head forward, eyes closed. This was their last vision in this life.

For Lena, events were now to accelerate into a blur, which she would never be able to reconstruct clearly in her memory: two or maybe three deafening explosions; the feel of warm liquid splashing on her face; the sight of one Russian falling backward and sliding down the sloping chamber wall into a sitting position, eyes open and a surprised look on his face; a second Russian sprawled, facedown, across the foot of von Ritter's bed; and a pink-white layer of smoke rising up toward the low ceiling against the reddened backdrop of sunset-washed walls. Then she was in his arms, crying. Together they fell back onto his pillow, and again she desperately wanted this to be the end but knew somehow that it was only the beginning of yet more horror.

This time, when he tried to push her away, she clung to him, gripping his belt and begging him to let her stay. Whispering assurances gently yet with all the force needed to accomplish his purpose, he disengaged the weeping woman and held her at arm's length, ignoring her pleas. As much as he, too, wanted to lie with her, to share one last moment of peace before the inevitable, he couldn't allow himself this one final indulgence. There was little time, and somehow he had to convince, beg, or intimidate this object of his longing to abandon him, but as he glared wildly into her sky-blue eyes, inspiration failed him. He couldn't let her in, nor could he find the strength to cast her off.

Time passed, and she seemed to recognize the uselessness of her struggle, so she ceased to resist. Large tears spilled down her cheeks, and she whispered softly, "Johann, please." He held firm. "Please let me go. Please."

It was reasonable to expect that the gunshots would be heard throughout the building, bringing a horde of Russians and instant death up to the tiny clock tower room, and von Ritter was racing against this inevitable moment. As he held Lena at arm's length, frantically searching for the words that would convince her to leave him forever, he didn't know that the enemy was not coming.

The gunshots didn't go unnoticed.

18

When Kurt Webber heard the drunk and crazed Russians arrive outside, he knew exactly what they were after and the danger they represented. Having decided on the nurse as his accomplice, her safety was all-important, and even as the wild laughter and shouting was still echoing outside of the building, he was pulling on his boots as fast as he could, ignoring the pain and muttering soft curses under his breath. Anxious as he was to find her, he was careful enough to take the extra time to put on his boots and tie them up tightly. When it came time to run, he wanted to be ready.

The sound of lustful shouts and footsteps stomping down the hall brought him abruptly to his feet, and with quickness and purpose honed in years of combat, he bolted to the door of the dorm room, grabbing his greatcoat as he went. With caution he opened it. A minute crack was sufficient to let him see the nurse and then two Russians as they passed the door and lumbered down the hall. He opened the door further just in time to see them disappear into the stairwell. Desperately he turned and cast his eyes about the room, looking for a weapon. Settling on the solid wooden chair in which Lena had sat those few nights ago, he grabbed it, raised it over his head, and in one movement brought it crashing down on the edge of the table. Files and splintered wood flew across the room. Webber picked up one of the pieces, a leg, tested its feel in his hand, and headed out the door.

He'd just reached the bottom of the stairs when the sharp explosions from above rumbled down the stairwell.

His heart sunk. "Shit, shit, shit," he muttered with each painful leap up the stairs. A fury was rising within him, fueling his ascent and blinding his better judgment. As he flew toward the open door, he heard sounds he didn't expect, crying and a low soothing voice. He stopped. It was a German voice. Caution returned, and he stealthily approached the doorway.

"Please let me go. Please." It was Lena's pleading that greeted him as he stepped into the opening and saw the destruction the young lieutenant had wrought. Surprise was immediately followed by admiration and respect.

"I apologize, Lieutenant. I misjudged you. I hope you can forgive me." Looking back at him were two pairs of eyes and the barrel of the lieutenant's handgun. Von Ritter returned Webber's smile as he lowered the gun.

"Think nothing of it, Sergeant. War is war."

"True, but for us the war is over, and I fear that the peace isn't going well." Webber ironically waved his hand over the dead Russians, and for a moment, a heavy stillness hung over the room.

It was then that Webber noticed the color. The granite sky had dispersed into a furrowed field of black, gray, and white, onto which the setting sun was painting a brilliant face of orange, red, and yellow. This puffy canvas in turn cast a fierce glow that filled the room and bathed the old plaster walls in a deep hue of sunset. The redness filled his senses. He could smell it, but it wasn't the work of the sun; it was the stench of blood oozing across and soaking into the old oak floorboards. He could feel it—the throbbing, suffocating evil that had infused the room. He saw Lena cover her mouth as if by doing so she might prevent the horror from entering. She closed her eyes, as if to squeeze the memory of this moment out of her head.

Webber immediately went to work, laboring over the corpses, pulling them away from the bed and swing of the door. He already had a good idea of what the future would bring.

"Lena." It was Johann's voice. "Lena, help him get them out of here. Quickly. There's little time."

Both men understood the situation perfectly.

Kurt Webber searched the dead Russians and recovered a handgun, a knife, and some loose cartridges. He was attempting to drag the first body out of the room, but the Russian was a big man, and Webber was still weak.

Grabbing the dead man's coat, Lena pulled, and together they managed to haul the reeking corpse out of the room and along the landing to the far corner near the opening to the stairwell. Without hesitating, they returned and soon had the second body resting beside the first.

As Lena turned to start back to von Ritter's room, Webber caught her by the wrist and, with a slight tug, spun her around to face him.

"We must go, immediately. There's no time to lose." His eyes were cold and determined. Seeing the hesitation in her face and guessing her thoughts, his next words were hard, blunt, and spoken for all of them to hear. He had no intention of letting her stay behind. "Others will be coming, and they'll have the same ideas as these two. If they find you, they will have their satisfaction, many of them and often, and then they will kill you. Don't doubt me. It's the law of war. Listen, the lieutenant in there is a brave man, but he is a dead man. He has no future. That's a fact. Your staying will only make it harder for him to do what he must do. I won't let you limit his options. So I give you two choices: either you come with me now, or I'll do you a favor and kill you right here." As he spoke, he leveled the handgun at the middle of her forehead. It held perfectly steady as he waited for a response.

It came as he expected from von Ritter.

"Sergeant, let me speak with her. Lena, come." In an instant she was at his side, and throwing her arms around his neck, she cried and begged that he let her die with him, but again he forced her away, and this time he knew what he had to say.

"Lena, my destiny is clear. All through my life, I've been following a course laid out by the gods. It's all so obvious, and now my mission is coming to its conclusion. It is time."

The sun had set, and the room was rapidly growing dark. Shapes and features were softening at the edges. It made it easier somehow. With one hand holding her firmly at arm's length, he reached with the other to the bedside table and picked up the second letter. It was sealed in an envelope, bearing a single name scrawled in von Ritter's functional handwriting: SS-ObersturmbannFührer Joachim Peiper.

The name held his gaze a few moments, and then he looked back at Lena.

"Go, close the door," he whispered, releasing her hand with a reassuring squeeze.

Lena responded immediately. On the landing Webber watched the door close, and he waited. With every fiber in his body tense, he waited and listened, straining for the sounds that would foretell the approach of the enemy. The cold granite tower remained strangely quiet, with only the muffled sounds of von Ritter and Lena's voices coming through the door. Once a small turret window rattled angrily somewhere down in the stairwell as another blast of wind smashed into the tower, which made him jump, but otherwise the world seemed to have forgotten them, and he waited. He wouldn't go without the nurse. He would wait.

She came out sooner than expected. She looked at him across the landing, and though it was quite dark now, he could still see the redness around her eyes from crying. They were ringed with sadness but no longer uncertain. He always wondered what the lieutenant had said to her, although he never asked. Leaving the door open behind her, she walked purposefully away, never looking back. As she passed Webber, she spoke in a low, steady voice.

"Follow me, Sergeant. I know where there are supplies that may prove valuable for our escape. I'll also need my coat and boots if I'm to be of any use to you. It's thirteen kilometers to the Oder by road, although Lieutenant von Ritter doubts we'll be traveling that way much."

Without further talk she was on her way down the stairs.

"Stop," barked Webber. He didn't like her reckless attitude. "Let me go ahead. You can tell me where to go." He peered into von Ritter's room. It was too dark now to distinguish anything but vague outlines. He snapped to attention and saluted smartly into the gloom.

"Good luck, Sergeant" came the lieutenant's voice, and Webber wheeled and started down the stairs. Lena followed, and their footsteps faded away slowly.

Von Ritter sat back against the wall, facing the open doorway. His handgun lay in his lap as he waited for the Russians. Soon it was pitch black.

He took a deep breath and closed his eyes. He was content, prepared. He drifted into a dream.

■ ■ ■

He rides high and straight on his battle charger. All around he can sense the movement of his warriors, gliding almost noiselessly with only the muffled sounds of cracking undergrowth and the nervous snorting of horses. Inside his polished armor, he is sweating as the adrenalin pumps through his veins. Soon they will emerge from the forest and come face-to-face with the Saxons, who had dared to trespass upon the lands of his liege and must now be punished. It is his great honor to lead the assault. Glory and a seat among the heroes of the ancestors lie just ahead. Proud and erect, he looks straight ahead, his strong body motionless on the high battle saddle.

His heart thumps like the pounding of storm-driven surf on jagged rocks. There, spread across the open space, is the enemy host, thousands of warriors, packed tightly into the sweeping bend in the river. The attack will start from the left, sucking the enemy in that direction. The second wave he'll lead into the heart of the enemy. The third wave will drive past the right flank to cut off the only escape route, a narrow wooden bridge that the Saxons have foolishly built to ford the river. They'll then be trapped on low ground without possibility of escape or reinforcement. Never before have the gods handed him such an opportunity.

Two messengers speed along the edge of the forest. A great clamor rises forth from the enemy below, who, seeing them, realizes the battle is at hand. His charger rears eagerly on its hind legs, and he soothes the massive beast with a firm pat on the side of its graceful neck. The animal responds with a sharp snort that sends a puff of warm steam into the cold air and begins to paw the ground as his rider waits patiently for the return of the messengers.

The mist is slowly clearing when suddenly the front ranks of the enemy open and a single Saxon knight emerges from their midst. He rides a huge, white, high-stepping charger, and his armor gleams and flashes in the low morning sun. The knight stops, glares up toward the forest, and then slowly rises in his stirrups until he is fully erect. He removes the gauntlet from his left hand, holds it for a moment above his head for all to clearly see, and in a single graceful movement, hurls it defiantly to the ground. Before the glove lands, the challenge is answered. Spurring his horse, he bolts into the light of the meadow, gallops a few meters forward to the ringing cheers of his own army, reins in to a controlled strut, and proceeds steadily toward his challenger. Again the gods have honored him and delivered the life of the enemy's champion. He reaches for and withdraws his sword, with which he ceremoniously salutes the unknown knight, and the next moment he's galloping down the hill at a terrible speed. He can already smell the blood of his enemy as it flows upon the land this intruder has so shamelessly violated.

■ ■ ■

Voices in the stairwell echoed into the bedchamber and shattered the dream, but the exhilaration lingered. Let them come. He was ready. He was Hagen, conqueror of the Saxons, slayer of the mighty Siegfried, keeper of the secret of the Nibelungen Hoard.

19

As Webber stepped out into the late afternoon, a chilly mist was rising and the sun, a faint round orange glow, was descending behind naked trees. He did a quick calculation. It was approaching the equinox so the sun was due west. He wanted to head north to Stettin, where he heard a bridge was still intact over the Oder River.

First they had to get away from the building, a wounded man and a woman. He was more concerned about the woman. He'd been through worse.

The school was built on a slight rise in a wooded area. The trees had been cleared around the building, and Webber estimated they would have to cross an open area of nearly twenty meters before reaching the seclusion of the woods. There was no one in sight, but his training and battle instincts drove him to caution. He whispered to Lena to wait and descended the short flight of concrete stairs. Hugging the brick wall, he worked his way to the corner of the building and peeked around. Past the far end he saw a half-track truck parked at the edge of the pebbled driveway, but no Russians. He returned to the bottom of the stairs and motioned Lena to come down. As she reached the ground, he grabbed her sleeve and guided her back against the wall.

"We've got two options, neither very good," he said. "We can wait here for more darkness, but that's an hour away and anything can happen, or we can run for the woods right now and hope no one sees us. We run, yes? We'll head over there." He pointed to their left where he had noticed a high stone wall just inside the edge of the woods; walls of stone meant protection.

"Follow me. Once we get to the trees, I'll take a moment to check behind us. You keep moving until you get to the wall or I say stop. Okay?"

The last word was more an order than a question.

Bringing the woman was both a rash promise to the fated officer and a questionable decision. Lena clutched the pillowcase she had used to carry the few medical supplies they picked up on the way out—aspirin, witch hazel, iodine, and most valuable of all, penicillin. She nodded, appearing calm and focused. Her eyes showed a bit too much white. Webber knew the look. He had seen it often in men, and he knew she was gathering herself for the moment when she would take an action completely against her instincts. A smile crossed his mind.

Kurt Webber had been in this war for six years. He knew what courage was and wasn't. He had nothing but scorn for those who didn't really know, like Goebbels, who had not been there to see it, to smell it, those who described it as some heroic mind-over-fear nonsense. Yes, fear plays a part, he thought, every part. Courage was nothing more than making the better choice when faced with fear coming from every direction, when your only option was to be afraid, and you still acted. Looking at it this way, most men were courageous, so why make a big deal about it? Why give medals for it? He could see the fear in Lena's eyes, and he knew she was about to be this thing.

"Don't worry about what may happen when we run for the trees," he said. "There's no one around waiting for us, so just run as fast as you can into the trees and head for the stone wall. I'll be close by. Okay, ready?"

Another nod.

"Go."

Webber reached the trees ahead of Lena and immediately crouched behind an old oak, all his senses now fully alert. He was in control, aware of everything at once—the damp blanket of a forest, the smell of decaying leaves, the rough bark against his hands, the caw of crows in the distance, punctuating the soft and constant sighing of the breeze passing through the higher branches. The throbbing of his shoulder and broken foot were forgotten. Quickly he scanned the building, checking off every window one by one, looking for faces looking back. There were none.

He turned his attention away from the building and, looking farther down the slope, saw Lena waiting for him by the wall as instructed. Perhaps she would not be a liability. From his vantage point, he could now see it was the corner of what was probably a fairly large, walled-in garden, and his practical mind, turning to the days ahead and the need for food, searched for and found a gate. With his good arm, he pulled the heavy overcoat tightly around his chest and headed off, beckoning Lena to follow.

The person in charge of this garden obviously did not care that chaos abounded outside the three-meter high walls and exercised his duties with a true Prussian spirit. The design and layout presented a serene orderliness, somewhat military in its precision, with perfectly exact rows, evenly installed from one end to the other. The walls supported a phalanx of geometrically espaliered fruit trees, clinging like crucified skeletons. Even the gray and white stocks of the previous summer's vegetables and flowers were cut low to the ground with the eye of a master barber. Off to their right, built against the perimeter wall, was a long, narrow structure, constructed with the same stones as the surrounding walls, punctuated with windows of opaque glass, and topped with a slanted roof of slate tiles. Webber immediately headed toward it. If there were anything of use to them, it would be there.

The structure ran the full length of the wall. Webber estimated about forty meters. It had three doors, one at each end and one in the center. The middle door, unlike the others that were plain and aged, was painted bright red, the color of energy and danger. It stood out like a ruby lying on a sidewalk and drew them there with the same power. As they came near, the curious attraction of this door irritated his mind like a pebble in a shoe. He reached for the knob, stopped, and withdrew his hand. He had a bad feeling about this anomaly to the somber canvas of the late winter scene. It was the feeling he often got patrolling cities where unseen snipers waited, where only an extra sense developed over time kept him alive. Now it was telling him not to go there. He listened.

"We'll check that door first," he said, pointing down toward the one on the right. Without further explanation, he walked along the front of the shed to the designated door.

Webber was aware that the day was rapidly waning, and he wanted to put some distance between them and that house with all those Russians, two of them dead. Equally concerning was the matter of finding shelter for the night, something as safe as possible and away from there. He picked up his pace, which sent a bolt of pain to his foot, causing him to clench his teeth and pass a nearly inaudible grunt between his lips. Lena made no comment. When Webber reached the door, he grabbed the knob, threw it open without hesitation, and entered.

The floor of the shed was sunken, and they had to descend two wooden steps to reach the brick surface. Under the windows there was a long, simply built workbench, which held an array of pots and wooden flats, neatly arranged. All were filled with fine loamy soil in preparation for the coming spring. Webber's interest was with the drawers. These he searched hoping to find anything that could be useful on their travels but drew a blank.

Wooden planks had been secured to the opposite wall, and a variety of garden tools hung there—shovels, hoes, rakes, and to Webber's satisfaction, a short-handled ax. He lifted it off its pegs and continued his hunt through the shed.

He saw what he was looking for. Running along either side of the center walkway were mounds nearly a meter high of tightly packed sand. He began digging into the mounds. Below the top layer of sand he reached the expected layer of straw, under which he knew would be stored carrots, potatoes, or beets.

A few minutes later, he'd dug up a sack full of carrots and potatoes. The problem was trying to carry it. The damage that happens when a tank is slammed by a 57 mm shell fired from a ZiS2 gun is substantial. A tank, no matter how well armored, will be moved when hit square on. Webber, who was on the opposite side from the attack, was smashed by a Panzer receiving such a blow. His clavicle broke in two places, the humerus bone dislocated from the glenohumeral joint, a number of ribs were cracked, and cartilage all over his upper body was torn. The three cracked metatarsals in his left foot added to the challenge. Now, his left arm was wrapped securely to his body, and the slightest exertion was painful on that side. Picking up a sack of vegetables was excruciating. Webber didn't argue when Lena took the sack away from him and handed him the pillowcase of medicines.

"Don't drop it," she said. The tone of her voice left no doubt that she was serious and brought a quizzical look to Webber's face. He could come to like this nurse.

They continued through the shed. In the dimming light he saw the booby trap. In the center of the room were two wooden sawhorses. Lashed on top, pointing directly at the red door—the door that had given him the uneasy feeling not too long ago—was the strangest gun Webber had ever seen. It was an ancient-looking shotgun with a barrel that was over a meter long and a massive bore. The stock was cracked and worn, the lock and hammer rusted. He guessed it was a long since retired elephant gun, a weapon that could do massive damage, especially at close range. There was a fine strand of wire attached to the trigger. This wire ran to the wall behind it, through a small pulley, and back to the red door.

Whether it was successful or not, he understood it was the death warrant for the gardener, and probably everyone else the Russians gathered for reprisal. He knew what happened to those who laid traps, and he knew the retaliation would not be swift or easy.

"Stupid fool," he muttered. He cautiously approached the device and surveyed the situation, seeking the best way to defuse it.

He had no way of knowing how sensitive the hammer mechanism might be, and the last thing he wanted to do was set off an immense explosion, calling forth the Russians. The wire, which had been wound around the trigger and twisted tight, would not be easy to unravel. He had nothing to cut it. He shifted his attention to the pulley. It was nailed to a wooden peg that was wedge-driven into the wall. Again, it would be too difficult to take apart safely. That left the door.

"Scheisse."

The idea of getting between the gun and the door did not appeal to him, and it was getting late. The one positive he detected was the slack between the pulley and the door, without which the trigger would pull too soon, before the door was open wide enough to make sure the targets were exposed. Looking closer, he could see the wire was attached to an eyebolt screwed into the face of the door. Maybe he could unscrew it and disconnect the trap.

Frozen with these thoughts, he paid little attention to Lena, who was silent and watchful behind him. He was about to step forward to get a better look at the door when, without a word, she walked straight to the relic, placed a thumb on the hammer, and, with the other hand, worked the trigger to release the tumbler, allowing the hammer to lower into the uncocked position.

"It's safe now," she said as she turned around and walked back to the sack on the floor.

Another man might have reacted poorly, suppressing an understandable feeling of stupidity and masking humiliation with anger. Webber was not such a man. A pragmatist by nature, he was open to any idea or action that led to the right result, no matter the origin. He was a man who gave credit where credit was due. He was not effusive with praise, so with a quick turn of his head and a nod at Lena, he was back to the task at hand: dismantling the trap.

When the gun was freed from the sawhorses, he took a moment to weigh it in his hand, feeling its heft and power. He tried to raise it to his shoulder, but with the use of only one arm, it was a pointless idea. He laid it down against the garden wall. Lena had already moved the sawhorses to the side of the room and finished coiling the wire. Then she slipped it easily off the trigger. Without being told, she knew what they were doing. The gardener's life may have been spared.

"Right then, it's time to go," said Webber, and he headed for the red door. This time he opened it without concern, and soon they were gone from the garden, threading through the trees toward the fading glow in the west.

His body ached, and his injuries affected his ability to function. He was unfamiliar with the terrain and worried that he had so little intelligence, but, if there was a better description of the chaos of war, he had not heard it yet.

It was dark now, a good thing. There was a long journey ahead of them, and Webber knew there were trials to come. The nurse had earned his respect, and he now considered his decision to bring her a good one. He actually liked her, and wondered about the letter she carried and the lieutenant who wrote it.

Together, they headed into the woods.

20

November 1989

"Give."

Kurt Webber, standing back in a corner, could see Christoph Mueller was totally baffled.

Dr. Braun pushed past the American, who seemed disconnected or preoccupied, standing motionless and holding the yellowed envelope in his hand, staring at the meaningless letters scrolled in faded ink. Webber took in the whispers and hurried movements of the nurses, but Christoph remained oblivious to the glances in his direction. Suspended moments passed before the doctor rose slowly and turned to face the American. All eyes were now locked in his direction.

Braun's voice was deep, a rumble like a passing trolley car.

Webber, who was behind the doctor, gathered a few thickly accented words like "sorry" and "sudden" and "relieved." He saw the young man's face take on the pallor of death, and beads of sweat appeared on his forehead. He began to sway and reached out for support. Braun grasped him by both arms and guided him to a steel chair at the foot of the bed. Carefully he pressed the American's head forward until it was nearly resting on his knees. Christoph exhaled with a low moan. Jesus, thought Webber, this is embarrassing.

Christoph passed out and would have fallen to the floor but for the doctor.

"That was impressive," said Webber. Braun turned and gave him a look to convey his displeasure.

"We'll have to put him in a room for the night," said Braun to the nurses. "He's had a long trip, and this must have been devastating for him."

Two burly nurses, one on each arm—like trainers helping an injured player off the field—lifted the unconscious American and carried him out of the room, his feet dragging along the tile floor. Webber, who followed, noticed the coarseness of their large arms and the obvious indifference toward their personal hygiene. Russians, he thought, though the pungent odor of the women seemed inconsistent with the gentle manner in which they maneuvered him through the wide, brightly lit corridor.

They took him to another room where, in the graying light, they carefully laid him on a bed, removed his shoes, and covered him with a rough woolen blanket. Even after they had left the room, closing the door behind them, their presence lingered. Brunhildas, he thought as he sat down and settled in to wait for Christoph Mueller, Lena's grandson, to wake. Alone now, he allowed himself to grieve.

21

Christoph awoke disoriented, with the pounding of a hundred-year headache, exhaustion still weighing on his eyes. He strained to get his bearings. The sagging springs and thinly stuffed mattress on which he lay added to his confusion, creating the impression of being wedged in the bottom of a shallow pit. Every direction he tried to move seemed uphill. He found his way out of this predicament by drawing his feet up under his knees, then pushing himself caterpillar-like into a sitting position. It was then that he sensed he wasn't alone in the room.

Gradually, adjusting to the dark, he began to make out the dim image of a face, out of focus, hovering, pale, and motionless, waiting. As he wrestled with this apparition, it spoke. The voice was throaty and heavily accented, so at first he didn't recognize that it was speaking English. When the face stopped speaking, Christoph's blank expression quickly extracted a second attempt.

"Mueller, you okay?" he heard it say as it moved a little closer.

The meaning of the words slowly took shape behind his aching eyes, and he became aware of a faint, blurry shape, the body to which the mask was attached.

"What's going on?" said Christoph, suddenly apprehensive.

He rolled as quickly as he could out of the bed, putting it between himself and the unknown visitor, and never taking his eyes off the resolving shape. For a few pregnant moments, there was a silent impasse. Now on his feet and slightly distanced from the cause of his discomfort, Christoph recognized the absurdity of the situation, and apprehension turned to embarrassment. Standing before him, obviously amused by his abrupt movement, was an elderly bald man, with a face that was lean and taut with deep-set eyes like bottomless holes. The smile didn't soften the fact that it was a hard face. As the two men stood silently on opposite sides of the bed, the tension eased from Christoph's body.

He forced a polite smile, thinking that this was all pretty unreal, being behind the Iron Curtain and all. He wondered what to say next, but it was the other man who spoke first. He talked in a thick German accent, his words like bullets fired with a staccato intensity, his dark eyes never leaving Christoph. The force of the words left no doubt of the serious nature of their content, even though much he couldn't follow.

"Relax, kid, didn't mean to spook you like that. We need some light in here."

Without waiting for a reply, and moving with quickness unbefitting his age, he turned and faded into the darkness. Christoph heard a faint click, and the dim yellow glow of the emergency button next to the bed was suddenly replaced by the cold white fluorescent glare of the recessed ceiling fixture. His attention was now fully on the lively little man who had darted back to his position on the other side of the bed.

He smiled at Christoph, and wrinkles like the prongs of a fork shot out from the corners of his eyes across his temples.

"My name is Kurt Webber. I knew your father."

Kurt Webber! It was a name from far away, from the days when his father was alive and he was a little boy. It was a name from the stories his father used to tell him, bedtime stories about his homeland, his childhood, and all the people left behind—magical stories of imaginary people who blended with all the other tales and fantasies of childhood. Kurt Webber, Onkel Kurt, had been one of those imaginary people, indistinguishable and inseparable from Hansel and Gretel, Iron Henry, and Old King Cole. He hadn't thought of these stories for a long time, not since his father's death, though some fragmented memories had stirred when the first letter arrived from his grandmother. Onkel Kurt had been so consistently present in those stories, so central to his father's life, so sharp a memory now. The name stabbed at his mind. He couldn't speak. Instead, he stared frozen in amazement, as if an image had just walked out of a movie screen into real life.

"What's up, kid, cat got your tongue?" Webber grinned. He loved to speak what he called American talk, as Christoph was to learn.

"Onkel Kurt?" Christoph finally whispered. The tone was drenched in awe.

For one fleeting moment, the corners of Kurt Webber's mouth twitched, the lines of age about his eyes deepened even more, and his black eyes seemed to reflect a minute glimmer, a brief gleam of sunlight on polished obsidian. Just as quickly it was gone, and the old man's face returned to a state of concentrated seriousness.

"Yep, that's me," he said. "I see your father in your face. He gave you his memories too. Das ist gut."

Christoph tried to formulate some kind of a reply, but Webber fired off another burst of words.

"I warned your papa about things, but maybe he don't always listen. Maybe he might live today. We gotta talk, and you gotta listen. You gotta believe what I'm gonna say. Where's the letter Lena gave you?"

Christoph's reaction was instant. Placing his hands on his hips and narrowing his eyes, his eyebrows forming a deep valley, he spoke with a voice drawn tight.

"What the hell? I'm confused. This pisses me off." He paused for a moment to gather his thoughts, a little surprised at himself. This was an uncharacteristic outburst. "I mean, like, I fly halfway around the world to see a grandmother I have never heard from before, and when I finally get here, does she smile or hold my hand or look in the least bit happy to see me? No. She gives me some antique letter, tells me to give it away, and dies. Now this."

Kurt Webber just stared at him.

With steadiness and control returning, Christoph continued. "Sorry, Onkel Kurt, but you wake me up in the middle of the night, and do you want to share our loss or ask me how I'm doing or extend a simple greeting? No. You want the letter. Excuse me, but if I've somehow lost my bearings and entered the wrong mystery novel, I'd like to correct my mistake and get back to normal life."

Another pause.

"She asked me to deliver the letter, and I'm going to do it. I'm going to find the person and deliver it."

Christoph stared at Webber and sagged a little. He was tired, and the passion he'd momentarily felt was dissolving, but in that sudden heat of anger, he'd set an unchartered course. It had jumped out of his mouth, maybe in spite, and now it was there in full view for examination, and a resolve was born.

He'd been feeling a bit lost for a while, bored with school and uncertain about what he wanted to do with his life. Maybe this was the thing he'd been waiting for, the answer to months of indecision, a sense of direction to fill a void that had existed since well before the end of his last semester and graduation.

Where was that letter?

Webber spoke again, a few sharp words. "Okay, okay. You're right. We'll deal with it later, ja?"

"Why? What's the big deal?"

The two stood facing each other as if waiting for the other to make the first move in an Old West gunfight. The young American was tall and lean with a fine, athletic-looking body. He stood there erect, legs slightly spread and hands on his hips, a vision of determination or, thought Webber, obstinacy. Webber, who was a head shorter, with a face battered by life, rested his fists on the bed, and composed an expression that declared he wasn't impressed.

"I don't want za damned letter," he said. "I'm only asking where it is. Obviously you got Lena's bloody will, kid. You know, I've worked with goats that were more cooperative than she was at times."

He chuckled and hardened again. "Let me tell you 'bout this letter; maybe then you get it. Can we sit?"

Christoph gestured to the nurse's chair and sat on the edge of his bed. Webber darted elf-like and sat facing him, leaning forward, his forearms resting on his knees. For a few moments, he looked intensely at the American, organizing his thoughts and assessing the young man in front of him. When he spoke the words came fast, recounting only what was necessary without embellishment.

"I was wounded at za end of za war and in a field hospital. Lena was one of za nurses. There was another patient, an SS lieutenant who lost a leg. Lena had taken to this man and made his recovery personal. I think she fell in love, if love is what you call it. It happened. It wasn't like her, no, but people did desperate things in za last days.

"He was Johann von Ritter, your grandfather. Your father's name too. He had a problem. In his heart there was a secret, something horrible, I think. He needed to fix this before he died. So, the letter, you see?

"I was there when he gave it to Lena. It was za last time they saw each other. Russians were inside za building. He killed two of dem. I'd thought he was a coward, an SS butcher, you know, who'd got some of his own medicine. But no, he was a real soldier. He knew he was gonna die, so he gave her za letter. I don't think he wanted her to have it, but no choice. He didn't know what burden he gave her.

"We got away from za hospital. He didn't. I wouldn't have made it without her. I had a busted foot, and she kept it okay. Took us a month to get to Berlin. But that's another story. I stay with her since."

His voice had trailed off as he spoke these last words, and for a moment the room closed in around his sadness. The old man's lungs involuntarily filled and exhaled with a silent shudder, and Christoph could see tears welling in his eyes. His grief lasted for an instant, and he went on with his account.

"In all za years since, we never talk of von Ritter or the letter, but I know she has it, and I know she never try to deliver it. She couldn't let go of it, I think."

As Webber's story of those long ago events ran on, Christoph grew increasingly excited. He stood and began to pace about the room. Webber's tale brought into focus the purpose of his grandmother's summons, and his determination to obey the last request was steeling as he imagined the scene and felt the heartbreak that his grandmother must have felt. He sensed the guilt too. All those years, it must have been tough. Von Ritter's last wish had to be honored, and it was his job now; he had to do it, and he would. Christoph felt nervous, aroused, like pre-game jitters.

Questions were forming in his mind, but he hesitated asking them. There was a lot to think about, like where in the hell was that letter? When he did his wimp act, it was in his hand; he was sure of that. So it was probably still in Lena's room.

To his relief, Webber stood, gave him a hasty bow, and headed for the bedroom door.

"Think about it, kid. I'll be back in za morning, and I'll take you over to Lena's place. Gute Nacht."

"Gute Nacht, Onkel Kurt."

Just like that, Webber was gone, leaving Christoph's head buzzing with the idea of the quest. Twenty minutes later, as he lay flat on his back, arms at his side and palms up, in a state of deep relaxation, he fell asleep.

When Webber left the room, he whirled around and nipped away down the wide corridor with the short, jerky steps of an old but energetic man. Right now he, too, had to think about the situation. A few minutes later, he was sitting in his car in the dark, lost in memories.

22

Inspector Klaus Krüger, retired six months from the *Bundeskriminalamt* (BKA), was in a rare good mood. Only in his late sixties, he hadn't adjusted well from a hectic career collecting and analyzing criminal intelligence to the dull certainty of retirement. Much of this new life vacillated between searching for significance and darker moments of prowling, like a caged leopard longing for the hunt. This night the Berlin Philharmonic Orchestra had again been brilliant, even without the leadership of his old friend Herbert von Karajan, the recently deceased maestro from Austria. The entertaining program included Johannes Brahms's Violin Concerto in D Major and Richard Strauss's *Ein Heldenleben*. His companion for the evening was the lovely Fraulein Langbehn, who had been as charming as always. It did his heart and psyche considerable good to have such an enjoyable evening with so desirable a young woman. Not that he had lustful desires toward the lady. Even in his younger days, he was never victimized by dangerous sexual urges, and what little drive he may have once had was now pretty much gone. His medical condition— the cancer that had been found in his prostate—made it almost impossible to perform, even if the urge did arise. What attracted him to Carlita was her bright and optimistic outlook, a stark contrast to the remnants of his generation, the *kriegskinder* generation, whose youth had been sacrificed on the altar of war. He really didn't prefer the company of these stony survivors and was always inclined to seek out the stimulation of a more vital demographic.

He was standing in the sprawling foyer waiting for Clarita to return from the powder room when his thoughts were interrupted by a deep cavernous sound he instantly recognized. Detective Erich Schneider's voice rumbled and echoed toward him like thunder in the mountains, a noise peculiar to the man even when he spoke softly as he was now. Krüger attributed this characteristic to his huge barrel chest and equally impressive neck through which air and sound must bounce and careen as it rose. So vast was this man's upper body that Krüger swore that words spoken were heard as a distant vibration and swallowed before they were ever fully enunciated.

"Inspector Krüger," boomed Schneider, "I'm sorry for intervening upon your leisure, but there's a matter of considerable importance."

Krüger and Schneider understood each other well. Except for his Prussian lineage, which made omission of the proper protocols quite impossible, Schneider need not have mentioned that something important was up, for the point was clearly established by the intrusion itself. He wouldn't have appeared for anything less than the highest urgency. Krüger nodded, quickly cast his eye in the direction of the ladies' powder room, and then led Schneider off to a quiet corner of the foyer.

"It's Lupus; he's jumped again."

Krüger's eyes widened then narrowed. "When?"

"About an hour ago."

"Who's on him?"

Schneider paused, then replied in a voice that seemed to drop even deeper. "No one. We don't have the resources anymore."

A dark shadow passed over the older man's countenance. Only bad things happened when the Lupus went into East Berlin, that and the other thing.

"Who else knows?"

"No one. I thought to advise you first." Schneider was huge but not tall. He stood with military rigidness, eye to eye with his former boss, waiting for his next instruction with Prussian patience. Krüger appeared lost in his thoughts for a moment before he spoke.

"Erich, keep this to yourself until the morning. If you pick up his trail again, let me know. Don't contact the East Germans. Instruct all checkpoints to be on the alert for his return. When he does return, pass him through with no more than the normal delay and get a tail back on him immediately. I want to be informed the instant we have a lock on him again. Can you check the log on all his calls today? Good, we'll touch base again tomorrow. Okay? And Erich?"

"Yes, Inspector?"

"Please, call me Klaus. I'm retired."

"Yes, Inspect…" He caught himself, then uncomfortably finished. "Klaus."

With the slightest of nods and no further words, Schneider disappeared into the crowd. Krüger watched him melt away and remained for a few moments, lost in his thoughts. Something was happening; there was always something happening when Lupus was involved. When he retired, he worried he'd spend his last days in unwanted peace. He wasn't a man suited for that, so he'd maintained a loose working relationship with Schneider, who was more than happy to oblige his former boss. Wolfgang Reisen, code name Lupus, was on the move again. This was one of the cases he'd left unresolved, and Schneider had agreed to keep him in the loop.

He turned and saw the lovely Clarita engaged in conversation with the daughter of a local politician, unconcerned by his temporary absence. He had time. Slowly he weaved his way through the crowd to the cloakroom and handed the clerk the claim ticket. The attendant returned with the coats, and as he handed them over the counter, he said, "Have a good evening, Herr Krüger."

Their eyes met.

"Thank you, I'm sure I will. There's a full moon over the East tonight." He didn't tip the attendant and returned to Clarita.

"I'm sorry, my dear, official business doesn't immediately cease when one retires. Come along, let's have supper."

The music had been superb, and the customary late-night supper, as always, would be delightful, yet Krüger knew he wouldn't recapture the pleasant feeling of the evening. The night had lost its magic. Lupus was on the loose. His head throbbed a little, and the ache deep in his back and hips seemed to grow more intense with the passing minutes. As they moved toward the exit, he guided their path past the cloakroom, just close enough to catch the slow, discrete nod from the attendant. The message had been delivered. There was a long night ahead. He wanted to get back to his apartment and rest.

23

Prenzlauer Berg sat to the northeast of the Mitte in East Berlin. It was the scene of ferocious and bloody street battles at the end of the war when the Russians were driving for the Nazi bunker and Adolf Hitler. Most of the buildings dated to the turn of the century; most were damaged and none were restored after the final orgasm of destruction. It was the most dismal, ugly area of decay and rubble, a forgotten land, and a dangerous place even for those who lived there. The socialist revolution hadn't reached Prenzlauer, with its dingy streets and smoky *Kneipen*, neighborhood bars where a person belonged or did not enter. Out of this cesspool of neglect, a new life form evolved: the *Gammler*, young, long-haired dropouts or punks who hung uselessly about Alexanderplatz in the day, wearing torn and ragged jeans and ill-fitting jackets, forever gossiping against the great socialist society, sneering and contemptuous and openly advocating a Western lifestyle. At night they slunk back into Prenzlauer to drink themselves drunk on cheap beer and sing forbidden rock songs. It was the same *Gammler* who'd fought the police and the Stasi recently, demanding the right to hear the music at the Wall. If there had to be one, Prenzlauer was the crime ghetto of the German

Democratic Republic. Nothing like the shoot-'em-up-and-leave-the-bodies-in-the-street ghettos of the West, but a place where it was wise to be cautious. The *Gammler* and the other rough inhabitants were always dangerous.

It was the desperate and forgotten nature of the neighborhood that brought him there now. It was an area he knew well. He was a frequent visitor, prowling for souls. He knew it was a section of the city where even the Stasi avoided going, and as a result, it was home to one of the few untapped call boxes in East Berlin. It was to this phone that he now arrived. He'd walked all the way from Friedrichstrasse station and was in a foul mood.

It wasn't his idea. Wolfgang Reisen had received a phone call from his mother earlier that evening. She was both excited and angry. The letter had appeared; the bitch had had it all along, and now she was dead. It's up to you, she'd said; you have to get it tonight. His reward was the bastard. Once he got the letter, he could do what he wanted with the bitch's grandson, his illegitimate cousin. She assured him this loathsome object was at the sanitarium where Lena Mueller died just hours before. Braun had called and told her he was there, and the letter had been in a Bible.

There was one more thing she needed him to do, which is why he was in a funk and negotiating the streets of Prenzlauer after midnight. The stupid Stasi agent she'd found a couple months ago and paid to search the bitch's apartment was now a liability.

He'd reported there was no such letter, not in that apartment. He was an expert, he claimed, and had left no place untouched. Drawers were opened, searched, and carefully closed; every book, every hat and shoe box was examined; carpets were rolled back; chairs were turned over; under the TV and behind the toilet were all included. He tapped walls for sounds of a possible cavity and examined floorboards for a possible hiding place.

Now that the letter was found, he had to be silenced. She'd contacted and told him to be at the designated phone to receive further instructions. He was due to arrive any minute.

A Trabant slowly approached and pulled up to the curb next to the phone. The driver turned off the motor and extinguished the lights. He lit a cigarette, and in the light of the match, Wolfgang saw him look at his wristwatch. In five minutes the phone would ring. The driver rolled down the window and settled back to wait.

Wolfgang took a deep breath and moved with the stealth of a hungry predator toward the unsuspecting Stasi.

"It was in the fucking Bible."

The suppressed Ruger Mark II .22 mm handgun fired quietly, making a sound like spit hitting the pavement. The slug made a small hole, sufficient at close range to kill yet lacking enough force to be messy. The bullet didn't exit the head but merely bounced around inside the skull. The Stasi's body slumped over the steering wheel. There was hardly any blood; a few drops trickled down the dead man's nose.

Ringing came from the call box. Wolfgang walked around the car and lifted the receiver. There was a tremor in his voice.

"It's done. I'm on my way to the bastard."

The receiver was replaced, and the shadowy figure of Wolfgang Reisen slunk back hurriedly to the car, opened the passenger door, reached across, and violently pulled the dead man out of the driver's seat and into the passenger's. It was no easy task. He shut the door, strode around to the driver's door, and entered. Moments later the Trabant was farting its way through the sodium-lit streets of East Berlin in the direction of the suburb of Beelitz. It would take him at least an hour to get to the sanatorium, and time was running out.

He drove through the deserted streets with as much caution as his aroused condition would allow. Inside the car, electricity crackled, and low, angry growls escaped between his slightly opened lips with the release of each heavy carnivore breath. His elegant fingers clutched the steering wheel, knuckles white from the pressure and forearms burning from the relentless contraction. Despite the coolness of the early morning air, sweat beaded on his forehead, running in small rivulets down his lean, smooth cheeks into the wispy black mustache that drooped around the corners of full, sensuous, pouting lips. Beneath the thick dark line of eyebrows that marked the edge of a slightly protruding supraorbital ridge were eyes of polished steel, the eyes of a wolf, shining out through the windshield, darting and alert. It was a face that defied definition, attracting some and recoiling others; a face that reflected the innermost emotions and instincts of the beholder; a face that was both beautiful and dreadful.

He seethed a messy turmoil of conflicting thoughts. The way he felt wasn't how it was supposed to be after a kill. There should be a pounding heart, a spiritual lightness, an exquisite feeling that he might explode with ecstasy at any second. It was the soul of his victim, the ethereal essence as it rushed forth to join with his. This should come on with a sudden exhilarating surge of power that made self-control nearly impossible. Tonight was bad; he felt sick and disgusted. Normally, it filled him with a primal urge to scream the news of this spiritual bonding, but not this time. There was no joy tonight. The whole experience was wrong.

As he drove through the night, he settled down and emerged from this hyper negative state of mind and was able to reflect. Slowly the throaty emissions lessened into mere rumblings, and the hands on the wheel relaxed. But the restless, seeking eyes never changed. There was more work to do.

It wasn't a good killing, not the way he liked. There should be time to prepare the donor so he could see and appreciate the wonderful transmigration about to occur. After a killing, with the joining of the souls, he should feel close to the pure substance of the ancient ones.

Mutti had ordered it. That was the difference with this one. He missed the buildup and hated leaving the donor so abruptly, without sufficient time to allow for the soothing joining of the souls. It had been too quick, and souls must have time. It was necessary to greet them and create a haven for easy assimilation. This brought the rapture. He liked order, structure. That was his personal trademark. He enjoyed positioning his subjects for the proper effect, and that took time and thought, but Mutti said there was no time for the proper ritual on this occasion. She'd prepared him for that. It was too dangerous to linger over the victim when the victim was Stasi.

He wasn't done yet this night. There was the letter to secure and the bastard cousin; he was looking forward to that. Until now Mutti had refused to permit the killing of this pox upon the von Ritter family. He'd waited months, and the disappointment hurt. It had caused a rare tension between them, which made him quite ill at the time. He couldn't bear to have Mutti upset or disappointed with him. So it was uplifting when this time she offered up the American.

He had to rush to finish before the Stasi agent was missed, because once that happened, getting back to the West could be difficult. The Stasi weren't used to having their own executed, and he expected a full-scale alert that would close off most escape routes. He looked over at the slumped figure. He seemed so useless, so pathetic, and it certainly made tonight more complicated, but a soul is a soul, he admitted, and his strength was that much greater for it.

With his mother there was no discussion or debate when it came to the "quest," as she called the long-sought-after letter, written by her brother long ago. It was hard to believe that it was finally about to reach its rightful owners. Mutti had told him they were the only ones in the world who could decipher its secret and claim some treasures it protected. It was their right.

He thought of the American often and the letter so dear to Mutti. He fantasized his death a hundred different ways and experienced the exhilaration of the moment with tantalizing vividness. He was a bastard, not a true von Ritter. He was the descendant of the seductress whore; he was the magnificent obsession. He'd pleaded with Mutti the last time, because, like his father before him, this one was also a desecration on the family's honor, a bastard's bastard, a vile leech that must be removed. Mother hadn't disagreed, but she said that the time was not right. There was the letter to be considered. He'd been too impetuous to understand. He hated the bastard with a passion so strong, so consuming, that it was almost sensual.

The lingering glow of the Stasi man's soul still tingled, heightening the anticipation, warming him for the approaching climax. The speed of his car rose slightly as the tension in his muscles inched the accelerator toward the floor as he approached the sanitarium. With effort he managed to slow down and enter the grounds under control. As he headed for the women's building, it was his mother who dominated his thoughts.

■ ■ ■

Demons and monsters exist in human form. Whether they are born or created by the environment is arguable. Wolfgang was not born into a happy home.

Kreimhilde von Ritter Reisen, "Hilde," loathed her husband as she did all men.

Dr. Paul Reisen arrived in August 1945 and was accepted into her home at a time when the need for security and protection was greater than the contempt she'd developed for the opposite sex during the degradations inflicted on the defeated. They married, but he never gave her the letter or revealed its existence. He did give her a son. For most of the boy's life, Hilde was indifferent to Reisen's son.

The boy's world was a seething pressure cooker. Throughout his earliest years, he was the troubled observer of persistent warfare between his parents, and he silently absorbed the taut and edgy atmosphere their endless battles fostered. He was shunned and ignored by his mother, who saw him as the constant and unpleasant reminder a woman's fate, while his Prussian father subjected him to a world of oppression. Paul and Hilde never touched the boy, not even as an infant. It was the one thing they had in common. Neither had the slightest inclination to share the least bit of intimacy or comfort, for comfort was anathema in the Reisen home. The only affection would come from the string of nannies employed to do the parents' business.

He was seven years old when the animals began to die, ten when he came to believe that the souls of his "donors" joined with his, fourteen when Hilde discovered his secret, and forty when she found out about the letters written by her brother. That was a few months ago when she was going through the papers of her recently deceased husband and learned his secret.

■ ■ ■

It took him nearly an hour to reach the sanitarium. Before he drove Bauer's car through the gates, he'd dumped the body in a stand of trees off the main road along a narrow lane. His mood began to change again. He was so close to his dream, the bastard cousin's soul.

24

Klaus Krüger sat patiently in his study, at ease in his favorite chair—a cordovan-colored leather armchair that he brought back with him from Italy many years ago. The comfort he enjoyed in this old chair was relative, considering the permanent pain that racked his back, compliments of the cancer moving through his body like an army on the march. Once dandelions get into your lawn, his doctor had said, you can try and cut them out, but their roots are deep and difficult to get at. You can poison them, but this can have side effects, or you can live with them. Krüger had chosen a fourth option, hormone therapy to reduce testosterone. He doubted it was working. The phrase "life is short" had real meaning for him now.

He checked his watch. It was after 5:00 a.m., and he'd been waiting for nearly three hours. Despite the early hour and the fact that he'd had little sleep, he wasn't tired. He needed less these days, and he often read until dawn with only occasional naps. His eyes drifted about the room. The study was the largest room in his apartment and the place he spent most of his time since retirement. His needs were few, and even when he entertained it was into this room that his guests were usually invited.

All the walls were lined with bookshelves packed with books, binders, papers, and magazines of every size and shape in jumbled disarray. One of his concessions to a relatively long life was the abandonment of any attempt to maintain an orderly system of stacking. It was a compromise between his love of order and logic, his age and health, and the restrictive confines of his limited Berlin apartment. He was a hopeless literary pack rat.

The floor was covered with a huge, ruby-red Boukarah rug and contained four pieces of furniture. In addition to the armchair, there was a small matching love seat and, to his left, a walnut writing desk and chair. On its polished leather writing surface meticulous order reigned. A large, black leather-bound blotter, centered perfectly, was flanked on one side by a black telephone and a small mantel clock, and on the other side, a black leather desk accessory box containing writing paper and matching envelopes with his name imprinted in black gothic script, a black Mont Blanc fountain pen, and a silver letter opener in the likeness of a small, elegant dagger. There was an inscription on the blade: *To KK, my confidant. HvK.* It was a gift from Herbert von Karajan. Centered on the desk was an antique lamp, set on an oval black marble base, with two black marble columns carved and gilded to create an ionic impression. The columns supported a long triangular-shaped shade painted a high black gloss on the outside and gold on the inside. It was this lamp that now provided a subdued illumination that kept the far corners of the study in soft shadow. The only sound was the steady ticking of the clock, which Krüger always found peaceful.

Over the years he'd kept a vigilant eye on Wolfgang Reisen, code name *Lupus.* The nephew of Lieutenant Johann von Ritter had settled some years ago into the collage that was West Berlin, an isolated world and the melting pot of Europe, attracting the cultural refugees from all nations. It was the great black hole from which escape often seemed impossible. They came in numbers, these outcasts, skinheads from Denmark, nihilists from Spain, escapees from the east side of the Wall who couldn't stand to be out of sight of the Tele-Tower of Alexanderplatz, West German students avoiding military service, and guest workers from Turkey who spoke fluent German and could never go home—all the disillusioned misfits and discontents of the world for whom the slums, bars, nightclubs, and government support programs provided the closest possible facsimile of comfort and acceptability.

Krüger himself was an exile; most Germans of his age were. He too had nowhere else to go. That's how it is when a spy comes in from the cold, and he was a special one.

It had been a while since he last contacted his masters, the Stasi— one of the benefits of retirement, he mused. Now that he no longer had direct access to most current information, his usefulness was almost nonexistent, so they left him alone. All employers were like that. Things went forward, and once he got off the train, it quickly disappeared down the track, forever. No matter how important and vital to their operations he once was, he was replaced and forgotten almost immediately. This didn't bother Krüger, who felt no attachment to his Stasi past nor the Gestapo life before that. He had always lived his life in the present, following the strange twists of destiny that had carried him along like a leaf drifting on the surface of a river, following the course of least resistance. This passive acceptance had allowed him a clear conscience as he traveled through a world darkened by lies, deception, and intrigue. He had no regrets and only a few pieces of unfinished business, which was why he now waited.

He'd kept in touch on a few matters. Wolfgang Reisen (Lupus) was one such concern.

A single ring of the telephone suddenly jarred him out of his solitude. The sound reverberated about the room before slowly fading away. Once again the steady ticking of the clock was the only sound. Krüger didn't pick up, and it didn't ring again. His wait was nearly over. Ten minutes later, the front door buzzer sounded. He pushed the release and moments later the door to the study opened, and a woman entered the room. She was unknown to Krüger, the latest in a line of Stasi handlers assigned to direct his activities. A woman, he thought, another sign of his diminished value.

She was tall and blond, perhaps natural, her hair cut in the modern post-punk style: short, layered, somewhat spiky, and parted to allow the left side to sweep down across one eye. She was well dressed in a tailored gray suit that accentuated her shapely assets, a delicately striped blouse, and a teal silk scarf fashioned around her neck to ensure its gracefulness was not obscured. She looked more like a junior executive for a Western bank than a Stasi agent, but that was the trend now. Gone were the days when the men he dealt with were bartenders, auto mechanics, and petty government employees—men who chose the lonely and dangerous life because they had lived and suffered under Hitler and believed in the communist gospel with their soul, men in black leather jackets and cheap shoes. Now there was a whole class of educated, perfumed agents, dressed up and more Western in their conduct than the regular inhabitants of Berlin. It seemed to Krüger that this new generation was too much at home in the West, shopping in the Ku'damm and sipping Kirshwasser late into the night in the Kreuzberg quarter where squatters, immigrants, and the young punk cult congregated in smoky, dilapidated buildings surrounded by the Wall. He wondered just how true their loyalty was to the party. Not that he was one to criticize. But he did worry about his own integrity when dealing with them.

The visitor carefully closed the door and proceeded to survey the room. The unpracticed lack of speed at which she performed this task reinforced Krüger's first impression. The young woman hadn't learned to see only what was necessary and important. Krüger waited patiently as she painstakingly scanned, extracted, prioritized, and analyzed the room. At least she didn't appear unduly nervous, which was a relief. He only hoped that she would be intelligent enough to listen to an old, retired agent of little perceived value. It would be easy for an inexperienced operative to dismiss him, especially if she wasn't familiar with the case history. Finally satisfied, she spoke.

"Sherlock?" she said in a smooth voice.

"Of course. Sit down, please." Krüger extended a hand toward the sofa.

"You have a message for me," said the woman after she sat down, crossed a pair of long legs, and threw an arm along the back of the sofa, assuming a position of casual relaxation.

"Yes," affirmed Krüger, "but you have the advantage over me. May I know with whom I'm speaking?"

"No. I will convey your message. You have to trust that."

Obviously policies had changed. A code name was always required in the past, and for good reason.

"My young friend, I'm a well-known person in Berlin. That you know my code name tells me nothing. I have friends, all of whom I know. You are not one of them. I have many enemies, only some of whom I know. This makes me cautious. You walk into my study in the middle of the night, claiming that I sent for you. I did not send for you. I don't even know you. I'm uncomfortable with people I don't know, who come into my house in the middle of the night."

When he finished, the Stasi agent was facing the barrel of a small handgun, a .38 caliber he'd kept in his lap.

"Perhaps you'd like to tell me who you are and why you're here. Otherwise I shall be left with no choice but to disable you and call the police. I'm a little out of practice, so I can't guarantee that you'll only be disabled. I'm waiting. Perhaps you could begin by telling me how you heard that I'd sent for you, and why."

The Stasi reacted well, showing neither fear nor surprise. She seemed to consider Krüger's words, looking away, like this happened all the time, before she spoke.

"You're right, Herr Sherlock. We must be able to converse with confidence. However, this doesn't change the fact that I remain nameless. We have no choice regarding this matter. I'm not authorized to identify the initiator of our exchange. I must assume the code name 'Sherlock' is you? I'm okay with telling you mine."

"I'm waiting."

"I'm Ainippe."

Krüger smiled and placed the handgun in his lap, leaving it in full view on top of the blanket. Ainippe, he thought, the swift mare that died in battle with Heracles.

"Good; let's talk about Lupus. Tell me, are you familiar with this file?"

"I'm not sure who you expected to meet with tonight. I was instructed to come here and get and report your message. I was provided your name, address, the contact signal, and code word 'Sherlock.' That's all I know. I don't even know who runs you. I'm not what you would call a handler. I don't run agents. Now if you'll be so good as to give me your message, I'd like to be on my way. It's getting close to morning, and I have a day job."

It was as he feared. For all they cared, he hardly existed. This seemed about as secure as making a direct phone call to Stasi headquarters.

He continued to watch the Stasi as he considered his options. An intriguing, perhaps foolhardy, possibility was swirling about in the distant regions of his mind, congealing, taking shape. The idea was completely out of character, and in years past he would have rejected it almost at once, but whom did he have to answer to anymore?

He took the leap and decided his course of action. He kept the sound of his voice steady as he addressed his visitor.

"Do you have something to write with or a tape recorder?" he asked.

"No. My memory is excellent. You can be assured that your message will be accurately transmitted."

"We'll see. I'm about to tell you a fairly comprehensive story, and Lupus is just a small part. You see my point?"

She shrugged, indicating that Krüger should proceed.

He didn't hurry. He took a slim, silver cigarette case out of his shirt pocket, opened it, and offered it to his visitor. When the woman declined, he took one out for himself and casually lit it. He rarely smoked anymore, but he needed time to contemplate. After he'd taken a couple of long pulls, he began.

"In March of 1945, as the Russian army under Marshal Zukor was amassing on the Oder River and the Allied bombers were demolishing our cities, everyone except Hitler knew the war was over, but no one could stop it. The army had tried in the July twentieth plot and lost thousands of its best officers for its efforts. Do you know what happened to the senior Wehrmacht officers who were the first arrested? The lucky ones were shot on the spot. Others were tortured into disclosing other names and were then left to die, impaled on meat hooks. They didn't teach you that in school, did they? Even Field Marshal Rommel was forced to commit suicide because the conspirators had contacted him. The military wasn't alone in seeking an end to the war. Some of Hitler's closest and most trusted henchmen were in on the act. Himmler, faithful little Heine, had been negotiating for a long time with the International Red Cross, through whom he had made proposals to the American general Eisenhower. In fact, he even released thousands of Jewish prisoners from the concentration camps in an effort to show some kind of good will, an extraordinary piece of self-deception, don't you think? He was also planning his escape, just as many others were.

"Things don't always turn out the way they're supposed to, but what can a man do? He takes life the way it comes at him and makes the best of it. When life gives you lemons, make lemonade, yes?

"At this time a Gestapo agent was summoned to Himmler's headquarters. This agent was a detective who'd worked directly for Himmler a few times. He had the knack, kept a low profile, and was careful to keep control of his own files. As a result, he wasn't well known.

"When he arrived at Himmler's headquarters, he was informed that a valuable and extremely secret cargo, a strongbox, had gone missing. His orders were to find it. He easily located the vehicle, one of Himmler's staff cars, which had been used by the officer in charge of this cargo. It was abandoned in the destination warehouse some days before. The SS officer, his driver, and the strongbox were gone. They've never been found.

"The Gestapo agent located the car in the middle of the night and unfortunately was caught in a British air raid, which demolished the warehouse and nearly killed him. He was left badly injured and unable to follow the trail."

The anxious-to-be-somewhere-else Stasi interjected at this point. "This is all quite interesting but rather old information. Perhaps you've found Himmler's strongbox?"

"No one, as far as I know, has found it yet. By the way, it was destined for Sweden. But let me ask you, given these facts, aren't you a little curious about this strongbox? Doesn't some kind of message go ricocheting about your brain when you consider the facts? The second most powerful man in the Third Reich, head of an organization that controlled vast sums of money and other forms of wealth—realizing the war was lost and knowing that his future wasn't looking good—attempted to send this trove out of the country as secretly as possible. Only four people other than Himmler knew about it, and two of these, the officer and his driver, disappeared with it. Whatever was in that box was hugely important to Himmler."

Krüger paused. He searched the young woman's face for some sign of understanding, but saw nothing.

"You know that others tried to get away; Bormann, Eichmann, and Mangelese attempted to escape at the end of the war. The inevitability of defeat was so obvious for so long that many networks were established and functioning for a long time before the end. The SS had a typically efficient organization, and hundreds of officers made their way out of the country. One favorite route was through Denmark and Sweden. Himmler himself was heading for Denmark and would probably have made it if he hadn't been such a fool."

Krüger lit another cigarette before proceeding.

"It would be reasonable to conclude that he intended to rendezvous with the strongbox in Sweden. Now put yourself in Himmler's place. The most wanted man in the world on the run. He had no close friends, and loyalty, well, who puts loyalty ahead of survival? In this situation what would you want to have: money, or better, negotiable wealth like gold or other valuables? Ah, now you look interested."

He could see the pretty Stasi was doing some quick mathematics, wondering no doubt how big the strongbox might be. At today's rates there could be a fortune buried somewhere, ready for the finding. The fish was checking out the bait.

"Actually, I was just wondering if this Gestapo agent was the man you call Lupus?" she asked.

"No. Lupus is an intriguing person, but we're getting ahead of ourselves. I thought you might be wondering who the people were that knew of Himmler's little secret."

The Stasi invited Krüger to continue with a hand gesture.

"As luck would have it during the aftermath, he meets Dr. Johannes Stumm, who had become police director for the whole of the Russian sector of Berlin. Stumm needed competent officers, and our Gestapo was convincing. There was no documentation to indicate that he had committed any atrocities or other crimes, and it helped that our former Gestapo agent was able to put the finger on a few other colleagues and SS men who had infiltrated the embryonic police force, including the police vice-president, Dr. Kionka.

"However, our man never got much of a start in his new job. The MVD heard about him. You know the MVD, the Russian Ministry of Internal Affairs?"

"Herr Sherlock, I studied recent history. I can bore you with my knowledge of the Russian security organizations, dating back to Cheka and OGUP. I know intimately the ups and downs of the NKVD and NKGB, and all the various heads, whose heads have rolled. Please go on."

"Excellent. The MVD wanted to take advantage of the turmoil to put as many agents in place as possible. They were ready to make deals. 'You work for us and we won't execute you' was one of their favorites. Our man was able to negotiate a good deal. He wound up training with the emerging foreign intelligence organization being created by Markus Wolf.

"For two or three months he had access to whatever records he wanted. He had little to go on, but, as I've said, he was good. Did I tell you about the man in Himmler's car?"

The Stasi, who had now forgotten her watch, shook her head.

"Well, when our Gestapo found Himmler's car, someone else was already there, someone with a key to the warehouse. It was confirmed later that this key was the one that had been issued to the missing SS officer, a Lieutenant von Ritter—Nazi records, particularly Himmler's, were extraordinary. Unfortunately, the bombing began before this man could be thoroughly questioned about the key. All this information disappeared into the rubble when the roof caved in."

"Was it von Ritter?" asked the Stasi. The fish was hooked, and all Krüger had to do was reel it in.

"No."

"Are you sure?"

"Positive. There was clear, definitive visual confirmation."

"By the Gestapo agent?"

Krüger nodded.

"Did this Gestapo agent know von Ritter?"

"Not personally, but he knew von Ritter's description. The man in the car was older, in his mid to late thirties. Von Ritter was young. There was no mistake."

"So the assumption was that this man had come into contact with von Ritter, and must have spoken with him sometime after his disappearance. How else could he have acquired the key and the knowledge of what it unlocked?"

"Precisely," exclaimed Krüger. "And that's what made the bombing inopportune. The strongbox couldn't be too far away, and the scent was fresh. But for the untimely interruption, this story might never have been told. But it wasn't completely terminal. Before the roof came down, our Gestapo had learned enough to give some shape to his subsequent investigation. A name, a division, a geographical limitation—this all helped to narrow his quest and provide the faintest of clues from which he was able to unravel an amazing story."

"A story that leads to Lupus."

"Sort of. A bizarre trail, to say the least, one that's known by few. Lupus is a fascinating person. He would have done exceedingly well in the Third Reich. As it is, he lives here in Berlin. He's intelligent, wealthy, and a murderous psychopath. We know of, or suspect, six murders he's committed, and it's safe to say that he would probably be in jail or some institute but for the problem of sustainable evidence. The fascinating thing for me, which I'll share with you, is his name."

Krüger paused, looking over at the Stasi to make sure the fish was still on the line. She was.

"Lupus's real name is Wolfgang Reisen," he said. "As we speak he is somewhere on the other side of the Wall. What makes this person so special is the curious fact that he's Johann von Ritter's nephew, the son of our dearly departed lieutenant's sister."

"Curious, to say the least, Herr Krüger, but why is this anything but a coincidence?"

"Excellent point. However, you should still call me Sherlock."

"Of course, my apologies."

"Naturally, investigating von Ritter's family is an obvious lead any detective would follow, which our Gestapo routinely did. He discovered that the sister, Hilde von Ritter, who was some years younger than her brother, was married in 1947 at the age of eighteen to Dr. Paul Reisen, a medical doctor teaching at the university in Munich, her hometown. Here lies the interesting part: when our Gestapo checked into Reisen's records, he found an intriguing piece of information. Reisen was a Wehrmacht doctor attached to the Army Group Vistula stationed in East Prussia in the final months before the sack of Berlin. He would therefore have been somewhere near the Oder River, near to and around the same time of Lieutenant von Ritter's disappearance. Curiouser and curiouser, wouldn't you think?"

"So, this doctor meets, perhaps treats, von Ritter who, while in his care, shares something regarding the strongbox with his physician. Von Ritter doesn't make it through the war, but the doctor does and makes a beeline, figuratively speaking, to the sister. Why would he do that? If von Ritter had told me where the box was, the last place I would go would be to his family. I'd keep it to myself. Correct?"

Krüger smiled and tilted his head. "Perhaps your first thought was accurate, and Reisen encountering Hilde von Ritter was pure coincidence."

Now it was Ainippe's turn to smile. She was enjoying this. "No, my dear Sherlock, I don't think you believe that. You think that if indeed von Ritter told Reisen about the box, he didn't disclose its hiding place. He might have, on the other hand, said that his sister knew where it was. So Reisen goes looking for her. Chances are she didn't know, dead end. In the meantime, they fall in love and marry. Too bad about the son."

Krüger slapped his knee, threw back his head, and laughed. "Ainippe, that's brilliant. You're wasting your time doing whatever it is you do, unless of course you're a detective, which I doubt. Your deductions seem Sherlockian, if I may say so. Unfortunately, I have to tell you they're actually Watsonian. There is an old joke about Holmes and Watson. It goes like this:

"Sherlock Holmes and Doc Watson go on a camping trip, set up their tent, and fall asleep. Some hours later, Holmes wakes his faithful friend. 'Watson, look up at the sky and tell me what you see.' Watson replies, 'I see millions of stars.' Holmes asks, 'What does that tell you?' Watson ponders for a minute, then intent to impress his mentor, says, 'Astronomically speaking, it tells me that there are millions of galaxies and potentially billions of planets. Astrologically, it tells me that Saturn is in Leo. Time wise, it appears to be approximately a quarter past three. Theologically, it's evident the Lord is all-powerful and we're small and insignificant. Meteorologically, it seems we'll be having a beautiful day tomorrow. What does it tell you, Holmes?'

"Holmes is silent for a moment, then speaks. 'Watson, you idiot, someone has stolen our tent.'"

When the laughing ended, Krüger leaned forward and said, "And so, Ainippe, while you're thinking along the right lines, you've missed one salient possibility. The sister couldn't have known where the box was at the time the paths of her future husband and brother crossed, so was it probable that von Ritter somehow subsequently tried to get the details to her?"

Ainippe thought about this. She couldn't fully imagine what the conditions must have been like on the eastern front, but she realized that a phone call was unlikely. The only thing she could think of was some kind of a messenger.

"Bravo. Excellent," exclaimed Krüger. "So, who do you think that messenger might have been?"

Ainippe's eyes widened and she nearly shouted her answer. "The doctor!"

"My dear woman, your talent is wasted on the Stasi."

"Let me think." Ainippe's mind was clearly racing. "If von Ritter told Reisen where the box was hidden, it's not likely that the doctor would have gone to find the sister. Why would he? So what did von Ritter reveal? What sent Reisen scurrying to find her?"

"Very good. Maybe von Ritter revealed nothing. Maybe he didn't trust the doctor. Just like you, he could have reasoned that if he told Reisen where the strongbox was, that would be the end of story. Now, consider this. For an SS officer to disobey a direct order from the second most powerful man in the Third Reich, effectively stealing something quite significant, well, this was a very, very desperate act, not one to be taken lightly. Von Ritter would be extremely careful to guard his secret and unlikely to reveal it to a stranger."

"Unless he feared the secret would die with him."

Krüger liked this woman more and more. Here was a mind that actually thought ahead, in search of a logical course of events. He wondered if she played chess and made a note to himself to challenge her someday.

"Why would that be so bad?" he asked. "Ah, maybe we can answer that question by exploring the young lieutenant's motives. It seems to me he took this drastic action for one of two reasons: greed or honor. In the first case, he sees the end of the war coming and seizes the opportunity to enrich himself for the peace ahead. Possible. However, I lean toward the second motivation. A young officer, a real patriot who has seen comrades die for the fatherland, discovers that a rat is fleeing the ship and decides to take action to foil little Heine's plan. In this scenario, it would be crucial to try and keep the truth alive, don't you agree?"

Ainippe could sit no longer. She stood and began to pace around the room. "Throughout this conversation I've been observing and taking in the contents in this room. I see the mementos and awards on the walls, bookshelves, and desk, signs of a career in police work, the indicators of a senior official. You haven't bothered to hide the fact that you are Klaus Krüger, a well-known federal investigator, and here I am, an unimportant, lowly tool for the Stasi who flirts and occasionally 'delivers' in return for what could be described as little more than gossip, which I accurately and objectively pass on to my handler. Why are you telling me all this? Are you a rogue agent? Or perhaps I'm being set up? If so, why? Or am I just a minor cog in some bigger operation? I won't be a puppet in whatever this affair might be."

Krüger, ignoring her outburst, went on with his narrative.

"I hoped you might be wondering how I came by this story, what the point of all this is, who needs to know, and why."

"I know who you are. I remember you from the Red Army days; you were often on the TV. Keep going."

Again Krüger had to smile. The game was becoming interesting.

"Knowing who I am should lend some credence to what I'm about to say. About three months ago, I was approached by an acquaintance to whom I owed a favor. He had a friend who also needed a favor. It always happens that way. This is the story I was told. This friend of my acquaintance wanted to get hold of some old family treasures—papers and letters stuck behind the Wall—held captive by a distant relative who refused to let them go. I was asked if I knew anyone who could find, extract, and deliver these documents to their rightful owner. I told my friend that I would see what I could do, but only on the condition that I knew the names of the two feuding family members involved. You see, if anything strange happened, I wanted to be ready. At first they were reluctant to provide this information, but eventually they came round. I suspect they weren't successful in finding anyone else who could help them.

"Here's where it gets interesting. The name of that mean old East German relative meant nothing to me at the time. On the other hand, the name of the person who wanted these papers hit me like a Max Schmeling uppercut. You know Schmeling?"

She shook her head. Krüger paused and studied his new accomplice. She looked composed, but the next few words brought her back to her feet with a jolt.

"The name was Hilde Reisen. Hilde von Ritter Reisen. Now what do you think she was after?"

Ainippe, who had continued to pace around the room, stopped in her tracks and turned to face Krüger, her hands resting on her hips. He found that attractive.

"Herr Krüger, the question is, who is this distant East German relative and how does he fit into the puzzle? Correct me if I'm wrong, but until you know this, you're wasting your time trying to guess what Hilde Reisen is after. It might be something quite innocent, yes?"

"Bravo, again. The same thought struck me, and I did investigate. The relative is a woman. Her name is Lena Mueller, a nurse living in Beelitz. That's a small town outside Potsdam. She works in a facility that treats the Russian military and high-up party members."

"But what's the connection? Did you find anything?"

"Nothing. I just wasn't that interested. I had other things on my mind." Like how long do I have to live, he thought. "But tonight, when I heard that Lupus had once again entered his favorite hunting grounds, it revived the dimming flame in this old man."

He smiled at the thought. Chasing the prey was something he enjoyed and missed.

"So, now that you've told me all this, what next?"

She sat, crossed her legs, and looked inquiringly at Krüger.

"First," instructed Krüger, "you must report to whoever sent you and inform him that Sherlock told you Lupus has gone east. That's all. Lupus has gone east. However, you need to delay delivering this message as long as possible.

"Next, and after delivering that message, but not before five o'clock tonight, you'll go to an executive suite that I lease and see what's in the fax machine there. That's where any further information or instructions will be. In the meantime, I have some thinking to do."

He scribbled an address on a sheet of yellow paper, took a key from his desk drawer, and handed it to the woman. He felt better than he had for a long time.

"And now, my dear Ainippe, I'm rather tired and must get some sleep. I won't show you to the door. Good-bye."

After Ainippe departed, he took a small key out of the center drawer and unlocked the bottom drawer to his right. From it he took a sheet of paper. It was a copy of the letter von Ritter had given Paul Reisen. He had coerced it from the doctor over ten years before, but the message contained in it was meaningless without another letter, the existence of which was a mystery, up until now. He admired von Ritter's clever devise and was amazed that it worked. The great wonder was that these letters both seemed to have the magical good fortune and the power of survival that allowed him this one last hunt.

25

After Ainippe's departure, Ernst Kepler sat motionless, pondering his spontaneous decision to draw her into this old business. He was a cautious man, but in the small hours of the morning he'd opened a tap, letting loose a flow of events that would follow its own course of least resistance. This was a remarkable divergence from his usual practice, in which a predictable path was assiduously planned and operations launched with the satisfaction, or at least the perception, of control. This aberration didn't cause any sense of alarm. Quite the opposite. There was a feeling of elation, as if he were in a flying dream where no danger existed. His parachute was the glorious independence when one had nothing to lose, the constant ache that throbbed across his back and hips a permanent reminder.

A smile creased his face as it occurred to him that after three decades of living two contrived lives at the same time, the real self—concealed, suppressed, unfulfilled, and biding its time like a sharp-eyed raptor high on its perch—had just taken wing. Leaning back in his chair, he closed his eyes. Retirement had left him empty, without tasks and duties to fill the hours, and he found himself exploring, not knowing what he sought.

His thoughts traveled back to his first meeting with Markus Wolf, code name Eckart or, as he was known in the West, the Silver Fox, who was the new head of the HVA, the international intelligence arm of the Stasi. Wolf had recruited him shortly after the war and later, in the middle of the massive brain drain era, sent him into the West, where he rather easily secured a position with the Berlin police under the new alias Klaus Krüger.

Kepler-Krüger became aware that the silence of the early morning had given way to the sounds of rain lashing at the study windows with a steady yet random rhythm. Released from his reminiscing, he rose and crossed the room to look into the antique oval mirror, enclosed in a gilded frame of lounging nudes. He observed without emotion that his journey had run a long course. Looking back at him was a well-worn face with reddened cheeks that sagged slightly into his jowls and puffy bags of pale flesh that underpinned his fading, colorless eyes. The nose had softened, and what had been a head of thick brown hair with a distinct widow's peak now, like a receding mountain glacier, had reversed direction, exposing a wide and slightly protruding forehead. It was a long way from 1953 when he "fled" the GDR.

The 'escape' had been planned by Markus Wolf and revealed to him during an interview in an office at the Institute of Economic Research, the front name for the fledgling foreign intelligence service that Wolf was building. This took place a week after they had met. For the first forty-five minutes, the tall, handsome head of foreign intelligence charmed Krüger, while minutely extracting his life story. After another hour had passed, he had agreed to the plan that would send him into the West.

It was simple, as all good plans must be. The socialist state didn't look favorably upon those who engaged in unlicensed private enterprise. Another agent, a graduate of the Karl Marx University, had apparently set up a private technical translation business and was looking for employees. The Stasi had found out about this and were about to have the criminal arrested, but Wolf, seeing an opportunity, arranged for Kepler, now Krüger, who was fluent in English and French, to become part of the enterprise. This led to his arrest, and he was labeled as politically untrustworthy, a necessary addition to a resume that already included a suggested Nazi past. With this kind of record, Wolf emphasized, "the West will receive you with open arms."

The opportunity came after the June 1953 uprising, when Russian tanks crushed East Germans protesting the state's decision to raise food prices and limit wages. This spurred a massive migration to the West, particularly among the intelligentsia. Wolf knew a good thing when he saw it and made use of this human flood to send Kepler and hundreds of other dormant spies across the border to await future instructions. That was a long time ago, and Kepler-Krüger sometimes wasn't sure who he truly was.

The sound of the rain had diminished. Krüger went to the window, pulled back the heavy burgundy-colored drapes, and looked out into the night, but all he saw were the liquid rivulets of water reflecting through the glass, flashing silver as they streaked down to the sill. He gave a small sigh as he thought it wouldn't be long before another long bleak winter hurled in from the north.

He reflected on how his life had been an amazing journey. He tried to remember who once told him that we walk a fine line on this journey, we survive altruistically, receiving both in kind and in quantity that which we give. *But be careful not to give more than the beneficiary can return.*

He turned and scanned his library, taking in the many landmarks he'd accumulated along the way: bookcases crammed with his favorite books, certificates and awards, mementos and gifts, and, most precious to him now, the many photographs. These were the people who had inhabited the spaces through which he had traveled, at least since the war. For him, the images were more than just captured moments. Among them was the irony of the three smiling faces of Willy Brandt, Günter

Guillaume, and Klaus Krüger enjoying a holiday in France, just days before Guillaume was exposed as a Stasi spy, triggering Brandt's resignation as chancellor, a tactical disaster for Wolf's intelligence machine.

Krüger no longer worried about survival or questioned the purpose of his life. He was done with living on the razor's edge, tracing the endless loop between the ying and the yang, the good and the evil, or the evil and the evil, depending on whom you believed.

He was certain, without reservation, that there was no god, because no source of benevolence could possibly have constructed Hitler or his war, or the great war before that, or the Black Plague, the Inquisition, and Khmer Rouge, but within the tiny theater where his play was about to close, he would perform that role.

He had found Ainippe quite amusing. His decision to let her into the von Ritter mystery was one of the fastest and possibly most reckless decisions he'd made in a long time, and now, looking back at it, he was still pleased he'd put into play this game he was inventing. He felt like the brothers Parker must have when they launched Monopoly. Best of all, he had no idea how it would be played or where it would take him, nor did he care.

He stood at the window and watched the colorless light of dawn testify that the night was over, and he realized how tired he felt, tired but content. He had a long and busy weekend ahead. He opened the drapes all the way, returned to his desk, turned out the lamp, and headed for the door. He would grab a short nap and await a call from Schneider.

26

Webber woke up, wide awake, every sense alert. He knew exactly where he was, as if he'd never been asleep. It was always this way, a habit. He often thought about this, but never figured out whether it was a something he'd learned or a natural predisposition that emerged in response to the constant, suffocating fear of war. He wasn't like that when he was young, back before the first bullet whistled past his head or the first bomb screamed its way to earth close enough to make the ground around him heave.

He remained motionless, listening. A pale, cold grayness glazed the surrounding world, the first hint of another day making the landscape seem a blur of dark shapes, like smeared ink stains on parchment. He smelled the earthy dampness and knew it had rained while he slept.

Mornings seem to come quicker every year, he thought.

How long had he been asleep? He figured it was around five thirty or six, so maybe three hours at the most, probably less. These days he never slept too long at a time; his body wouldn't allow that. It ached to lie in one position too long, and it hurt even more to move; and he always needed to pee, like now.

With the painful reminder of how old age rewards those who endure, he pulled himself out of the car and hobbled toward the sanitarium. It was a building that always made him think of a nineteenth-century German version of some fantastic Dickensian estate.

As he approached the building, the image of the car turning the corner with one taillight came uninvited and went. He couldn't say why, but a feeling of apprehension came over him. Casting his eyes about the gloomy surroundings, he saw nothing to explain the disconcerting visitation.

At the main entrance of the women's sanitarium, he climbed a short flight of concrete stairs and passed between two white Corinthian columns rising from red brick pedestals to support an ornate awning of mixed architectural design. It was all decorated with Victorian gingerbread cutouts and topped with a bizarre steeple, reminiscent of the spike on the top of a Prussian helmet. A few steps more and he entered the deserted reception vestibule. From there he went up the main staircase—a wide, winding affair with elaborate iron railings—to the second floor, where he turned and headed down the long corridor with a high arched ceiling, cold tile flooring, and wrought iron windows overlooking the sanitarium grounds. He stopped at the fourth door, Christoph's room. All the way from his car to where he now stood, the feeling of dread clung to him, and now, noticing that the door was ajar, his dismay took flight. He was certain he had shut the door when he left a few hours earlier. Throwing it open, he darted into the darkened bedroom.

There was someone in the bed, motionless. Without hesitation Webber lunged through the darkness and began shaking the American. To his relief the body moved.

"What time is it?"

"Doesn't matter; it's morning and you need to get up and go for a drive with me. We're gonna go to Lena's apartment. I don't like it here. It's crawling with Russians."

"Russians?"

"Russians. They never left. It's a Russian hospital. Get up."

"My grandmother worked for the Russians?"

"Of course; she was an excellent nurse. You do what you have to. Here, get dressed."

Christoph looked like he'd been scolded for not doing something, without any idea what. He thinks I'm crazy, thought Webber.

It took twenty minutes of constant harassment before Webber finally pushed Christoph out the door. Still buttoning his shirt, with his backpack over his shoulder, he followed the strange little German down the corridor.

As they came out of the building, they were greeted by waves of mist, floating like ghostly spirits across the grounds, disappearing into the trees without a sound. Webber's short body leaned forward as he hurried to his car, tilting side to side in the way he'd adapted to account for the toes lost in the last frozen winter. Behind him the tall American glided effortlessly. Together, they made a strange comic vision, a prince and his fool out for a stroll on a soggy morning.

Soon they were heading southwest along der Strasse nach Fichterwalde, a straight narrow road that sliced through the woods toward the town of Beelitz. As they got closer, trees gave way to open fields—some cultivated, some pasture—providing the first suggestion of color to the terrain. The day seemed brighter despite the continuing rain. Webber's 1970s vintage Lada, a Russian-made import, a piece of junk he'd restored to decent condition, soon entered the sleeping town and stopped outside a plain white building, one in a long row of equally bland, attached two- and three-story structures that lined both sides of the street.

"Welcome to Poststrasse. This is where your father lived."

"Why did he leave?" asked Christoph.

They were sitting across from one another sipping coffee. Webber looked out the window as if searching for an answer in the angry blanket of clouds boiling across the expansive skies. He recalled a similar kind of day when another young man, a son to him, said good-bye and, with a laugh, closed the door of this very apartment behind him. Webber was a hardened man, a realist, who understood that every separation, every farewell, or every departure might be the last one. It was his habit to make few friends and never closely bond with anyone. Whenever he went away or left someone, his parting phrase was "See you, maybe." Even with Lena, throughout the forty years of their relationship, they maintained a platonic distance sustained through polite protocol and unspoken etiquette, and now, just hours after her death, his emotional response was nil. It was different with Johann. He raised that boy.

"Because I told him to," he finally replied. "I told him he didn't fit here; he was too curious, too smart, too likely to make waves. He wanted to be an engineer; he was gonna make a better world. I told him za state would crush him. He believed me."

The two men were silent for a moment. The little Christoph knew about life in East Germany was typical for his generation. Their athletes excelled, though probably with chemical assistance, and their culture represented all the evils of communism, economic stagnation, spying, and cheating at sports, stuff like that.

Webber stared into his coffee and reflected. Sometimes, he thought, a man has to look back to understand what lies ahead. His intent had been to open Johann's eyes to the reality of life in the GDR for his own good. Instead, he drove the boy away. Now, here in Lena's apartment was the son of the son, the prodigal son, who was lost and is found. What was the right thing to do this time?

His reverie was broken by a sudden thought: the Bible, the letter.

"Where is za letter?"

"I have it here in my backpack. I'm not changing my mind about finding the guy, you know, especially, like, after everything that happened last night. Really weird, and you don't know the half of it."

As soon as he said this, Christoph wished he could suck the words out of the air back into his mouth. There was something he didn't want to talk about.

"What do you mean?" asked Webber, his voice raising.

The tone of the question was intended to make Christoph feel uncomfortable, on the spot.

"Well, after you left last night," he responded, "I realized I didn't have the letter. I remembered I had it in my hand right before I passed out. I must have dropped it."

He went on to say that he found his backpack, but not the letter, and he concluded it must still be in Lena's room. He figured he could find his way back there, so he went ahead and sure enough found it, no problem.

"The weird thing," Christoph went on, "was finding the body still there in the bed. Shouldn't she be in a refrigerator or something?"

"Who knows?" said Webber with a slight roll of his eyes. "In this country, in this hospital, there could be any number of reasons. The doctor didn't fill in za forms, or za correct forms; za staff was changing and nobody said anything; za refrigerator was full; they simply forgot her; nobody cared, she wasn't Russian. There are plenty of possibilities. She'll be found sooner or later."

"Someone sure found her last night," said Christoph, and he told Webber the story.

He'd crept barefoot along the sanitarium corridor, dimly lit and silent except for the faint sound of rain outside. He found the room and entered like a burglar, or a schoolboy sneaking out of detention. At least he felt that way. Once inside, he closed the door as softly as he could. The emergency button provided enough light. The first thing he noticed was the body lying on the bed under a sheet. He had no desire to see it, so he went straight to the task of finding the letter. He wanted to get out of there as quickly as possible. He reckoned that it would be in the

Bible, which was still on the table next to the bed, but it wasn't there. He thought he might have dropped it. He got down on his hands and knees.

Sure enough, the letter had come to rest just under the bed, where it went unnoticed after his fainting episode. He heaved a sigh of relief and was about to get up when he heard the sound of the door opening.

"Don't ask why, but I rolled under the bed to hide, lying flat on my stomach, arms tucked under my body, trying not to breathe, listening. I remember thinking what the hell was I doing, hiding under this bed like a boy caught in a girl's dorm? Then it occurred to me that the lights hadn't been turned on. Why was that? Maybe I was actually alone. I waited and listened but heard nothing. I was about to admit I was being stupid and move out of the hiding place when I heard it, a soft shuffling sound, shoe leather sliding across the floor, inches away from my head. That really freaked me out. There was someone in the room, someone with a reason to be cautious. Your warning flashed in my mind, and I was scared, and for good reason."

The silent intruder was moving. Christoph explained how he followed the progress around the bed until it reached the very spot where he'd just been kneeling. His retreat under the bed had left his head facing in that direction, and he could now see a faint illumination, bobbing and flickering around the edge of the dangling sheet, hanging unevenly above the floor. A flashlight. From the steady movement of the shadows thrown by the light source, he could tell that a search was being conducted. He heard the sound of pages being turned, slowly at first and then faster, until, with a sudden snap, the book, Lena's Bible, was slammed shut. This was immediately followed by the sound of the Bible being thumped on the table with a curse.

"Scheisse."

It was barely a whisper, but the chilling edge of fury cut through the air. The intruder was a man, and Christoph knew he was looking for the letter, which he'd expected to find in the Bible.

The next few moments seemed endless. His heart began to pound a little harder, and he could feel the sweat oozing from all his pores, sticky from the nervous energy that was building, waiting for the unseen's next move. When it came, he nearly gasped in surprise.

It was another loud thump. This time the whole bed shook in sync with another vicious curse.

"He punched the body. Boy, did that make my heart speed up another notch."

Finally the light danced around the bed, and he heard the door to the corridor close softly.

He remained motionless long after the last faint click of the door latch, not trusting that the intruder had really left the room. Fearful of making even the slightest sound, he'd slowed his breathing so dramatically that oxygen debt was beginning to have an effect on him. And still he refused to allow his lungs to fill. Darkness seemed to close in around his mind.

"That's when I finally got out of there."

He listened. The hum from deep within building was all he heard, so he rolled out from under the bed and, without a glance back, letter in hand, crossed to the door, cautiously peered up and down the corridor, and stepped out onto the black-and-white octagon tiles.

"There is evil in that letter; I know it. It just laid there, and no one noticed it," said Webber. "I'm not surprised. Friday evening, the patient was dead with no further needs and would keep until the morning. So, pull up the sheet, time to go home. Can I see it, the letter?"

Christoph was also curious to take a look at the object that had come into his possession, an unexpected inheritance that seemed in perfect harmony with the bizarre sanitarium in Beelitz, East Germany, and the strange death of his grandmother. It was an eerie message from the past, which had already had an effect on him, an effect heightened by the peculiar Onkel Kurt. As he stood to retrieve his backpack, he decided to share one last oddity of the night with Webber.

"You know, when I said last night was weird, I mean the building, too, like, it was silent and empty. It seemed like there was no one there, at least until I was coming back to my room with the letter. I'd just turned the corner into that big open landing at the top of the stairs when I'm pretty sure I saw someone leaving my room. It was dark, and he could have come out of another door, but I don't think so. Anyway, he turned the other way and disappeared down the corridor. I didn't get the impression he was a doctor or any kind of hospital staff; he wasn't wearing a uniform."

The memory of the Trabant, which had already flashed in Webber's mind, came back again. This was another of a few connected happenings that had bothered him over the last few months, all of which he was certain were pointing at that old and loathsome letter.

"I knew Lena had it. Over the years, usually when reading her Bible in za evenings, I'd see her take it and just hold it, thinking. I knew za trouble it gave her. We never spoke of it, or about za time when it vas written. This is who we are. When we shared company, those things never happened, and whenever za letter came out, I pretended not to see, not my business. If Lena ever wanted to talk about it, well, that was up to her. That was za deal; za letter played no part in our friendship, just another person's keepsake, a memory of a happy moment in a long ordeal of misery."

But things started to change about a year ago, he thought, right around the time of Lena's first stroke.

Webber watched and waited for Christoph to finish rummaging through the backpack, thinking that this was is useful device, like a woman's purse, but invented to hold all the mysterious things a man might need to carry. Christoph sat down and looked closely at the envelope for the first time. The paper was old and yellowing, like a leaf turning in the fall. Somehow the glue that had been licked decades ago still seemed to be doing its job, and the seal was secure. He turned it over and tried to read the name of the intended recipient, but the Germanic handwriting was beyond him. He handed it over to Webber.

"What does it say?"

Webber took his glasses out of his shirt pocket and squinted in his effort to make out the faded name. "Standartenführer Joachim Peiper," he murmured as if by just saying the name recognition might follow.

"Does that mean anything to you?"

"No. Could be anyone. This was a colonel, probably Waffen-SS, like von Ritter."

"How do we find him?"

"Probably dead."

"Maybe, but I need to try. Maybe there's a library where we can do a little research. Shouldn't be too hard, should it?"

Webber looked up from the envelope, wondering if the American was a dumb ass or just naive. Giving him the benefit, he patiently explained how a person didn't just go around the GDR asking about dead Nazis, especially a foreigner who just arrived. That was a certain ticket to Normannenstrasse, the Stasi headquarters, but Christoph wouldn't be put off and tried again.

"Come on, Onkel Kurt, I'm amped. What a mystery. You got to be a little interested; a message from a long dead ancestor, isn't that cool?" he implored. But Webber's eyes were cold and unmoving, two black marbles. Unperturbed, the younger man pressed on.

"One way or another I'm going to search for this guy, and if it's too hot to do it here, so be it. I'll be going back to the hotel at the airport, and I doubt there's any creepy danger in West Berlin."

The idea of Christoph going back to the West, taking the damned letter with him, sent conflicting thoughts buzzing in Webber's head. A protective instinct was affecting his feelings. Maybe it was the kid's determination to do the right thing. This reminded him of Lena. Or maybe it was his optimistic outlook, reminiscent of his father. Whatever it was, to let him go seemed right but somehow also wrong. Webber sensed real danger in whatever the boy did, and simply crossing the border wouldn't make that go away. He worried that the kid would be exposed to who knows what and he wouldn't be there to help, not that he'd be able to do much, old and decrepit as he was. If Christoph went now, he wouldn't be able to join him until he got the necessary papers. That wouldn't be until Monday, when state offices opened again, and getting permission to cross the border could be a bureaucratic minefield, even for an old pensioner like him. He didn't cross often or know what it would take, but he'd probably have to apply for an exit visa, pay a substantial fee, and undergo an interrogation from the police to make sure he had the required "urgent family business," which was the formal reason for such a request. He knew he could swing it, but it would take time. These things always took time.

He also knew there was no way Christoph could stay on until he got his papers. There really wasn't an option.

"Do you know how you're getting back?"

Christoph hadn't given this a thought.

"Well, my suitcase should be at the hotel that was set up for me. It's near the airport, but I don't know where. Hold on, I've got it in my pack."

Once again Christoph dived into the backpack and emerged with a battered manila envelope, out of which he pulled an array of papers, brochures, and what looked like an airplane ticket. He shuffled through and found what he was looking for.

"Hotel Bärlin, Scharnweberstraße 17."

Webber wasn't listening; he'd made up his mind and was already thinking ahead. He didn't know or remember much about West Berlin, but he would do what he could to make sure Christoph got back to the hotel. He knew it would be easy once he got through the border crossing, and the best place to do that would be Friedrichstrasse station.

Once across he would have no problem finding a way to a hotel near the airport. If he couldn't figure out how to get there on the U-Bahn, there would be taxis.

"I'll take you to Friedrichstrasse station. Foreigners can cross there, and you can probably take za underground right to za airport. I think it's za U6 line, but you can always find someone to ask. If not, take a taxi. You're American; you can probably afford it, ja?"

Christoph pointed out that was exactly how he came, so no problem.

"Once I drop you off, I'll see vat I can find out about this Peiper. Let's go now."

27

It was still dark when Sabine Goetz, Ainippe, stepped through the massive oak entry door of Krüger's apartment building. To the east there was a faint amber glow suggesting the imminent arrival of the sun, which would soon rise into the layers of filthy air, an ever-present reminder of the GDR's reliance on the soft brown coal gouged from the Lausitz lignite pits in towns like Cottbus and the aptly named Bitterfeld. For a moment she stood motionless on the pavement absorbed in her thoughts, vaguely aware of the hollow echoes of the stirring city.

She decided to walk to the Neue Nationalgalerie where she had some work to do that morning. Located at the Kultureforum, south of the Tiergarten, and a few blocks from the Wall, the Neue Nationalgalerie was home to masterpieces of the likes of Picasso, Miro, Kandinsky, and other twentieth-century artists. As a technical assistant in museum documentation with the Institute for Museum Research, much of her time was spent at this gallery, where the planned lack of viewing area made regular rotation of exhibits necessary. Each new program required precise documentation to meet the strict standards set by the institute. It was Sabine's task to oversee, advise, and ensure adherence. She loved her work. It was absorbing and individual. She worked alone. It was also a perfect cover for a spy.

Sabine's recruitment by the Stasi had been simple and swift, following a standard methodology: lured by a Romeo agent, entrapped by a small bit of extortion, and sealed with threats of harm to family members back in the GDR. Conversion was secured by a seemingly harmless task. She was an easy catch. Once hooked, she was slowly reeled in.

It was her destiny, a stop along a path entered long before.

You could say it started in the summer of 1962; Sabine wasn't yet two years old when her father, Robert Goetz, had had enough. He was a professor of Germanistics in the Herder-Institut at the University of Leipzig, and his intellectual curiosity had reached an impasse with the narrow vocational approach around which the GDR designed its university curriculums. This was particularly problematic for a man in his position, as the Herder-Institut was one of the mainstays of the GDR's foreign cultural policy and subjected to extreme scrutiny and surveillance by the state and party leadership. Individual faculty members were liable to be penalized for failing to toe the party line, and senior-level and managerial positions were often awarded based on political criteria rather than professional aptitude. The Stasi was conspicuously present at the Herder-Institut.

Robert Goetz gradually determined that it was time to go west and join the flow of intelligentsia crossing the border, which was rapidly closing. It could still be done relatively safely because of the advanced generations of walls, fences, guard towers, and patrols of the no-man lands that now separated the two countries. Back then there were holes, even though Berlin had been walled the previous year. This event convinced Goetz to take action before it was too late.

Sabine was too young to remember the night of their escape, but the story was etched in her memory by the many times she heard one of her parents tell the tale. It was forever the most important piece of family lore, and eventually she came to believe the details as firsthand; she could actually recall the images, the sights, and the sounds.

The point he'd selected for crossing was a steep ravine carved by a small creek. Three strands of barbed wire left a meter-high opening at the bottom where the water trickled below. The banks on either side that were covered with shrubs and rocks provided further concealment. The most difficult part was getting down the inclines, and that was not so hard. Once down to the creek bed, all that remained was to wade into the stream and duck under the wire. Finally, a short dash across the twenty meters of cleared space and into the trees again and they were free, out of breath, but free.

Robert Goetz immediately settled his family in Cologne, where he secured a teaching position at the university. Sabine's early years were unremarkable, but as time passed and she reached adolescence, the great escape came to be her own imagined adventure, increasingly more real to her. But a longing grew in her heart. Her youthful fantasies were a search for excitement and fulfillment, and this flaw gave the Stasi its opportunity.

It was 1977 and she was just eighteen, open and eager to fly when she entered the Free University in Berlin to study art.

The Free University was located in the upscale Dahlem district, about ten kilometers southwest of the center of Berlin, in the American sector. Dahlem was also the home of the US Army Berlin (USAB), and it was no surprise that an attractive German fraulein would eventually catch the eye of an American or two.

She met Captain Robert "Bobbie" Basingham in a small café near the university. He was assigned to the US Military Liaison Mission (USMLM), which, pursuant to reciprocal agreements with the Soviet Union, sent units traveling around East Germany pretty much at will for the purpose of monitoring and furthering better relationships between the Soviet-controlled country and Western occupation forces. In reality, as they were virtually above the law, these personnel performed the accepted role of intelligence gathering. The same freedom was granted the Soviets. He became her first lover. Their relationship, though brief, was the simple twist of fate that sent her into the arms of the Stasi.

The relationship was torrid. It lasted three months and ended when Basingham's tour was over and he returned to the States, but Sabine was ready to move on anyway.

It was at this time that Peter Buckner, her future handler, came along. It was fertile ground for a spy recruiter: an attractive woman in a relationship with an American intelligence officer. What more could he want?

Jan Metzger, one of Buckner's agents, was responsible for trolling, and it was he who found Sabine. He hung out at the café where Sabine and her friends hung out and soon infiltrated the group. While he was a bit of a mystery to them, an artist, or so he claimed, none of them had even seen any of his work. He would sit on the fringes of their chatter and sketch endlessly on a pad. No one could explain how or when he came to be part of this clique. The same could be said of all of them. They just happened. Looking back to those days, Sabine figured he'd been lurking around the university before she arrived, prowling she now knew for the right target: her.

Metzger fit the image of a young struggling artist, but she was still surprised late one afternoon when her companions drifted away and only Sabine and Metzger were left. It was then that the attack was launched. It came out of the blue.

"Sabine, I want to paint you. Would you sit for me?"

The idea was astounding and intriguing. Metzger, in the few months she'd known him, seldom spoke directly to her and certainly never expressed nor communicated any particular interest in her. The stark intimacy of the request was so audacious she felt like laughing, but something in his pleading brown eyes, wide and puppylike, suppressed that urge. "You want to paint me?"

Sabine took the bait.

"When?"

"Now?"

Metzger's studio was on the fifth floor of an apartment building on a narrow street in the Kreuzberg district. Far across the city from the wide, tree-lined streets of gentile Dahlem, Kreuzberg was an area of Berlin Sabine had never visited. It had a reputation, or perhaps an aura, that warned her to beware while pulling her, daring her to venture in. Surrounded on three sides by the Wall and heavily damaged in the war, the housing there was a mix of rundown survivors slated for demolition, as well as buildings quickly constructed on the cheap, mostly owned by absentee landlords. To make things worse, the government, exercising the wisdom with which governments are endowed, imposed rent controls, further dampening any motivation to invest in the district. This made it the natural home of immigrants—mostly Turkish guest workers, young squatters, and other deviant types—all stuffed into this neglected fringe. By the time Sabine arrived in Berlin, it was a diverse and vibrant ethnic ghetto, just the kind of neighborhood where she'd expect a penniless artist to live.

It seemed like entering a foreign land. The streets were lined with a continuous façade of new and old buildings, ugly and butted tightly together, all decorated from the ground to the top of the first floor with an unbroken band of colorful graffiti, as if a gigantic magical paint roller had been drawn down one side and up the other.

They walked the three or four blocks to Metzger's building in silence, leaning into a biting wind that swept along the sidewalk, funneled between the monolithic walls of apartments and closed shops. Was she crazy? She thought she probably was, coming here with this guy she didn't really know without telling anyone, such a long way from her cozy suburban and university existence, to pose maybe. What if he had other ideas? A couple times she nearly stopped, almost turning around and heading home. But something lured her forward. Somewhere in the back of her mind a voice was whispering, "Adventure."

His building was ancient and dilapidated. From the street Sabine could see windows with broken or missing panes, peeling paint, cracked lintels, and crumbling masonry everywhere. The whole edifice sagged like an old crone, giving the impression that a strong breeze could easily cause it to collapse. Metzger grabbed a large rusted handle and, placing his foot against the adjacent wall, tugged on the crooked front door, which opened with a groan.

"It's free," he shrugged as he stepped through.

Inside it was dark and damp, and a rush of moldy air escaped past them when the door opened as if the very soul of the place was escaping. Metzger pulled a flashlight from his jacket pocket. He flipped the switch and shadows came to life, phantoms swaying in counterpoint to the movement of his hand as he led the way to the stairs through a filthy cavernous lobby, littered with wreckage and copious piles of garbage. It smelled like something had died there, a long time ago.

Whatever enthusiasm she might have harbored had vanished by the time they had negotiated the five flights of stairs to the landing, where the door to Metzger's apartment, new and solid looking, stood out from the dinginess of its surroundings. She was certain she wanted to leave.

"Jan, I'm not into this. It's a stupid idea," she said firmly. "How can you live in this place?"

She had to get out of there somehow. There was no possibility that she'd "sit" for him in this dump.

To her surprise Metzger provided the way out.

"Okay, want to go to SO36? It's just around the corner. Bowie and Iggy Pop play there a lot; let's go see."

Sabine had heard of this place, a notorious punk rock nightclub where stupid young men drank themselves silly, bashed about frothing and spitting, and generally behaved obnoxiously, while high-energy

monotonous music with low artistic content by talentless bands—with
anarchistic or just plain foul names like SYPH and Snot Puke—blasted
around a huge, dark, stinking industrial cavern. It was a place to be
avoided, so it was a surprise to Sabine to hear that such famous people
as Bowie and Iggy Pop would perform there.

They left the apartment headed for SO36. The night hadn't lost any
of its bitter sharpness, and the short walk north along Mariannenstrasse
was accompanied by flying debris, newspaper, and other litter. The sidewalk was a minefield of broken glass and other trash, forcing Sabine to
tread cautiously, her head down into the wind, thinking this had better
be good. They reached Heinrichplatz and turned west on Oranienstrasse.
A white paper cup tumbled past her. Ahead, she saw the neon sign an-
nouncing the nightclub.

There was a crowd in front of the entrance, all wearing the uniform
of the punk culture: black, torn, metallic. The sidewalk was littered with
paper cups like the one that had bounced down the road. A dark figure
lay against a nearby storefront, ignored by the mingling nightclub goers.
A pool of vomit spread out beside its head. From inside the building,
Sabine could hear the thunderous, pounding bass rhythm echoing out
of the entrance. She had a bad feeling. This wasn't going to be good, she
thought.

"*Mittagspause.*"

"What?" said Sabine.

"It's *Mittagspause* playing tonight," shouted Metzger. "They're a bit
monotonous, but good to bash around to."

He was leading her toward the entrance through the Mohawks, tat-
toos, and metal piercings when it happened. Sabine saw him stumble
and fall forward into a guy with spiky blond hair. Suddenly everyone
around her seemed to be pushing toward Metzger, and the air was filled
with shouts and curses. Sabine, terrified, was bumped and pushed, and
Metzger disappeared. A scream was welling in her throat when a strong

hand gripped her arm, and she felt herself being guided away from the melee.

He led Sabine to a café and brought a couple coffees to the couch where she'd settled.

His name was Peter Buckner. He was tall and rangy and reminded her of the American actor Lee Marvin as a young man, with long wavy hair the color of coffee with cream, but it was the full lips that curled up so slightly at the corners that captured her attention. When he spoke, it was a deep, melodic sound that flowed and enveloped her, and filled her head with a soft buzzing. She didn't remember what they talked about. It didn't matter; the voice had her, and she wanted those lips.

When she woke up the next morning and felt the warmth of his body spooning against hers, she thought she was in love. That lasted about thirty minutes.

Peter Buckner awoke and rolled over. He reached out and grabbed a couple cigarettes from the bedside table, lit them, and passed one to Sabine. He exhaled a large cloud of bluish smoke at the ceiling and watched it dissipate, deep in thought. When he spoke, it was with that magical tone again, but soon the words turned stunningly blunt.

"Sabine, I'd like you to do something for me."

"Again?" purred Sabine as she rolled over and slid her hand between his legs.

"That too, perhaps," said Buckner, "but I have in mind something else, though, a little task."

"Sure, anything. I'm all yours." She snuggled closer, pushing against his thigh as her hand began to stroke slowly.

"I'm a collector. I collect information for people. I have a client who seeks some information that you may be able to provide."

"Just ask," said Sabine with a smile.

Buckner took another hit on his cigarette and blew a series of perfect rings into the room.

"You're acquainted with a guy named Robert Basingham, an American, yes?"

Sabine's hand stopped in midstroke and withdrew sharply. She felt like a rattlesnake had bitten her. She sat up and looked hard at the man she'd just met ten hours ago. In that instant she understood. Buckner looked straight ahead, unperturbed.

"How do you know about me and Bobbie?"

"Like I said, I am a collector of information."

"So that's what this is all about. Go to hell, you bastard."

Sabine jumped out of bed and started to gather her clothes. Buckner said nothing and lit another cigarette as she stormed into the bathroom, slamming the door behind her. Five minutes later she came out, dressed. For a moment she stood at the foot of the bed trying to think of something to say, her eyes red and teary, but it was Buckner who spoke first.

"Your father, Robert Goetz, is presently visiting relatives in Leipzig, yes?"

The anger that had shattered the happiness of the night flushed away, replaced with stunning disbelief. She groped for understanding, trying to make sense of what was happening here. The knowledge about her relationship with Bobbie was public, easy to find, and her reaction to that was mostly a feeling of loss, a beautiful relationship nipped in the bud. But this was different; it was frightening. Someone had invaded her private life. This stranger knew things that only an intrusive and purposeful surveillance could have revealed. Who was he? What did he want from her? Her legs felt weak. She felt sick.

"I think you'd better sit down," said Buckner, indicating toward the foot of the bed. "It'll make it easier for you to concentrate on what I'm about to say."

To make sure nothing happened to her father, all she had to do was meet with another agent who would ask a few questions about her American boyfriend, simple. Of course, the interview would be confidential, and afterward she could go on with her life. Nobody would know about it.

That was ten years ago, and she was still going to bed for the Stasi. Peter Buckner was a shrewd man who played Sabine like Menuhin on a violin. He tapped into her wanderlust for adventure and made her believe in the beginning that spying would satisfy this longing, and for a while it did. As the years passed, the costs to her soul mounted, and her reputation sank. Her associates seemed to like her, but whispered about her loose behavior and seldom invited her into any intimacy. The American whose habits, thoughts, and secrets she gave up in the first interview was the last relationship of any duration. Now approaching thirty, she sensed a cold, lonely future and anguished. Her heart wanted to find a safe harbor, a mate, a family, but she knew the chances were slim while in the clutches of Buckner and his Stasi masters.

She had just about given up hope, resigned to her fate, when Klaus Krüger offered her a lifeline. She couldn't start to think how this might play out, but she knew it might be her only chance.

She walked briskly through the wakening streets of Berlin. Her pager vibrated. It was Buckner. For once Peter can wait, she thought. Even the grayness of the morning seemed brighter than usual. There was lightness in the air and in her step. She looked forward to when she would see what lay in the policeman's fax machine.

28

Christoph and Webber moved through the streets of East Berlin. They'd been silent for a while. Webber was thinking about the car he'd owned for three years. He loved it as if it was his daughter. It was a 1978 Vaz-2101 he'd bartered in return for working free in an auto repair shop. It had been sitting in the shop yard to be stripped for parts, but like many things in the GDR, that could be a long way off. The shop owner was happy to get rid of it. At the time Webber thought it might take ten years to finish the rehabilitation project, but now he wasn't sure. He'd probably die first. The challenge was finding parts.

"How'd you learn to speak English?" asked Christoph.

Webber didn't respond immediately, thinking back. He wasn't sentimental; no one who survived the war, or the peace, was sentimental. He wasn't sure he wanted to talk about it, and he wasn't much of a talker anyway.

"To za victor, the spoils" was all he said.

"Huh?"

"You won. You had all za spoils. When a man has nothing, he does what he has to do."

"What do you mean?"

Webber looked at Christoph and realized he had no idea. Growing up in the security of the United States, he could never start to imagine what those years were like. He didn't want to talk about it. Those days were long gone, and there was no reason to bring them back. They were best forgotten. He wanted to put an end to this discussion.

"I learned English when Yanks and Brits were in charge; they didn't have to learn German, and they didn't want to; they were the winners. It's the losers who change. You crawl to their feet and beg if you have to. I don't think you can get that."

Christoph considered this and then quipped, "So you were smart enough to learn the lingo and cut down on the groveling; makes sense. You don't seem the type to lick boots. That's it, *nicht wahr*?"

The kid was trying to flatter him, an old no-bullshit survivor. Webber couldn't help but smile. It was okay.

"*Das ist wahr*," saluted Webber. Then he decided to tell his tale to the young American, and the tale flowed.

When Russians made their push to the Oder, he was with the Army Group Weichsel outside Stettin. It was March 1945. A Russian bomb got him, but he survived with a few wounds, enough to evacuate him to a hospital behind the front. That's where he met Lena and Christoph's grandfather. He'd had a leg amputated. He never got out. He was a brave man.

He couldn't be evacuated or escape. He died there, but he convinced Lena to save herself, and they got away from the building. She had two things with her: Christoph's father inside and that damned letter.

They'd arrived at the outskirts of Berlin on April 19, the same day that the Russian offensive, under Zhukov, wrapped up the battle for the Seelow Heights to the east of the city.

"I remember looking across za street at the Tiergarten. The forest was an ugly mass of burned-out stumps and bomb craters filled with muddy water. Everywhere buildings were ripped open. You could see za insides like giant dollhouses, people's lives on display.

"I'd forgotten this, but as I looked, there in the middle of this destruction, I saw za rhododendron bushes. They were in full bloom, so I asked, what is reality? So clear in my head right now."

For a while Webber was silent, his mind transported far away. He looked at Christoph, his black eyes shining.

"Life is a sequence, and a man makes decision's along the way, but fate holds the upper hand. It's dumb luck that decides where the bomb drops or whose path he crosses as he travels, ja? I wouldn't be here if I hadn't run into Len Carpenter."

They got away from an American bombing raid in a randomly picked cellar. That's where they met this Englishman. Len Carpenter was a prisoner of war who worked as a laborer. He'd been a captive for more than four years and had simply merged with the city. He spoke German and was a survivor. He had the peace all figured out.

"He'd separated the cellar to create an area that was his alone. It was furnished and tidy, and za other tenants seemed to accept this arrangement so long as they were able to join him when the sirens sounded. His door vas always open, he joked.

"We stayed with Lenny. In fact, neither Lena nor I left the cellar for weeks.

"Lenny had a pretty good idea of what to expect when the Ivans got there. He'd been preparing for a long time. He was ready. He had been a bricklayer before the war and used salvaged bricks to construct a false wall in the back of the cellar with a concealed door; very clever. It took him a long time to build because he could only sneak in a few bricks at a time. Behind it he stored stuff for when there was nothing: cans of food, gas and motor oil, soap, blankets, and cigarettes, lots of stuff like that. It was also a hiding place when the Russians came hunting for frauleins.

"You know, I sometimes wonder what happened to Lenny. Went home in forty-seven and I never heard of him again."

Lenny taught him English. He did such a good job with Webber that he was inspired to open the LC Academy of English. He made up signs and leaflets that he spread around Berlin and soon had a whole floor of the building dedicated to the lessons.

"Like I said, za vanquished learn the language of za conquerors."

"How long did it take to get things back to normal?"

Webber fell into a sudden and violent fit of laughing. Tears poured out of his eyes, which took Christoph by surprise. He didn't see anything funny about his question. It took Webber a long time to collect himself, during which the car weaved along the street drunkenly. Finally, he was able to talk.

"Kid, you're cute. Stupid question. You can't get to a place that doesn't exist. Look around; think about it."

Christoph still didn't think it was that humorous.

"You don't have to get philosophical with me. It was a simple question, but if you don't want to go there, I get it."

"Okay, okay," responded Webber with a conciliatory tone. "Let's talk about normal. Normal is nothing but doing what you have to do, and there are only two things in this world that you have to do: eat and die. You do what you have to do to eat, and you die when you die. There's no guilt in doing what you have to do. Once you get this, you know that it's always normal."

There was silence in the car for a few blocks, and then Webber spoke again.

"You could buy anything with cigarettes, the new normal. So I started traveling around the city, mostly in the American sector, picking up cigarette butts. They called guys like me *kippensammler*, butt collectors. I didn't care. I was eating. I was a sergeant in the war and good at leading small groups. After a while, I got a few women to work with me, and they processed the tobacco into full-sized cigarettes. This way they made currency. It was profitable. Seven butts made one cigarette. I survived.

"It's not that different now. I see Turks all the time at za Intershop in Friedrichstrasse station. They pay two marks at any station in za West and take za S-Bahn across za border, get off, walk along the platform, buy duty-free cigarettes, alcohol, and coffee, cheaper than in za West, then jump back on za train. One guy can make za trip a number of times in a day. Once home in za West, they make a profit in za black market. Add that to their unemployment money, and it's pretty good. You do what you have to do. Ya?"

It was a long drive from Beelitz to Friedrichstrasse station because they had to circle east around the wall that imprisoned West Berlin. They were finally on Friedrichstrasse, heading north toward the station, when traffic stopped. Webber had never seen this many cars, and on a Saturday at that. There were throngs of people, and a carnival atmosphere hung about the street, with signs and banners everywhere. Free Press for Free People, No Violence, Forty Years Are Enough, Open the Doors to Wandlitz. This last sign amazed Webber. Wandlitz was the secured, heavily guarded region where all the apparatchiks lived and was off limits for ordinary Germans. They were in the middle of a revolution, and that was making it a problem to get to the station. Driving the remaining few blocks was going to take forever, and it was starting to drizzle again.

"Out you get; you'll have to walk the rest of za way. When you get to za station, go past it to za north end. There's a special building there you go to if you're traveling west—a big blue building, mostly glass. There'll be a separate checkpoint for you. Should be no problem."

Christoph hesitated. "Okay. How will we keep in touch?"

Webber thought for a moment. "You can call the sanitarium and talk with Dr. Braun. If I learn anything, I'll call za hotel. In any case, I should be able to cross over on Monday. They don't care about old farts like me."

"Okay, ciao."

Webber watched Christoph disappear into the crowd. He leaned back and lit another Club cigarette. It was going to be a long wait, but it gave him time to think. To the right, high above the city, he could see the Tele-Tower with its revolving globe. The world was changing, he thought, and the past was being forced into the open.

Who the fuck was Peiper?

29

The ringing was far off in the distance at first, but grew louder and closer, like something was coming his way in the dark. Finally the sound filtered through the layers of his consciousness, and Kepler awoke. He rolled over to reach out and grab the phone next to his bed. It was Schneider.

"What time is it?"

"Two minutes after twelve o'clock noon, Inspector" was the precise answer, stated crisply.

Kepler yawned and rested back on the pillow. He struggled to shake the sleep from his body.

"I'm not an inspector or anything anymore. Can't you call me Klaus?"

"Okay, Inspector," replied Schneider without any hint that he got the absurdity.

"Schneider, that's what I like about you. Accurate and predictable," he said.

Colorless but efficient, he thought.

"You never surprise me, nor, I must add, have you ever failed me. How do you like working for Waner?"

He had no idea why he asked this. Hans Waner had been promoted over Schneider to Kepler's old position. Maybe it was spite for being awakened from a deep sleep.

"Different," replied Schneider flatly, unaware of the slight. "I have two bits of information that you should know."

"Fire away," said Kepler, now alert. He recognized the tone in Schneider's voice and expected important news.

Both items set off little explosions in his head.

"One, there had been a number of phone calls the previous night to and from the Hilde Reisen's residence." Schneider listed the few of interest.

"19:43 incoming from East Germany. Beelitz. We tracked the number to a hospital located there.

"19:47 outgoing to Lupus's number in Berlin.

"19:58 outgoing to an unlisted number in East Berlin.

"20:02 outgoing to Lupus

"01:22 outgoing to a public pay phone in East Berlin, the Prenzlau district."

It was the next item that yanked Kepler into an upright position, sending a jolt radiating through his lower back.

"Two, this is why I called you. We just got word from our source in the East that one of their agents was found dead a short time ago. A couple early morning strollers found him. He was shot in the head."

"Too bad. It didn't happen over here, did it?" Kepler was pretty sure what the answer was before Schneider's reply.

"No. You'll appreciate this. The body was found in a wooded area just outside Beelitz, less than two kilometers from the hospital where the call to Hilde Reisen came from. Lupus doesn't usually pick this kind of victim."

"Or shoot them in the head or dump them without ceremony. It just doesn't sound like him."

Things were moving faster than he'd envisioned. He thought for a moment, trying to decide whether to ask another question. He hesitated, wanting to be careful not to alert Schneider to concerns he need not know. It was more than enough that he relied on his old associate at all. Any inkling that "Krüger" had dealings in the East, besides those worked through Schneider, could lead to the detective putting too many things together. The loyal Schneider was humorless and official in his attitude, but he was smart too, a good detective.

"Remind me, what time was it when Lupus went through the checkpoint?"

"20:46. Friedrichstrasse." Schneider had the time ready in his head, anticipating the question. "Coincidence?"

"You know I usually don't believe in coincidence. Do we know when this agent died? I mean, the fellow could have been lying there for days, weeks. Did they provide the details?"

"Not yet. They're somewhat distracted right now. There's another antigovernment demonstration going on. By the way, an old friend of ours was on TV this morning, Markus Wolf. He was making a speech to the crowd in Alexanderplatz. He looked nervous, and they jeered him. Strange, don't you think?"

Very strange, thought Kepler. The man who recruited him, trained him, and sent him west to spy for the great communist state suddenly retires and starts fraternizing with the dissidents. What the hell was going on over there? Kepler had more immediate matters to consider, and he needed time to think, to play with all the puzzle parts bouncing around in his head, to assemble some kind of image that made sense. Was that agent the one he suspected, and why would Lupus do him in? If it wasn't a coincidence, and the agent was the one he'd set up for Hilde Reisen, then the odds were high that it was him. What did that mean?

Was there a secret drifting around the GDR, which had taken up residence in Beelitz? Who made the call to Hilde Reisen? That's something he needed to find out, but not through Schneider. Another thought occurred to him.

"Has Lupus crossed back yet?"

There was a momentary pause. "I'll have to check on that" was the reply. Kepler thought he detected a slight tone of embarrassment; no doubt Schneider felt he should have been prepared for that question.

"Okay, get back to me when you have it. You ought to get a tail on him."

Schneider paused before responding. Kepler knew this was a big request from a retired friend and mentor.

"I'll see what we can do. It'll be hard; we're stretched pretty thin with all the excitement going on over the Wall. There are a lot of visitors coming, press and media from all over the world, and on top of that the CIA has asked us for help. I won't be able to put a full team on him, but that might not be needed, just a couple men trading off perhaps. I'll let you know."

With that, the conversation ended, and Kepler hung up.

He needed to think. There were a number of scenarios already forming, but they all had one common element, one starting point: the call to Hilde Reisen the night before. Did this open the next chapter in a long story? And, like every good book, would events start slowly, then build momentum toward the denouement?

He carefully lowered himself back onto the pillow and closed his eyes.

The possible scenarios were many, but the activity of the last few weeks all pointed to the same fact. A sleeping dragon had been awakened. Knowing about this "family member" who, it would seem, possessed papers sought by Hilde was enough to confirm the assassin of the Stasi agent last night was likely Wolfgang Reisen.

Lena Mueller lived in Beelitz, a nurse at the Beelitz-Heilstatten Sanitarium. The phone call last night to Hilde came from there. The connection was clear. He wondered if Mueller was in on it. Maybe she knew of the second letter. Killing an agent of the most lethal security organization in the world was no small matter, and one had to assume the benefits greatly exceeded the risk. So, if she was in possession of information regarding the secret strongbox, she was in great danger, or worse.

Further, if the Stasi was killed because of what he found or knew, then everyone in the chain of knowledge was in equal danger, including Klaus Krüger.

A stunning thought exploded in his mind. It was so obvious. The fact that Lena Mueller was a nurse created a possible link to Paul Reisen. Had their paths crossed? Could she be an old friend of the von Ritter family, someone von Ritter might also have sent a message to?

Somehow Lena Mueller needed to be contacted and interviewed.

For a moment he pondered his motives. What was he doing? His prostate condition was worsening, and he knew his time was short, but with his impromptu decision with the beautiful agent, for the first time since his retirement he was mildly excited—invigorated, in fact—and determined to make his death wait its turn.

He leaned back and closed his eyes.

Outside, a gray day dragged on. People trudged through their daily chores, politicians exhorted and lied, sinners and saints behaved as they must, Lupus was on the prowl, and somewhere, just maybe, a strongbox lay hidden with unimaginable secrets, awaiting discovery.

His thoughts were racing.

He'd tracked down Dr. Paul Reisen over ten years ago and confronted him about von Ritter. Reisen was not a good liar and quickly confessed to the letter addressed to von Ritter's sister, now his wife. He'd never shown it to her; he couldn't explain why. Kepler had his own thoughts on that. Kepler convinced Reisen to give him a copy, promising to never tell Hilde. He told no one.

He knew Paul Reisen was dead; his passing had happened a couple months ago. He was sure Hilde found the first letter, perhaps in a safe, a buried file, taped to the bottom of a drawer, or in a diary. Who knows? Didn't matter. But the discovery set the wheels in motion, which seemed to be heading toward Lena Mueller. He wished he'd devoted more effort to finding out about her and hoped it wasn't too late.

Lupus hadn't returned yet.

Gradually, like shadows creeping up a wall at sunset, he slipped out of his ruminations and became aware of the ticking of the old wall clock, a Gustav Becker. But he'd made a decision and determined his next step.

It was also time to talk to Lena Mueller. His final call was to the Beelitz-Heilstatten Sanitarium.

When the operator came on, Kepler asked to speak with Nurse Mueller if she was on duty. There was a slight pause.

"May I ask who's calling?"

There was a hint of concern in the voice, and Kepler, who was prepared with a good story, replied, "My name is Klaus Krüger. I'm a friend and need to speak to her on a personal matter."

Another pause.

"Please hold."

The operator departed, leaving the soft fuzz of static in his ear. He waited nearly five minutes, then a click, and a man's voice came on.

"Hello. This is Dr. Dieter Braun. Who are you, Herr Krüger?"

Kepler wrote down the doctor's name, while he decided which version he would tell. It was clear from the tone of the voice that the speaker was guarded and a bit aggressive, so his instinct told him to go with "Inspector Krüger."

"I'm Inspector Klaus Krüger with the *Bundeskriminalamt*. I'm calling from Wiesbaden. There's a case about which Lena Mueller may have information that can help us with our investigations. We're working with your authorities on this, as East German citizens may be involved. May I speak with her?"

This time it was Dieter Braun's turn to pause. When he spoke, his voice was low with a slight tremble.

"Lena Mueller died yesterday."

Fascinating, thought Kepler, as all sorts of possibilities immediately arose, and the next question leaped from his lips.

"I'm sorry to hear that. When did it happen?"

"The official time was twenty-one minutes past five; I was the attending physician. She had struggled for a long time, multiple strokes, but the fight went out of her when her grandson finally arrived from the States. She passed away right after he got there, like that's all she held on for."

Braun hesitated for a moment and then added, "What was it you wanted to discuss with her, if I may ask?"

Another puzzle piece was now placed on the table.

Lena Mueller, the person of interest to Hilde Reisen, dies, and a couple hours later a phone call from the hospital is made to the Reisen residence, followed immediately with a call to Lupus, no doubt from Hilde. Within an hour Lupus crosses into East Berlin. In the early morning hours, long after people should be asleep, the Reisen residence places a call to East Berlin, to a public pay phone, and finally later that morning a Stasi agent, possibly the one hired by Hilde, is found murdered a short distance from the hospital where Lena Mueller's corpse is still warm. Quite a sequence. Someone at the hospital was in cahoots with Hilde Reisen, reporting to her about Lena Mueller. Krüger had a pretty good idea that the voice now on the other end of the phone line was the one. It was time to put the good doctor on the spot.

"Dr. Braun, do you know Paul Reisen?"

A long silence, Kepler could sense wheels turning.

"I met him in 1979," admitted Braun. "I was participating in a cultural exchange to the Federal Republic, a medical symposium, and met Paul Reisen."

"Where?"

"It took place in West Berlin. He was accompanied by Mrs. Reisen, who spent most of her time shopping. He was an older, cynical capitalist, and I a young, disillusioned communist. We struck up an acquaintance, each of us opening a door to misery equal or greater than the other's. The exchange was soothing to both, and after we parted we kept in touch."

At first it was formal and professional, added Braun, two physicians sharing the innuendos of their craft, a natural process as old as human endeavor, and dry enough to quickly lose the interest of those who intercepted and scanned for ideas dangerous to the state.

A year after the symposium, Braun wrote to Reisen and happened to mention the highly competent and skilled nurse, Lena Mueller, who was such a joy to work with while surrounded by condescending Russians.

"Almost immediately I noticed a change in the nature of correspondence. There was a sudden shift from the professional to the personal, which was fine with me as it fed my discontent."

"Discontent?" interjected Kepler.

"Well, I'd rather not get into that. Let's just say it's difficult working with Russians."

"Understood. Can you describe for me what you meant when you said Reisen became more personal?"

"He shared his feelings, stories about his family and friends, and gradually his worldview. I felt he was drawing me into something that seemed like friendship. I was wary at first. You have to be careful dealing with outsiders."

"Did he ever mention Lena Meuller again?"

"Yes, often. Over time a string of references evolved into an ongoing discussion of Nurse Mueller. At some point he even vaguely recalled another nurse whom he remembered from the war that reminded him of her."

Braun was beginning to wonder who this West German policeman really was and why the interest in deceased Lena Mueller.

"Why all this interest in Dr. Reisen and Lena?"

"I can't tell you too much. Reisen died a few months ago, and we believe he was acquainted with Lena Mueller."

"I wasn't aware that he'd died. Our communications weren't terribly frequent, you see. I'm sorry to hear it. Was there some issue around his death?"

Kepler ignored the question. If he was right that Braun was the one who called Hilde last night, then Braun was lying, and if he was lying, he wanted to find out why.

"During the time you knew Paul Reisen, did you get to know his family or anything about them?"

"I met his wife once, the same weekend I first met Paul. I believe there's a son too. But that's all I know."

"So, while Reisen became somewhat personal, it sounds like your attitude remained on a professional level?"

"Right. He was a trauma specialist with a lot of experience from the war. He possessed a wealth of knowledge and was happy to share. You see, this hospital gets a number of Russians wounded in the Afghanistan fiasco, and Dr. Reisen was a wonderful resource."

"You don't happen to know for sure if he was acquainted with Lena Mueller? She was a Wehrmacht nurse during the war, and we have reason to believe they may have served together at some point."

"I can see the possibility. But I don't know a lot about her wartime service. She didn't talk about those days. In fact, she didn't socialize at all, so I know little about her other than her work here at the sanitarium. She was an excellent nurse."

Braun's reply was obviously evasive.

"And she never mentioned Paul Reisen?"

"Never."

"Interesting," Kepler said, oozing skepticism, and Braun reacted immediately.

"Okay, that's not altogether true." Dr. Dieter Braun was a bad liar too, and a wave of relief swept over him as he decided to be straight with this policeman. Perhaps it was the cultural fear of authority all East Germans experienced.

"As I said, Paul knew Lena worked with me. He told me he thought he'd served with her on the eastern front at the end of the war. He was interested in her but asked that I not tell her about him. He didn't think she'd care either way. Every now and then she'd come up in our conversations. That's about it. I was evasive just now out of professional courtesy. You understand."

"Perfectly. What about Reisen's wife? Did you ever speak with her?"

"A few times."

"When was the last time?"

Kepler sensed he was almost there and was pushing harder now. He didn't wait for Braun's answer.

"It was last night, wasn't it? You called her to tell her that Lena Mueller had died. I'm sure our investigation will show there were any number of calls between here and Hilde Reisen's residence since Paul Reisen died. I think Hilde Reisen had a strong interest in Lena Mueller. Am I right so far?" Kepler's voice turned steely. "Why don't you tell me the whole story?"

For the next ten minutes Braun did the talking. He told Kepler everything. He recounted how he learned of Reisen's death from his wife, Hilde, who then expressed far more interest in Lena Mueller than her husband. He also confessed that the son, whose name was Wolfgang, had visited the sanitarium a couple times since the second stroke, but never actually talked with Lena. When Braun finished talking, Kepler remained silent as he entered a few more notes on his yellow pad and arranged in his mind the follow-up questions. There weren't too many.

"Doesn't it seem curious, the interest the Reisens have in such a distant connection?" asked Kepler.

"Not really. The inner border has created a lot of these types of inquiries." Many that the people try to keep as secret as possible, thought Braun. Hilde's concern wasn't unusual.

"Is there anyone else at the hospital who might have known Dr. Reisen?"

Braun thought for a few moments. Kepler waited patiently.

"Lena had one friend whom I believe she knew as far back as the war; at least that's what I've heard. He's been a constant presence around here during these final months. He's an old soldier. It's possible he knew Dr. Reisen, though that's a long shot."

"What's his name?"

"Webber, Kurt Webber. He's a crusty old coot."

"Does he work at the hospital?"

"No. He's a retired pensioner."

"How well do you know him?"

"We don't socialize, if that's what you mean, and when we've spoken, it's always been about Lena. You hear things about people, but not much is known about him. Like I said, he's an old soldier, but I don't know anything about what he's done since the war. I just know he and Lena were very close."

"When was the last time you talked to him?"

"He was here last night. Not sure when he arrived. I was away picking up Lena's grandson at Friedrichstrasse. He was in the room when she died and came to see me later in the evening to discuss the disposition of the remains."

"You mentioned that Lena's grandson is there."

"Yes. Lena was obsessed about getting him to come. That's not unusual for a dying person. I'm sure he was the only living relative she had, and she'd never seen him before. He was born in America."

Kepler made another note as Braun continued.

"His name's Christopher Mueller. At her request, I sent him a number of letters and then made a phone call before I was able to convince him to come. He lives in California. I arranged for his flight; Lena paid for it and a hotel over near Tegel. Like I said, he landed yesterday and came straight to Friedrichstrasse."

"You said she died right after he got there; did you mean there at the hospital?"

"Right. It was strange to say the least. She died and he fainted. We put him in a room for the night, and he left this morning with Webber."

"Where'd they go?"

"Not sure. Maybe Webber took him back to his hotel, or at least to a crossing point. There was no need for him to stay. Lena got her wish to see him, and…"

Braun paused, deciding if he should say more. Why not, he thought. If he told the Reisen woman, why not tell this policeman?

"You know, it was a strange encounter. She had a letter that she kept in her Bible. I'm convinced that the only reason she wanted the grandson to come was to give him this letter."

Kepler's heart skipped a beat. The Reisen letter wasn't enough to lead him to the strongbox. It needed a second letter. This letter is what Hilde was looking for, and now an unsuspecting American had it. All manner of thoughts were buzzing in his head, but there was one more question for the doctor.

"Have you told Hilde Reisen about this letter?"

Kepler already knew the answer to that question and realized the American grandson was in grave danger. He was also perfectly aware that he, too, would have to be careful from here on.

When he hung up, he jotted down a few additional notes, rose, and walked over to his fax machine.

30

Hilde Reisen had been awake for nearly an hour when the gentle knocking on her bedroom door announced the arrival of her housekeeper, Frau Kunze. Seven days a week it was the same: the three soft knocks, the slow unlatching of the door, the quiet click as the door closed again, the muted rattle of coffeepot and cup on the polished teak bed tray as it was carefully placed on the English Pembroke table, and then the sudden explosion of light as the heavy, flowered drapes were drawn to the side of the south-facing window with experienced flair. Down a long meadow, with a view to the jagged Alps in the distance, Frau Kunze could see a blanket of white mist that lay there lightly like fallen clouds, and when she opened the window to let in the morning air, the rat-ta-ta-tat song of chaffinches filtered into the room, declaring that all was well in the world.

"Guten Morgen, Frau Reisen. Haben Sie gut geschlafen (Did you sleep well)?"

Most mornings Hilde Reisen would combat the attack of light with pillow and eiderdown, but this day, to Frau Kunze's surprise, the lady of the house was already sitting up, a pink, satin-covered bolster propped behind her.

"My coffee, quickly."

The harsh command from the bed shattered the moment. Frau Kunze turned away from the window, smiled kindly toward her mistress, and attended to the coffee. She was used to her employer's haughty temper, but this morning, as she placed the bed tray in front of Hilde, there was a distinct sense of agitation about her. As Frau Kunze filled the cup with the rich brown coffee, Hilde snatched the napkin off the tray, snapped it open, and laid it over her dressing gown.

"That will be all, Marta. You can start to fill the tub and then go."

Marta Kunze nodded and headed for the bathroom, a bit unsettled by this deviation from the usual morning routine. Normally, she would have other small chores to complete before departing, but it was clear that Hilde Reisen had something on her mind. A few minutes latter, with the water running into the tub, she opened the bedroom door and was about to leave when Hilde spoke again.

"Please send Luddy to see me."

Marta nodded and left.

Ludwig Lang was the latest chauffeur hired for Hilde's carnal pleasures as much as anything particular to driving a Mercedes. Her chauffeurs usually lasted a month or two, but Luddy was different. He'd been servicing her now since early summer with energy, stamina, and a willingness to perform creatively.

Hilde took a sip of coffee, placed the cup back on the tray, and stretched her arms toward the ceiling, allowing a feeling of sensual expectation to course through her body. She checked the clock. Wolfgang's call should come any second, she thought happily.

When it rang, she started, despite expecting it, her nerves a bundle of excitement. She had the receiver to her ear before the first ring died away.

"Wolfgang?"

For what seemed a long time, there was silence on the other end, but she could feel his presence, and she knew something was wrong.

"Wolfgang, what's happened? You have the letter?"

When he finally replied, his voice had the tone of a dog in trouble with its owner, subservient and whiny. It trembled as he spoke.

"No, Mutti. I went to the bitch's room, but it wasn't there. Then I went to the room they put the bastard in, but it was empty. I waited hours until the doctor got there, but he didn't know anything."

"But, but, but. Wolfgang, my dear, buts never get anything done. You've made me quite upset; it's not like you to be so useless. Are you sure you had the right room?"

"Yes, Mutti, I went back with the doctor. He was surprised the bastard was gone too. He didn't know where."

"I'm extremely disappointed in you, Wolfgang, and you know how I get when you let me down, yes?"

There was a long pause, then a scarcely audible "Yes, Mutti."

"Where are you now?" snapped Hilde.

"At the sanitarium."

"Is Dr. Braun still there?"

"Yes, Mutti."

"He arranged the bastard's visit, including, I'm sure, a hotel somewhere. Find out where."

"I did," returned Wolfgang eagerly. "He's booked in a hotel by Tegel; let's see, it's the Hotel Bärlin."

"So go there, find him, and get that letter. No letter, no bastard for you, right, Wolfgang?"

"Yes, Mutti."

"Tell me about the Stasi."

"Dead, Mutti."

"Where?"

"In some woods."

Hilde heard a voice in the background. She could tell that Wolfgang quickly muffled the handset, and she waited. A few seconds passed before his voice came back.

"Sorry, Mutti, that was the doctor. I should go now."

"Wolfgang."

"Yes, Mutti?"

"Just get the letter."

With that, Hilde replaced the receiver. At the same moment there was a knock on the bedroom door. It opened to reveal a handsome man, with dark hair and a chiseled face.

"Good morning, Madame. You sent for me?"

"Ah, Luddy, yes, come in. Go turn off the bath water and come back. I've had a trying morning."

When Hilde Reisen had finished with Luddy and dismissed him, she slipped into the luxuriating waters of her bath, closed her eyes, and inhaled the perfume of the imported oils. She contemplated without pleasure the arrival of the letter she hoped Wolfie would soon be bringing back, the missing part of a puzzle she didn't even know existed just a few months ago. Hopefully Wolfie wouldn't mess this one up.

Hilde rose and stepped out of the bath, quickly dried herself—avoiding her reflection in the full-length mirror—and slipped into a white satin robe and matching slippers. She felt electric.

She went to her eighteenth-century Bavarian writing desk by the large bay window, from which she could look out into the garden. She sat down and opened the center drawer. From a blank white envelope she extracted a facsimile of the letter from Johann. The original was locked away in the library safe. She had read her brother's last words a hundred times, but today there was new excitement that came with the expectation that soon it would all have meaning.

"I have written already to an old friend, and if he gets the letter, you may expect him to contact you. Together, you may be able to locate the hoard.

"I am unhappy to be putting this burden on you, but have no better idea."

For weeks she was sickened with anger intertwined with hate after she'd discovered the letter. It was buried in an old wooden filing cabinet among papers she was preparing to dispatch to the landfill. If she'd known while Paul Reisen was alive that he'd kept her brother's dying message from her, she would have killed him. At least she would have had Wolfgang do it.

The message in the letter was a disconnected jumble, a bunch of separate clues, like puzzle pieces spread across a table.

It was after agonizing and getting nowhere that she'd finally approached Wolfgang with this secret. It was a desperate decision. Hilde loathed the idea, but it turned out to be a good one. It was Wolfgang who tenaciously plowed through his father's private papers, then his office records, and finally his father's library where he struck gold: a diary. Everything fell into place, and the hunt was on.

It was up to wicked Wolfgang, tormented and unreliable as he was. She had no other plan.

31

People of all ages were streaming out of the entrance as Christoph approached the Friedrichstrasse U-Bahn station. The atmosphere was high-spirited and merry, and it struck him that it was just like the day he'd joined in the celebration of the fiftieth anniversary of the Golden Gate Bridge, a couple years before. That was an experience. The city of San Francisco had decided to reenact the opening day celebration in May of 1937, when thousands of people were allowed to walk across. This time half a million turned up, flooding onto the bridge from both directions at the same time, meeting and stopping at the center. It was one happy party. Inspired by the memory, he turned from the station and converged with the masses.

The demonstration sucked him in and carried him into Alexanderplatz. It was the Golden Gate Bridge all over again, without the swaying. Hundreds of thousands crammed into the cavernous square, chanting and carrying banners. He knew he was at a protest but had no idea what it was about. He'd never actually been involved in a protest, and this one didn't match his idea of what a protest was like. It was peaceful, joyful, a family affair. The chanting was full of exuberance rather than anger. It was more like a crowd at a pregame rally. One by one, speakers took turns reading from prepared notes, all meaningless to him. The crowd cheered throughout, until one speaker appeared. Even before this man stood at the microphones, the crowd's cheers turned to shrill whistling, which continued sporadically through his speech. It was then that Christoph felt a nudge in his ribs, and he turned to face a massive apparition.

Uwe Hilbert was a bear of a man, over six feet tall, with a barrel chest; wild, dense black hair that descended into an equally impressive beard; and a booming voice that emerged from deep in his throat like distant thunder. He was a big man with a big personality.

"Ziemlich Muttig von ihm, hierher zu kommen, meinst du nicht?"

Christoph just stared back.

"English?"

"Huh? No, American. *Ich spreche kein Deutsch.*" He shrugged apologetically.

"American? Are you press?"

"Nope, just visiting." Around him the crowd started whistling again, drawing the big man's attention back to the stage.

"I was praising that man for being brave to come here. He's apparatchik, not poet." He laughed, and it sounded like the rumble of a bass drum struck in a cave. "He's saying, 'We hear you; we will change; trust us.' And he's trying, as you say, to kiss our asses. But you can hear the citizens don't believe him. My name is Uwe Hilbert." He held out a huge hand.

Christoph took the hand, which was surprisingly soft. "Christoph Mueller."

He insisted that Christoph join him for beer at his drinking place, a bar he called Hackepeter. When Christoph heard the name, he'd stifled the urge to laugh out of politeness. However, later that night after many beers, he cracked up unabashedly when Uwe explained that *hackepeter* was a spicy German dish of raw minced pork mixed with garlic, adding with a dead serious expression that it translated into English as "chopped Peter, very tasty."

From the street, the Hackepeter was just another indistinguishable storefront on the corner of two streets, its name blandly displayed in black letters painted on a white background above the double-door entry. Inside, it was equally unexciting. Long and narrow, its brown walls and peeling plastic vinyl countertops, dimly lit under a permanent cloud of cigarette smoke, conspired to greet a first-time visitor with an impression of tired gloom. This night the place was crowded and the atmosphere was loud and festive.

Uwe Hilbert led the way. He carved an opening, like a pulling guard, right up to the bar, where he pushed other patrons aside to make room for his new American friend before roaring at the bartender, "Zwei pils, wir sind durstig hier (two pils, we're thirsty here)!"

"It's easier to scare people than to make them see," bellowed Uwe as he slammed his glass down on the table. The room went quiet. "They want us to be faithful; they force us to be faithful; they scare us to be faithful. But, my American friend, faith is a thing that can make truth out of anything. Faith is not logic or reason or arguments and evidence. Faith is good for making people do things. Faith is the biggest tool of control ever invented. I have no faith in the apparatchiks of the Socialist Unity Party."

Everyone in the bar was now looking at them. Christoph suddenly felt exposed. Uwe, whose eyes burned with passion and not a little pilsner beer, let his gaze drift away from Christoph and scanned the room. Suddenly he broke out in roaring laughter. He leaned forward and whispered, "It's a good thing no one speaks English, eh? They'd think I'm Stasi. And you know something? Speaking of truth, half of them are probably working for the Stasi."

Gradually the other patrons returned to whatever it was they were doing before Uwe's outburst.

"They do think I'm Stasi?" he asked after draining his glass of beer. "It's because I, like Shakespeare's queen, 'doth protest too much.' No innocent citizen in his right mind would speak as brazenly as I do, ergo, I must be Stasi."

"Are you?"

The big German pulled back and allowed a hurt look to momentarily spread across his face, followed instantly by another outburst of gaiety. "Welcome to the GDR, where the game we all play is called 'Who's Stasi?' Everyone is 'IM,' secret informers. We're a nation of spies. That, my friend, is what today was all about. No one wants the end to communism, and we can all live with the Wall. It's our crazy, misdirected, and senile leaders, and the Stasi, who have to go. *Keine Lügen; neue Leute.* No lies; new people. That's what the banners were demanding."

"So you don't think Mr. Gorbachev should tear down this wall?"

"Ha. Who is this Gorbachev? Is he a German? Does he tell us what we should do? Your president who said that was uninformed, or just ignorant, perhaps. The Wall is a fact, like Hadrian's and China's. It will be studied by anthropologists."

Christoph laughed. "You know, Reagan also said that 'facts are stupid things,' though he should have said they were stubborn things, which is what one of our first presidents actually said."

"'Words without thoughts to heaven never go.' That's Shakespeare," boasted Uwe. "I like you, Yankee. I accept you as a friend." Uwe offered his hand for a high five, and Christoph hit it. "So tell me, why were you at the demonstration if you're not press? Perhaps you're the spy?"

"No, no, I'm not a spy. Like I said, I came here to see my grandmother, who died yesterday. It's a bit weird, really."

"'It is a tale told by an idiot, full of sound and fury, signifying nothing.' That's Macbeth. Please tell."

Christoph gave him the whole story. Uwe listened. The other patrons of the Hackepeter watched knowingly out of the corners of their eyes. When he'd finished, it was after eleven o'clock and Christoph felt the need to pull himself away and head for the hotel on the other side of the Wall. Uwe offered him a ride on his motorcycle to Friedrichstrasse. It was no bother, and to walk would take forty-five minutes.

It was an old Ural 650 with a passenger seat that reminded Christoph of pictures he'd seen of metal farm tractor seats in the days of the dust bowl and the Depression. It pretty much felt that way, too. The journey only took a little more than ten minutes, but he was happy to climb off, thank his new friend, and say good-bye.

"Perhaps we meet again, you never know," said Uwe.

"That would be great. How do I get hold of you?"

His new German friend revved the Ural and let out the clutch. He shouted over his shoulder, "Kommen sie in die Hackepeter."

It was past one o'clock in the morning when Christoph finally walked into the Hotel Bärlin and rang the silver bell at the reception desk. He was exhausted.

■ ■ ■

Uwe Hilbert was in a hurry to file a report on this American encounter to keep his handlers happy. He knew this American's story of a mysterious letter out of the past was unusual enough to actually engender a response from the clowns sequestered inside the Stasi headquarters.

32

It was Saturday afternoon when Sabine finally went to contact Peter.

By this time the crowds in Alexanderplatz had dispersed to their homes, pubs, cafés, or train stations, and Christoph Mueller sat in a warm pub with new East German friends he'd met at the demonstration.

Bruckner was pissed off. "Where the fuck have you been?"

"On important, secret agent mission," she quipped.

In the past she would have passively absorbed his abusive language; however, today she laughed, which added to his annoyance but stimulated a worm of concern. It wasn't like her. Something was wrong.

"Don't get cute with me. The Firm, for some god-awful reason, has been all over me. They're not happy. You were to visit this guy, get a message, and report back. I should have heard from you in the morning. I paged you five times. Did you sleep with this guy or just give him a blow job?"

"Battery died," she said, ignoring his insult. "Why do you think it was a man?"

He was about to say something but changed his mind, kept his temper under control.

"So what's the message?"

"Lupus crossed over yesterday evening."

"That's it? 'Lupus crossed over yesterday evening'?"

"Lupus crossed over yesterday evening; that's it."

He heard the mocking tone and could feel her smile. His consternation grew. Events were spinning wildly. What was going on? Could this be part of the bigger picture? The old equilibrium was in a major wobble that might not correct itself? Was the iron fist fatigued; could it be cracking? If it did, where did that leave him? All this flashed through his mind as he pondered a response. In the background he heard Nena singing "99 Luftballons" on a radio nearby, no doubt a DJ's tribute to the happenings in the GDR, where the troubles and dissatisfaction that seemed to coalesce around the Gorbechev visit for the GDR's fortieth anniversary celebrations had in recent weeks spun into a vortex that was spinning faster and faster. The East German machine was stressed and challenged as its people, with increasing boldness, demanded change. The news was full of stories about a new wave of refugees seeking passage to the West and demonstrations in Dresden, Leipzig, and now Berlin. Today he heard that as many as half a million had gathered in Alexanderplatz.

"Where are you now?"

"At a pay phone, where else?"

Buckner realized how stupid his question was. He forced his thoughts to focus on the task at hand.

"Okay, I'm going to send this message ahead. Be available in case there's a response and further instructions."

"I was up in the middle of the night, remember? I'm tired and I'm going home. Page me only if you really need to."

Sabine hung up.

Buckner stood transfixed, staring at the telephone box, deep in thought. A couple minutes passed. He moved to an adjacent phone, called the designated number, and recited the meaningless message into a recorder. This was all wrong, and he'd made up his mind. Ignoring protocol, he placed another call from the same phone, issued a brief set of instructions, and went home for the night. He was sure Sabine was up to something, and whatever it was he was going to know. Tonight someone else would tail her. He had an engagement with a very desirable woman that, even in these upsetting times, he wasn't about to miss.

He placed one more phone call and then walked slowly home. Traffic was light on Martin-Luther Strasse as he approached and turned onto Freisingerstrasse, where his apartment was located. The trees that grew in the center median were almost skeletons, the last brown leaves clinging against their inevitable future, and the gnarly trunks punctuating the forlorn impression. He continued down the pavement feeling much the same.

He was certain he was somehow being set up, but why, and what could he have done or not done? The answer could be as whimsical as it was practical. He never knew what they were after. That was one of their basic tools. With each step his paranoia grew.

As the weight of these thoughts bore down upon him, he became increasingly determined to take action rather than wait for the ax to fall. Putting a tail on Sabine was the first step. Whether her involvement was implicit or direct, she was the one avenue he had to explore. If she moved, he would follow. In the meantime, he had a night of pleasure ahead, and he did his best to turn his thoughts back in that direction.

33

Ernst Kepler, like Kurt Webber, was a survivor.

While most of his life he refused to attach moral values to a person's behavior, he was always astute when it came to looking for and recognizing danger and wickedness in another's motives. So it was with the Reisens.

It was time to call Hilde. He wrote down a list of questions as they occurred to him. Slowly a strategy took shape for the interview. He would present the simple facts and proceed from there. The authorities in the GDR found a murdered Stasi agent. The agent's phone was tapped. He wouldn't reveal that hers was also tapped, but calls were identified as coming to and from her residence. The East German authorities had contacted the BKA with a request to follow up. That would be the opening. He would avoid, if possible, getting into Wolfgang and what he knew about him, but if he had to, he would go there.

"Inspector Krüger, what can I do for you?"

The voice was all sweetness with a condescending edge and an undertone of annoyance. Kepler recognized the passive-aggressive characteristics and knew this was the context in which the interview was going to proceed. He'd been there a thousand times.

"Please, call me Klaus. I apologize for this intrusion; it couldn't be helped, as you'll see."

"Please."

"I'm with the Serious and Organized Crime Division of the BKA. The kind of criminal activity we deal with doesn't recognize borders, so we're part of an extensive policing network that also traverses borders. This includes our friends in the GDR. Late last night we received at our headquarters in Wiesbaden a request from our eastern colleagues to do some follow-up on information they had relating to an apparent crime."

"And why does this bring you to me?" asked Hilde, with just the right amount of innocent curiosity.

"That will become clear in a minute. First, I'd like to know about your house staff."

"My staff?"

"Bear with me."

"I have four: Marta, my housekeeper; Ludwig, the chauffeur; Bernard, the gardener; and Otto, the gamekeeper. Otto doesn't do much anymore. He's seventy-eight, but I keep him on."

"Do they all live in the house?"

"No, only Marta. Luddy has a room over the garage, and Bernard and Otto have cottages. Why is this relevant?"

Ignoring her question for the moment, Kepler proceeded with his line of questioning.

"What are your house rules regarding making phone calls?"

"There are none. Why do you want to know?"

"Very well, as you probably know, our neighbor's state security agency keeps a pretty close eye on its citizens to protect them from any capitalist infections. The Stasi's job is to know everything about everyone, using any means it chooses. It knows who visited whom; who are friends at work, at school, in the bar; and whom their citizens telephoned. I can't say I agree with this state of affairs; however, as a policeman who succeeds by gathering information, I do keep my contacts. This protection takes many forms, including, as I mentioned, the interception of phone calls."

"What's your point, Inspector?"

"They tell us that a call was made from your phone on Friday night to a number in East Berlin. The number belonged to a man who turned up dead yesterday. Shot in the head."

Kepler cracked out the word "head," *in den Kopf geschossen*, hoping to get a reaction. He wasn't disappointed.

Her voice, which had been pleasant and accommodating, took on a hard edge. Excellent, he thought, she's conjuring a lie.

"Are you accusing one of my household of murder? That's ridiculous. I can assure you that none of them have been across the border in a long time. I can vouch for every one of them."

"Mrs. Reisen, I'm not accusing anyone. I'm trying to clear up this one little detail, which probably has no implications, but nonetheless needs an explanation," soothed Kepler, even as he prepared to insert a wedge into the small opening she'd just provided. "Why would you think I was interested in knowing if someone from your house had gone across the border?"

"Inspector Krüger," she replied, "you out of the blue accuse, or at least insinuate, that someone here has committed murder in East Germany. How would this person do that without going there?"

"As I said, I'm only trying to clear up a few points."

"A few points? A second ago it was one little point."

"Well, yes, you see there's another call we need to discuss, but one at a time. With your permission, I'd like to question each of your household staff to find out who made the call in question."

"That won't be necessary. I made that call. I dialed a wrong number and hung up as soon as I realized it. If you don't already know the length of the call, I'm sure you can confirm it was connected only a few seconds."

"Well, that explains that one. Our Stasi friends can cross it off their list."

"I'm glad I was able to clear that up for you."

"There were others."

It had been a guess, a shot in the dark, just to get a reaction. She could have denied any knowledge, but instead she made up a story, which could easily be unraveled. Wrong phone numbers were usually the result of just a single missed digit, so what was the number she was actually attempting to call? Did she then redial? Since the wrong number was to an East German area code, she would have to explain how that happened. Who was she really trying to call? He would come back to that in a bit.

She had to be wondering if the call from Dr. Braun was listed there.

"According to my information, you, or someone here, received an earlier call from East Germany on Friday evening, to be exact, at 19:43, which lasted three and a half minutes. Would you know anything about that one?"

There was silence. He knew facts were being aligned, connections forged, contradictions analyzed. Something was out of balance and not adding up. She knew what it was.

"Did you in fact receive the first call?"

Hilde Reisen did not hesitate this time. "Yes, I did get a call around that time, from an old friend of my husband's," she admitted. "A doctor."

"Three minutes isn't a very long conversation for an old friend," he suggested.

"As I said, he was a friend of my husband's. He didn't call to chat."

"So why did he call? I'm sure the Stasi would like to know that, you know, to dispel other possibilities."

"A mutual acquaintance had died," said Hilde, "and he thought I should know."

It was time to strike, decided Kepler. "This mutual acquaintance wouldn't happen to have known your husband during the war?"

He let another silence linger.

"I can see you're puzzled. I think we should talk, candidly."

Another ten minutes passed before the call ended.

It was a dangerous game he was playing, not that he cared that much as far as his own safety was concerned. It really didn't matter what happened to him. His future was already sealed. It would be nice if he lived long enough to enjoy some of it.

He crossed his study to where the fax machine sat on a small table, and sent more notes to the beautiful Stasi agent.

■ ■ ■

Later that afternoon, Sabine arrived at the address Krüger had provided and let herself into his small office. As she closed the door behind her, she heard the familiar sound of a fax machine receiving and answering a call. Moments later she was sitting at his desk reading through the documents. She could barely contain her excitement as the words leaped from the pages. She read through Kruger's notes and reread a few times the faxed copy of the letter from Johann von Ritter to his sister written four decades ago.

It was mysterious and intriguing; it left her hanging. There was no doubt that the second letter, now likely in the possession of the American, was the critical key. Further, she realized that even if she got hold of both letters, the message might remain elusive without the special knowledge of the "old friend" von Ritter mentioned. Eventually she looked at her watch. She would grab some lunch, head over to the Hotel Bärlin where Kruger's notes indicated he was staying, and make contact with this Christoph Mueller. She smiled; this was truly the adventure of a lifetime.

34

Mutti's call came just after he arrived back at his apartment. He could tell something had happened, something bad. Mutti's voice had a tone that he'd never heard before, a hint of desperation. It was like the sound of the pleas he loved to coax from his donors, as he gently squeezed their throats and freed their souls. But from the mouth of his mother, it gave him a feeling like spiders crawling around the back of his neck.

"Did you get the letter?"

"He never showed up at the hotel."

"I was afraid of that."

He braced himself for the coming firestorm of angry cross-examination, but all he got was a long silence. He was about to say something when Hilde finally spoke.

"Wolfgang, listen to me. There are complications we, you, have to deal with."

When he hung up, Wolfgang Reisen was shaking. The call had made a bad situation worse. He paced, caged in the small Kreuzberg apartment, and his agitation filled the air like an invisible, malevolent presence. Small snorts and grunts escaped through clenched teeth; a knot, tight as a bare-knuckle fighter's fist, grabbed his stomach; and his unstable mood seethed back and forth from mercurial anger to abject despondency. His thoughts were in turmoil. It had been like that ever since Mutti called and sent him to do the Stasi guy and get the letter. He'd done everything he could, but now Mutti was treating him as if he was a little boy who'd done something bad, like pinching sweets or failing to kiss a decrepit grandmother. He hated her when she was like that. She knew he loved her and obeyed her and always tried his best for her, but she was using him. She knew he lusted to free that bastard's soul. It wasn't his fault he couldn't find the loathsome American and the stupid letter.

He was sure of one thing; when the time came, he would make the bastard pay. He would extract the soul slowly. He'd do it right, not like last night.

What the hell did it matter that the idiot Stasi knew about Lena once they had the letter?

No, it wasn't his fault.

The American seemed like a phantom. He was nowhere to be found. Even the fat doctor didn't know his whereabouts. Wolfgang had missed him at the sanitarium, slept a couple hours in the miserable Trabant, confirmed with Dr. Braun that Christoph was no longer there, and received no sympathy from his mother or rewarding words either for dispatching the Stasi.

After leaving the sanitarium, he'd returned to Berlin, taking the long route around the Wall, east to Treptow, before turning north and crossing the Spree on the Elsen Bridge. He ditched the car near the Frankfurterallee U-Bahn, where he bought a ticket to travel the short distance to Friedrichstrasse. He joined a surprisingly large and festive crowd squeezing down onto the platform, which he learned was on its way to Alexanderplatz for the demonstration. After four completely packed trains came and went without any space for new passengers to embark, Wolfgang climbed out of the station and took off walking. Friedrichstrasse was a six-kilometer hike.

Unlike the streets of Berlin, the lines of border crossers were short and moved fairly quickly to the Formica counters, where green-uniformed border guards checked visas and passports. Wolfgang eyed the guards with forced nonchalance. They appeared to be in a perpetual state of boredom. Even so, he felt his heart race as it always did at this point, and he felt small beads of sweat roll down the back of his neck. It was always this way on the western trip. His breathing was shallow as he handed over his papers, and when the guard gave him a cursory look, stamped the visa, and pressed the button to open the gray steel doors to the platforms, relief flushed through his body. In his eagerness to move on, he didn't notice the Turkish-looking man standing outside the Intershop kiosk, wearing cheap jeans and a gray sweatshirt that said "California University."

From Friedrichstrasse he took the U6 to Kurt Schumacher Platz. When he came out onto the street, it was late into another dull afternoon. The Hotel Bärlin, where Dr. Braun said the American was staying, was just a block away. He was sure he could feel the presence of the bastard.

Once again he was wrong.

Christoph Mueller hadn't checked in, but the young woman at the reception desk confided that a suitcase had arrived the day before, and a call was received earlier that day, confirming he would be arriving in the afternoon. The rain had stopped, so he settled into a chair at the small café located across the plaza from the hotel, where he could observe the hotel entrance. He didn't know what the bastard looked like, but reckoned he would recognize an American male around twenty-one years old when he saw one. He was tired, frustrated, and hungry, but like a hunter he would await his prey.

Hours wore on, the bastard didn't show, and he went home.

"Fucking bastard; fucking, fucking bastard," he muttered. "Where the fuck is he?"

The whole world had turned ugly. He looked at his watch. He couldn't procrastinate any longer. He had to go back to the Hotel Bärlin, but Mutti ordered him to do another job first. She gave him strict instructions and an address. It had to do with retrieving a copy of his father's letter.

"Scheisse," he muttered as he opened the apartment door, "it's a fucking cop this time."

35

Ernst Kepler was aching. The cancer began three years ago with a dull, hardly noticeable twinge in his side, which he attributed to age—just a touch of arthritis. He didn't suspect that a whole new community was propagating. Rogue cells from the primary tumor in his prostate had escaped into his bloodstream and traveled to his hipbone, attracted by proteins secreted by the marrow. His doctor referred to these as "receptors" called cytokines. Cytokines sounded to him like space invaders, and perhaps they were. Once there, the renegade cells found a homey environment, settled in, and began to multiply, growing new blood vessels to obtain the oxygen and food they needed to survive. Slowly the pain worked its way around to his back and increased in intensity as new tumors formed, now attaching themselves to the spine, repeating the process over and over with increasing speed. By the time he grudgingly went to see his physician, it was too late. Now he imagined a virtual colony of death crawling around his insides, like termites in a rotting house, eating away at the structure, making it brittle and dangerously fragile. His bones ached. It was just a matter of time.

Despite the pain he decided to go for a short walk. He needed to get away from the claustrophobic study and think. It was the delicate matter of time that he pondered. Time hadn't been a concern until yesterday. He was ready to die. Then the sad serial killer and beautiful Stasi agent had come along. He still couldn't fathom it. He'd had no intent the other night of doing anything more than passing on the information that Lupus was in East Berlin. Now what? Why now? There was so little time. How long until Hilde Reisen attempted to strike back? What should his next step be and when?

A searing bolt shot across his lower back, and he froze as a tight-jawed grunt passed his lips. He fell back against a tree. He took slow deep breaths as he waited for the pain to ease. It was getting worse, goddamit, and quickly.

After a few minutes, it still didn't get better, so he braced himself to once again endure getting back and inside, where the morphine was waiting. He felt sick to his stomach as the throbbing spasms continued to rack his body. With excruciating effort he managed to continue down the street. Bunched over and twisted, he shuffled toward the entrance of the building. There was a heavy mist filling the air, and he pulled his hat down to shield his eyes. He didn't notice the dark figure that glided silently up behind him. It wasn't until he found the lock and with a shaky hand inserted the key that he felt this presence. Through the pain Kepler instantly knew it was a gun that jabbed him between the shoulder blades, and he knew the gunman.

"This is a gun," a voice whispered, removing any doubt. Additional pressure was applied to his back as if necessary to fully communicate the situation. "Open the door."

"Of course, Herr Reisen. I was expecting you sooner or later, perhaps not this soon. Take that thing off my back, and please come in."

The lobby lights snapped on as Kepler stepped into the dark entrance hall, where, laboring under the weight of pain, he started to lead his assailant past the main stairs to the door of his apartment. He never got there. As suddenly as the lights came on, they went out for Kepler.

Wolfgang Reisen stood over the prone body and watched the blood seep onto the tile floor from the gash in the policeman's head where the butt of the gun had struck. It was a blow full of rage. Twice more he struck to make sure.

Moments later Lupus left the building. Leaning into the damp breeze, his hair drooping, wet and stringy from the moisture, he hurried bedraggled along the sidewalk, its surface now reflecting the light of the street lamps like mirrors set into the pavement. People he passed, had they looked closely, would have noticed his tears and the foamy slobber drooling from his mouth. They might even have heard soft sobbing as he disappeared down the street carrying the leather briefcase he'd wrenched from the hand of the battered policeman.

His spirit was broken. He wanted to go home. The bastard would have to wait until the next day.

■ ■ ■

Across the street, one of Schneider's men followed at an appropriate distance. In the pocket of his overcoat, a notebook held the address of the building Lupus had just briefly visited and the time. These details, along with the observation that the subject now had a brown briefcase in his possession, were entered into his report when he was relieved later that night. He confirmed that Lupus went to his apartment and didn't emerge again.

36

Sabine returned to her apartment with Inspector Krüger's notes and the letter. She read through them over and over. She called the Hotel Bärlin three times; his suitcase was there, but Christoph Mueller had not checked in yet. She gave up after the last call around ten o'clock and went to bed. She couldn't sleep. She got out of bed and tried to read, but couldn't concentrate. She poured a stiff scotch, turned on the television, and tried to watch a repeat of an old *Verstehen Sie Spaß?* but the candid foibles of unsuspecting citizens quickly lost her interest. Sometime in the early hours of the morning she finally dozed off on the couch and slept fitfully. It was after ten o'clock when she woke, feeling like hell.

After a cool shower, she called the hotel. This time the news was good. He'd arrived late the night before.

She'd got to thinking about first impressions and decided she'd need the right ensemble for her planned "accidental" encounter with the American, so she went shopping. It was midday when she entered the hotel and crossed the reception lobby, her high heels sending echoes into the air. She headed for the row of house phones and wondered why they needed such an array. The Hotel Bärlin couldn't have that many guests. German efficiency, she decided. She picked up one of the hand-sets and placed a room call.

"Please, will you connect me to the room of Mr. Christopher Mueller?"

The phone rang three times before it was answered by a tentative voice. "Hello?"

"Mr. Mueller."

"Yep, that's me."

"Mr. Mueller, this is the reception desk. I'm sorry for this inconve-nience, but we need to take another imprint of your credit card. When you checked in, the reader caught the edge of the carbon paper, twisting it so the number didn't transfer completely. There's no rush, but next time you're in the lobby, could you come by the reception desk, and we'll do it correctly."

"No problem. I'll be right down."

Good boy, thought Sabine. Now we'll see what you look like. She hung up the phone, found a seat from where she could watch the desk, and, opening a dog-eared copy of *Die Welt*, she started to browse through the pages. The big news was the massive demonstration for political re-form in East Berlin at Alexanderplatz that had taken place the day be-fore. What caught her eye and grabbed her attention for a moment was the list of speakers, which, as one would expect, included celebrities and dissidents, but also a name that brought a silent exclamation to her lips: none other than Markus Wolf. He was nervous and his hands trembled when the crowd booed, reported the paper.

In the corner of her eye, she caught the elevator door opening and, without moving her head, turned her attention that way. A man emerged and walked toward the desk.

He reminded her of Dennis Wilson, her favorite Beach Boy, but be-fore the beard. It was the shaggy hair, bushy eyebrows, and pronounced, slightly protruding chin, creased with a faint dimple, that brought the comparison to mind—these and the well-balanced features of this handsome American. From the moment she saw him, she was sure it was Mueller. He was wearing Levi jeans and a white dress shirt, the sleeves rolled up to the middle of his forearms, and leather sandals without socks. He moved from elevator to desk with a casual swagger that displayed a lack of self-consciousness, very un-European, and a refreshing change from the body language she expected of a good-looking man. This assignment gets better all the time, she mused.

She watched the misunderstanding unfold and was pleased to note that Mueller showed no irritation nor anger as the reception clerk formally and properly assured him that there was no problem with the credit card imprint and that no one from the hotel had called him. Sabine stood and slowly approached the desk, coming to a stop just behind him and slightly to the elevator side, so when he turned to leave, he had to look at her. Brief eye contact and a twitch of a smile, and she knew when their paths crossed again, by coincidence of course, he would remember her, and it would be Mueller who made the first move.

Before he got out of hearing range, she inquired, just loud enough, if the meeting room was ready to see yet, and as he entered the elevator, she didn't miss his quick glance back in her direction. The shopping excursion was paying off. Yes, this was going to be easy.

She excused herself at the desk and left the hotel. Now it was waiting time. He would have to leave the hotel sooner or later, and when he did, she would be watching.

She'd developed the fundamental skills that a spy needed to succeed, including the ability to wait things out and not to push too hard or move too soon. She found a seat in the window of the characterless café just across the small plaza in front of the hotel and waited. Mean clouds tumbled across the sky and slowly turned from gray to black.

It was approaching one o'clock when Christoph came out through the glass door. He had on a dark sport coat for his outing, which to

Sabine's eye looked more traditional than fashionable. Only the occasional vehicle now passed through the intersection, which on any day but Sunday would be choked with the heavy activity generated by the nearby airport. He paused, getting his bearings, and then turned to his left and set off at a relaxed pace. Sabine stood and prepared to follow, hoping he was on his way to a restaurant. That would make staging a coincidental second encounter easy. When she reached the doorway of the café, she froze. A motion in the shadows of the ivy-clad archways that enclosed the plaza caught her eye—a flash of light, maybe something like the reflection from a belt buckle—and a dark figure emerged from the gloom, black and stealthy, moving like a beast hunting in the night, sensing the air, the smell of its prey hot on its nostrils. The figure paused for a moment before stalking ahead and disappearing around the corner in pursuit of the scent. She had no doubt who the intended victim was.

"Fuck." The expletive escaped her lips as she bolted across the wide plaza, kicking off her shoes with their spike heels and picking up speed as she went. There was no way a street punk was going to blow this one. She slipped her purse off her shoulder, prepared to use it if necessary.

She reached the corner in seconds, but when she rounded it, she was met with another surprise. They were gone, vanished. All she saw was an empty sidewalk and a lonely car coming in her direction. For an instant she was seized with a feeling of panic; surely nothing bad could have happened in such a short time. There must be an explanation.

The street was lined with buildings fronted with small retail shops. Proceeding now with caution, she wandered along, checking each establishment with forced aimlessness, as if just passing the time. A pharmacy and a hairdresser's shop were closed for the day and dark inside, but the third establishment was a tiny bistro with a red awning that overhung a couple of metal tables with matching chairs. To her relief, through the doorway she saw Christoph. He was obviously waiting for someone to seat him. She continued to stroll by, troubled by the disappearance of the other one, the shadow. Where'd he go?

Next to the bistro, a narrow passageway led under the second story of the building. A painted blue sign bearing a white "P" above the opening indicated it was the entrance to a parking lot, and as she walked in front of it, a gust of air tussled her hair and sent leaves and paper wrappings out into the street. Glancing to her left, she saw him again just as the shape dissolved into the gloom. Good riddance, she thought, and turned to meet the American with rising excitement at the prospect. Then she remembered her shoes.

Sabine returned to the plaza, slipped on her heels, and turned back. She'd enjoyed deciding what to wear for this first encounter with Mueller. She wanted to be just right for the American and decided to be herself, and ignoring the possible chill of November, she wore a casual black pantsuit—a long-sleeved double-breasted jerkin, cut quite low and revealingly in front, with stylish shoulders and matching custom-cut pants that clung comfortably around her best attributes before cascading loosely to the ground. In this outfit she felt relaxed and alluring. It was a winner. The final decision was what to wear underneath, and she decided on nothing.

As she entered the bistro, every eye in the place, all ten of them, turned in her direction. For a split second it seemed that the choice of ensemble might not have been the right one. In the tight and cluttered surroundings of plastic and vinyl, she felt like a fish out of water standing there—a fox in the henhouse, Claudia Schiffer in a Boy Scouts' camp—but, just as quickly, all the diners in unison, as if carefully orchestrated, turned back to what they were doing before her appearance. Everyone but Christopher Mueller, who recognized the woman he had seen in the hotel that afternoon. His gaze lingered.

Sabine knew Americans. She'd already decided to be friendly, warm, and accessible when he made his move. With calculation, she allowed their eyes to connect briefly, just before the proprietor arrived to greet her, passing between them and breaking the link. It was all going well, she thought, and when she was gestured to the table next to him, she knew she had it made. As she expected, it only took him a few minutes to speak to her.

"Excuse me, do you speak English?"

"Yes, of course."

A few minutes later they were together at her table, digging into plates of schweinebraten and spätzle.

"Didn't I see you in the hotel this afternoon?" asked Christoph between mouthfuls.

"Probably, I have been there much of the day."

"So you're visiting Berlin too?"

"No, I live here. I was checking out the hotel in advance of some visitors who are coming on business. They're Hungarians, and their budget is small. But even so, I think that hotel won't do."

"Yep, it's pretty crappy, that's for sure. I mean, the rooms are nice, and its convenient being so close to the airport, but it's got to be the noisiest place in the world. The airplanes are ridiculous as they come in to land, and all day long the traffic never stops. I didn't get much sleep last night."

In case he needed any proof, another plane thundered past, stopping conversation in the same way as all the previous planes, which seemed to come every minute or so.

"There are fewer after midnight," he added and smiled, "but then it's like a Chinese water torture."

"Chinese water torture?" asked Sabine, thinking his was a nice smile.

"Well, I don't know if it's really Chinese, but you tie up the victim so he can't move, then drip water on his forehead until he goes crazy, or confesses. I've got five more nights here, and I'm pretty sure I'm going crazy."

"You should go somewhere else."

"Can't. It's already paid for, and I'm waiting for a friend whom I can't get hold of. He doesn't have a phone, and I don't know exactly when he's coming."

Sabine gave a little laugh. "Sorry, but it sounds like your typical travel vacation."

This time it was Christoph's turn to laugh. "I wish it was a vacation. I've been here since Friday, and it's been anything but a vacation. More like falling into a rabbit hole, if you know what I mean."

"Sleepless nights aren't the whole story then?"

"Far from it. It's been pretty weird. Wanna hear?" He hoped she did.

Sabine couldn't have asked for more. It was like shooting fish in a barrel, she thought, an American phrase she had learned from her old boyfriend. She leaned forward, resting her chin on the back of her hands, a calculated move that drew him a little closer as he recited the bizarre occurrences of the last couple days.

"I'm sorry. That must have been a shock," she said as he described the death of his grandmother.

"Well, yeah."

Christoph looked up and was captured by her eyes; they were the pale-blue color of Paul Newman's, with the gemlike quality of a Charlotte Rampling. The thought occurred to him that if he gazed too long, he might never be able to pull away. Suddenly he had the urge to tell this woman everything, but he wasn't about to open up, not now, particularly when he wasn't sure yet if they were flirting or whether it was just those eyes.

It was Sabine who broke his spell.

"So, your grandmother lived here in Berlin?"

"No, she lived in a town called Beelitz in East Germany. She worked in a hospital for Russians, and that's where she was a patient. She died on Friday."

Sabine became interested. She was after that letter, and she intended to use all her charms to get it. It seemed there was more to the story than she'd been told.

"How is it that you have a Communist grandmother? I hope I'm not intruding."

He was pleased she asked, thinking she cared, so he began at the beginning.

For the next twenty minutes, he told her the thumbnail version of the story of his life.

He was twelve, he told Sabine without emotion, living the life of a typical middle-class American, when the dream burned up on a late summer night in 1978.

"I'd gone over to a friend's house to spend the night—an 'over-nighter' we call it. The farmhouse burned to the ground with my parents in it. The report called it arson, but no one was ever caught."

For Sabine it was turning in to a night of surprises, and Krüger's simple mission—meet, befriend, secure the letter, exit—was morphing into something different as Sabine listened to the tale. She had set out as the huntress, just like a hundred times before, but Christoph and his narrative was worming its way into a long-buried part of her, a part that remained unattained and elusive. It was the part about a life of adventure, a silly dream that had made it possible for her to be easily fooled into becoming a cheap informer, a glorified hooker. She was so tired of that now. As she listened to Christoph in this low-rent restaurant, she felt herself drawn by a feeling, like the pilot of a lost ship in a pitch-black storm who has located the beacon of a lonely lighthouse blinking in the empty darkness, not quite sure where it was steering him, but certain it was better than the present situation. It was hope.

If the summons to Krüger's apartment was the door at the end of a long oppressive passage, Christopher Mueller might just be the key that unlocked it, and whatever kind of world might lie on the other side, she thought, it was certainly better than the present.

She made her decision and set a course for the lighthouse.

"My God, that's terrible. You must have been demolished."

"I don't know about 'demolished,' but I guess it's tough anytime to be wrenched by that kind of life-changing event. I mean, I had a lousy year. Middle school was crappy anyway, you know, everyone going through changes. The big problem was nobody quite knew how to react. They didn't know how to deal with it, and they kind of gave me too much space, when what I really needed was to feel normal. But I got over it. I mean, I still miss them every now and then, but, well, you know."

He seemed to run out of words, as if embarrassed by his explanation as lacking a suitable quantity of angst and sadness.

Sabine sensed his mood and saw her opportunity. Long ago she had discovered that a cocktail of a little panegyric and a lot of good looks was the easiest way into a man's soul, or wallet, or bed.

"I think people dwell on misfortune because it's expected. That's weakness to me. A strong person moves on. I think that's the way with you, yes?"

The flattery worked to perfection. Christoph, who had never dwelt much on this tragedy, at least not in recent years, immediately rose to the bait. With a shy smile curling around the corner of his lips, he brought his eyes up to meet hers. At that moment Sabine walked willingly into his life.

"Yes, I'm sure you are," reinforced Sabine before he could speak, returning his gaze, locking on like a guided missile. "That's why you don't complain about one-star hotels or fret much over the death of your grandmother."

Christoph seemed to recognize the flattery but liked it just the same, particularly from her. His eyes went soft and dreamy, and his smile grew to show his perfect, orthodontic teeth.

"I guess if you gaze too long into an abyss, the abyss will gaze back into you."

Sabine laughed; she knew the quote.

"Nietzsche. Do you know the whole quote?" she parried.

"You got me there. That's all I remember. I memorized it just for moments like this," he confessed with a slight rising of his eyebrows and a cute grin.

Sabine's eyes never wavered. "It goes, 'Whoever fights with monsters should see to it that he does not become a monster in the process. And if you gaze long into an abyss, the abyss will gaze back into you.' Be careful, Mr. Mueller." As she delivered this mock warning, the thought of Lupus crossed her mind.

At that moment she detected a sudden change in his expression, as if a cloud had passed in front of the sun. His entire face dropped slightly and took on a texture of concern and query. It was as if he had read her thoughts and conjured up the countenance of the beast. He was looking past her, out the window of the restaurant. She turned but saw nothing that would have caused this reaction, just a quiet street with a couple trees on the far side, their naked branches swaying in a gentle breeze. A bus went by, and she turned back to Christoph and gave a little shrug and a quizzical look that said, "What was that all about?"

"Well, I told you this has been a weird visit, but I haven't gotten into all of it yet; I kind of got carried away with my life story. Part of all the weirdness is the feeling I'm being watched. I thought it was happening again, but I guess I'm just a little paranoid."

Sabine allowed a soft laugh to escape her lips.

"Welcome to Germany. I wouldn't worry too much about that. Your arrival in East Germany may have excited the Stasi. If you're being watched, it will be them. They're addicted to knowing everything about everyone. They watch everyone all the time, even here."

"Yeah, I guess so. Onkel Kurt told me someone's been watching my grandmother, even secretly searching her apartment. That's crazy. Well, I thought I just saw a guy watching me. But I'm not sure. Probably just a passerby."

Sabine wasn't so sure, remembering the shadowy figure.

"Who's Onkel Kurt?"

"Kurt Webber, a friend of my grandmother, who knew my dad. I just met him yesterday. He sees conspiracy everywhere. Not cool."

"But a fact of life there."

"I guess."

Christoph returned to his tale. "I was hanging out at the beach when I got the first letter from the hospital telling me my grandmother was ill. That was about a month ago. Then another one came from Onkel Kurt. Like I said, he's a longtime friend of my grandmother. Not really an uncle, that's just what my dad called him. This letter included a plane ticket and other instructions. What the heck, I wasn't doing anything, so here I am. And, like I said, I just made it."

If this had been another project, Sabine would have steadily worked the conversation around to the letter. Her objective would have been to confirm he had it and find out where it was, all done with an attitude of complete indifference. She would do whatever was necessary to get it and get away, but not tonight. All she wanted was to keep talking, like normal people, letting the discourse travel where it would, sharing stories, comparing ideas, and getting to know each other while enjoying the company, and so they talked.

He told her what it was like growing up in California—the swim teams, the school teams, Halloween, the beach. She told him about her life, the escape from which she admitted for the first time to have no firsthand memory, her years at the Free University, the punk scene in Berlin, and her love of hiking and camping, "very German." She described the job at the Neue Nationalgalerie and promised to take him there. He thought that was brilliant. They discussed the political upheavals that seemed to be happening in Europe, the flight to the West, the increasingly bold demonstrations, and the seemingly impotent response from the authorities. They lost track of time and were amazed when the lights went dim and the proprietor told them he wanted to close and go home for the afternoon. They split the bill at Sabine's insistence and left the restaurant.

They were silent as they rounded the corner and entered the small plaza, each contemplating how to suggest the next move, to hold on to the mood and keep from saying good-bye. Christoph opened the lobby door; Sabine entered and turned to face him.

"Christoph," she said with firm resolve, "I hope I'm not being too forward; I think I'm not. I have an extra bedroom at my apartment, and, well, you have a poor hotel here. I know it's been arranged and paid for you, but really, it's bad. I think you should check out and come be my guest. You'll have a much better stay the next few days in Berlin."

She expected a polite refusal and was ready to push back, but that never happened.

"Hey, I'm down with that," he chirped, looking at the sky, his words fighting through the roar of another 747 coming in to land. "Let's bounce." And they both laughed. It had been a very long time since Sabine last laughed.

She stayed in the reception area while Christoph went up to his room to collect his things. She wrote a note and handed it to the desk clerk. It was addressed to "Onkel Kurt Webber." A few minutes later they left through the back passage that led out to the parking lot, where she guided him to a shiny red 1982 BMW 318i.

"Very cool," admired Christoph as he slid into the passenger's seat.

"Very," agreed Sabine as she let out the clutch, backed the car out of the parking space, and wheeled it toward the exit to the street.

■ ■ ■

Lupus, who never saw them leave, remained diligent and patient, watching the hotel entrance for another hour before he finally gave up. He wasn't prepared to risk an attack with her in there. Unbelievable, he growled. The bastard would have to have gone and picked up a fucking whore. He'd have to wait and return in the morning. No doubt they would not be early risers.

He descended into the subway, his mind blank, worn out, and scattered like the bristles of an old toothbrush.

■ ■ ■

Another tailing shadow followed with more notes in his book to transcribe, which he would do as soon as he handed off to the next officer. It would be interesting reading. Lupus was not the only subject being watched. Officer Lothar Kahn identified what he thought was a stalker interested in the woman who picked up the guy that Lupus was following—maybe her husband? He considered contacting Schneider but decided it could wait for the report.

37

His pager vibrated. Peter Buckner looked at his watch before picking it up and reading the number five on the display. About time, he thought. He stood, snatched his jacket off the back of a chair, and headed for the door, then stopped.

"Fuck it," he said to no one and tossed the jacket back on to the chair.

Everything was changing; the machine was breaking down, and he was feeling increasingly exposed and vulnerable. He'd sent numerous signals to his handler and still had no response. It was time to look after things his way. He sat down and, violating protocol, made the call to the designated public phone right there in his apartment.

"Speak," he snapped when the connection was made, "and make it brief. What's she up to?"

"Okay, okay. She went to a hotel near Tegel, Hotel Bärlin, where she picked up an American who was staying there."

"Picked up?"

"Right. She had this guy in mind. She stalked him."

"How do you know?"

"Trust me, I know a stalker when I see one."

"So who is this guy?"

"An American, name Christopher Mueller. After she took him home, I doubled back to the hotel. Someone in the GDR made his reservation, and he checked in late last night. He was booked for a week."

"Shit. What the fuck's going on?"

"I don't have a clue, but I need to go get some rest. Surveillance isn't something I do, you know. By the way, as of ten minutes ago, he's still there."

"Right. I'll take it from here." Buckner hung up. "What the fuck's going on?"

Sabine was his agent, and he decided her assignments. It was clear someone else was running her now. He lit another cigarette. He wasn't going to let himself get hung out to dry. He'd seen it happen to others, and he had a huge aversion to the possibility of prison again. No way was Peter Buckner going to be set up. He looked at his watch. He decided to postpone a confrontation with Sabine Goetz until the morning. He'd get to the bottom of this little caper.

38

As the city of Berlin slowly woke up to Monday morning, no one could have predicted that by the end of the week the Wall would fall and the Stasi would be on the run. Nothing that had happened was enough in the minds of the citizens on either side of the Wall to inspire the slightest hope that forty years of communist rule would soon end, and in the blink of an eye—not the protests in Dresden and Leipzig, not the sudden resignation of General Secretary Erich Honecker, not the flood of East Germans escaping to the West through Hungary, not even the million East Germans who packed into Alexanderplatz on Saturday, none of these.

Berliners went about their daily routine as they would any Monday morning.

Shortly after eight o'clock, four of them, almost at the exact same moment, walked out of their homes. Peter Buckner's objective was Sabine's apartment. Wolfgang Reisen's was the Hotel Bärlin. Sabine Goetz and Detective Erich Schneider headed for their respective offices.

■ ■ ■

Buckner rode his 1980 BMW R100RS, a sparkling steel-blue café racer-style motorcycle, maneuvering through the streets with finesse, the seventy-horsepower boxer twin motor leaving a throaty growl in its wake. It was chilly, and his belted black leather jacket was buttoned up to his neck. A white silk scarf flapped and danced over his shoulder, and a pair of split-lens goggles flashed reflections like miniature signal projectors sending out Morse code messages. His hair, cropped and bleached blond, fashioned after the Sting character in *Quadrophenia*, streaked backward like short grass on the steppes blasted by autumn winds. He loved this machine, more than any human. She always responded and obeyed. Together, they were one being—no mysteries or secrets, no tantrums, unlike women.

He knew Sabine's morning routine, so it was a surprise when the American opened the door. He was wearing a brown T-shirt and khaki pants. He was barefoot and had that sloppy, casual look that Buckner disliked instantly. It was apparent he'd not been awake long.

"Ist Sabine hier?" asked Buckner.

"No, uh, nein."

"You're English?" asked Buckner, as if he didn't know.

"American. I'm visiting." Christoph yawned. "Sabine's not here. I heard her leave about fifteen minutes ago."

"That's unusual. She's early. I usually have coffee with her before she leaves for work," lied Buckner.

"Hey, c'mon in then," said Christoph, stepping back and opening the door. "I've just been trying to figure out the coffee machine. Do you know how it works?"

"Of course. It makes espresso. You like?"

"Like Turkish coffee, real strong in little cups?"

Buckner fought hard to keep out of his voice the distain he felt due to this sad ignorance, not that this Yank would recognize it. "Yes, very similar." He condescended, wishing his English vocabulary were larger.

Fifteen minutes later the two men sat in the stark, all-white living room, sipping espresso from white porcelain cups. One slouched easily; the other assumed a calculated position, designed to express control. Two cups later Buckner was ready to leave. He'd learned as much as the Yank could tell him, but it did nothing to lessen his anxiety. A letter, this was the whole deal, and it worried him to hear that it was now in Sabine's possession. The idiot had given it to her so she could try and find someone who could identify the addressee. By now it was probably already in the hands of whoever had recruited her on Friday night. He thought he might ride over to the Neue Nationalgalerie and confront her anyway, but dismissed the idea. He'd never been comfortable as a spy and was always fearful of crossing the Firm. He sat astride the BMW trying to decide whether he should try to contact his handler again.

■ ■ ■

Around the time Buckner was pondering his future outside Sabine's apartment, a call came into Schneider's phone. He had just settled down at his desk to read through the papers and documents that filled his in-basket. He hadn't gotten to the surveillance reports yet. It was his boss, Waner, and the news was bad. Klaus Krüger had been attacked in his home and was in a coma. Lupus was the first thought that came into Schneider's mind.

"An attack? What happened?" asked Schneider, expecting to hear that it was a small caliber bullet in the head. To his surprise, Waner described what sounded like a common assault and battery for the purpose of robbery. It had happened in the lobby of his building. He'd been hit repeatedly in the head with a hard, round object, could have been a pipe or a gun barrel, something like that.

"Any witnesses?"

"No."

"Who's on it?"

"I spoke to Schertz. The Schupo have the building secured, and he's got a Kripo detective from the fourth directorate named Noll on it. Know him?"

"No," replied Schneider. "Is it okay with you if I get involved?"

"That's why I called. I already cleared it with Schertz. I want to make sure it's just a robbery we're dealing with here."

Georg Schertz was the chief of police for Berlin and had a good working relationship with the BKA, unlike some others.

"I'll keep a low profile. Does Noll know we're involved?"

"Yes."

"Then I'd like to go to the crime scene immediately. I assume there's someone with Inspector Krüger, and I can get updates on his condition."

"Yes."

Minutes later, Detective Erich Schneider was descending to an awaiting squad car. The surveillance report on Lupus sat, unread, in the in-basket.

■ ■ ■

Sabine arrived at the Neue Nationalgalerie before nine o'clock. It was quiet at first, and she took advantage of this to read through Krüger's notes again. Twice more she read the photocopy of the letter from Johann von Ritter to his sister, hoping some hidden message would jump out at her. She tried to make sense of the phrase near the end, which seemed a bit out of place:

HIER RUHT IN GOTT

UNSER LIEBER SOHN

Was he referring to himself, anticipating his own death, when he wrote, "Here with God lies our dear son?" Why, she wondered, the big capital letters? There had to be some significance, but what?

Soon others began to gather. The buzz of early morning conversation grew into something centered on the massive demonstration in the East on Saturday. West German TV had covered it extensively. Sabine, who hadn't had the chance to keep up with the news, was amazed to hear the details. A million East Germans gathered peacefully to hear radical speakers, and the government just stood by; so did the police and Stasi. What was happening? Had glasnost descended overnight?

"All dictatorships fail, monarchs like the kaisers, totalitarian states like the Nazis, and now the GDR under the Commies; they all fail. It's already under way, isn't it?"

The speaker was Günther Herzog, an art historian who was a frequent presence at the museum and whose knowledge and interests, he was always ready to remind his audience, went well beyond the confines of art. Sabine, who'd been looking out the glass wall over the enclosed sculpture garden that spanned the entire west side of the building, turned to join the conversation. She recognized the onset of one of his famous opinion blasts. Before he was able to launch his treatise, Sabine cut in.

"Günther, speaking of Nazis, I have a friend who's doing some research for a novel she's writing, and asked me if I knew anyone with in-depth knowledge on the Waffen-SS. It just occurred to me that you might have some expertise."

"Well, I am familiar with much of the history of the war and have a general knowledge of what the Waffen-SS contribution was, but..." Herzog paused, took off his glasses, and proceeded to examine the lenses in the morning light while he searched for a positive way to express his actual lack of expertise. Then he remembered someone. "But if your friend really wants to delve into the minutiae, there's this Englishman I know who lives here in Berlin. He's the ultimate Nazi hobbyist. I'd guess he has more knowledge than any academic historian, and he knows it. He's a real nut, *Verstücke*."

"Sounds perfect. My friend's also a character. They're bound to get on. Can you arrange for an introduction?"

Herzog let out a merry laugh. "You don't need an introduction. He loves visitors, anytime. I'll call him for you though."

Ten minutes later Sabine called her apartment and spoke with Christoph. Nettleton would meet them in an hour.

■ ■ ■

The trip from the Kreuzberg district to Tegel airport was never a quick one, but this morning, of all mornings, it was worse than usual. Wolfgang Reisen was already stretched to the snapping point, and now this. He'd been unable to sleep as hostile and anxious thoughts, fighting like angry boxers, circled in his head and refused to leave. Instead of the high he loved, the emotional drug fix he got when the killing was done right, the rushed and impersonal killings had left him flat, depressed. His joy was to see the eyes fade and roll up. It was like setting a soul free to mingle and join with his. Now, as he stood surrounded by Berliners heading to work or to school or to daily chores, a relentless pounding filled his sinuses, and his eyes burned and tears squeezed from their corners. He felt like his head might explode. Mutti was taking advantage of him. He knew it, but what could he do? She didn't have to make him do the Stasi guy, and she should never have given the policeman his father's letter. That cudgeling was barbaric. The brutality made him sick. Why was she doing these things? All he wanted was the bastard, and Mutti had promised he could have him. He would do it right with the bastard—slowly, painlessly, with respect for the soul. It almost seemed that the bastard knew what was going on and was playing with him. He'd better be at the hotel.

It was going on ten o'clock when he finally arrived.

"You missed him," said the man at the reception desk. "He checked out yesterday."

He repeated the clerk's statement as if testing it to see if it were true. How could this be happening to him?

"He checked out? But he was supposed to meet me here. Did he leave a message as to where he went?"

"Yes, he did. It's right here." The clerk reached under the counter and retrieved a sheet of paper. "May I ask you your name?"

The clerk wasn't being secretive about it, and Wolfgang caught enough of the name on the note.

"Webber."

"Kurt Webber?" asked the clerk obligingly.

"Yes."

He unfolded the sheet and smiled. It gave a phone number where the bastard could be contacted. He asked the clerk if there was a public phone and was soon sitting inside a glass-enclosed booth. He sat there for a few moments looking at the numbers, thinking through what he would say, and then he began to dial. Before he'd finished, a sharp pounding on the glass gave him a jolt. He looked up from the paper with a start and came face-to-face with an apparition glaring angrily at him. At the same instant, the door was pushed open.

"Who the fuck are you?" growled the intruder.

39

Maybe it was old age, but Kurt Webber had come to terms with life in the GDR. He was comfortable within its constraints; things were predictable, and the pace was right. The failed achievements of the party, decaying buildings, constant shortages of everything, and phony propaganda didn't bother him. He seldom went into West Berlin, despite the fairly easy access given to pensioners. On the other side of the Wall, the out-of-control, multicultural chaos of the city was oppressive and foreign, a jungle. It took something like the letter and his concern for Christoph to get him to make the journey.

He was on guard and a little wound up by the time he arrived at the hotel and approached the reception desk.

"You too," remarked the clerk when Webber asked for Christoph Mueller.

"What do you mean, 'me too'?" shot back Webber.

"Another person just asked for him, but Mr. Mueller checked out last night."

"What? I was to meet him here."

"That's what the other guy said."

Webber pondered the situation for a moment. Christoph wouldn't leave without telling him, and what other guy?

"Did he leave me a message? My name is Kurt Webber."

A look of surprise spread across the clerk's face. "Excuse me, but the other guy, just a minute ago, said he was Kurt Webber."

"God dammit, I'm Kurt Webber. What guy?" Before the clerk could answer, a bad thought struck. "Was there a message? Did you give it to him? You did, didn't you?"

Webber saw the answer in his expression.

"What did he look like? Where'd he go?" he snapped.

"He's right over there, in the telephone booth."

Webber trotted across the lobby, pounded on the glass, and pushed open the door.

"Who the fuck are you?"

What happened next took Webber by surprise. He had just enough time to absorb and recognize a few details—the dark hair, a moustache, scared eyes—before the imposter slammed into him and sent him tumbling on to his back. His head struck the floor hard, and lights streaked across his vision like miniature comets. He laid there only a few seconds, but by the time he'd pushed himself up and regained his feet, the imposter was gone. He felt woozy and was aware of people looking at him. Someone approached and asked him something, but he couldn't make sense of what was being said. Slowly the confusion in his head drained away. He'd been concussed, but it could have been worse, he thought.

"I'm okay. I'll be all right," he assured the small group that had gathered around him. He reached down to pick up his cap lying on the floor, and he noticed the sheet of paper on the small ledge inside the phone booth.

"No, no, don't call the police," he said when the hotel clerk made the suggestion. "I'm sure it was just a stupid young man in a hurry. I'm fine."

"That was the guy who said he was you," volunteered the clerk, and then added cleverly, "of course, if you are you."

Webber started to walk away, the message from Sabine now in his hand. As he passed the clerk, he muttered, *"Blödes Arschloch."* Moments later he left the hotel, heading for the U-Bahn.

■ ■ ■

Wolfgang ran, hardly aware of his surroundings, as if passing through a dark tunnel. His breathing was labored, and his lungs burned. He was vaguely aware of crossing a street, cars blowing their horns, accompanied by the sound of screeching tires. Far in the distance, at the end of this desperate corridor, he could see a sign, *U Kurt Schumacher Platz*, large white letters on a blue background, calling him like a beacon in a storm. Now, caught in the turbulence of churning emotions, the unwavering sign was all that mattered; once he got there, he would be safe. Below, off the streets, he could try to figure out the thing that was crushing down on him. He arrived at the top of the entrance and then descended the stairs, the blue and white sign floating up and away. He found himself sitting on a wire bench staring at the white tiled walls of the underground, the name of the station coming into focus in large black letters. He didn't know how long he'd been sitting there, his mind blank, but slowly he managed to gather his thoughts.

Again he'd been thwarted. Each time he'd be so close; each time another stranger would appear, as if through a trap door from the empyrean, sent by some guardian to save the bastard. He wanted out of this nightmare, but the more he fumed, the more he wanted the bastard. The bastard was everything now. Collecting the bastard's soul would release him from this ordeal. Fuck the letter; that was Mutti's thing.

Where was the bastard? Where was the note with the phone number? Fuck, it never ends. He couldn't go back there now.

At that moment he saw Kurt Webber at the bottom of the stairs. He sprang to his feet and ducked behind a large concrete column, his heart racing again.

■ ■ ■

Webber needed to think. He was more worried now about Christoph than before. He knew his assailant; he'd seen him before at the hospital. He was after the damned letter. In the frozen steppes, he'd been hunted by wolves and knew what he was seeing. Crossing the plaza, he scoured the landscape but didn't see the predator. He headed for the street away from the hotel. As he waited for the streetlight to change, he looked at the note for the first time. On one side his name was written. The "Onkel" reassured him. He turned it over, and the message was a phone number and the instruction to "call me." Nothing more. With a sense of urgency, he looked around to see if a public phone might be somewhere near and saw the U-Bahn station. There would be one there. Down on the platform, he found what he was looking for.

The phone at the other end rang five times, and then a woman's voice came on. As soon as Webber realized it was a recording, he hung up. He wasn't used to leaving messages and had to work out in his mind what he would say. He called again and this time left a message.

He hung up and left the station. At the top of the stairs, he once again looked across the plaza in case the son of a bitch who was stalking Christoph was around. He didn't think to look behind him. Seeing nothing, he set off walking. His destination was the food court in the KaDeWe. It would take him a couple of hours, but it wasn't raining, and the exercise would do him good. In Webber's mind, the KaDeWe food court was one of the great wonders of the twentieth century. He was ready for a good meal, and he'd wait there for Christoph.

■ ■ ■

Lupus stalked his prey across the city. His objective was clear, and his mind was settled and sharp once again. He was back in his element.

40

Christoph Mueller was having the time of his life.

He couldn't believe his luck meeting Sabine—what a hottie, and nice, too; a lot less the German than her friend Peter, who reminded him of Klaus Kinski. She'd just called to tell him an expert had been located who might be able to help him find Peiper.

As he waited for the taxi she'd said would pick him up, he wandered about her apartment, whistling and thinking how random it had all been, starting with the first letter from Dr. Braun. The memory of his first night—passing out, the dream, and his humiliating cowering under the stiffening corpse of his curious foreign ancestor—had faded. Saturday was the turnaround. He'd definitely seek out Uwe when he got the chance. That was a great time.

Outside, a car horn hooted. Christoph looked out the window; it was the taxi. Life was good.

■ ■ ■

R. Headley Nettleton lived in a small, second-floor studio apartment in the Schöneberg district on a quiet, tree-lined street. The building was new, modern, bright, and airy, much like Sabine's. When the door opened, the round, balding head of the English transplant appeared, dominated by two magnified gray-green eyeballs, blinking through thick lenses set in square tortoiseshell frames that peered out at his visitors like something in a Lewis Carroll dream.

Moments later they stepped into another world.

No other race found as much fascination in the Third Reich as the English. Perhaps they were simply sucked into the vacuum created by the reluctance on the part of Germans, who for their part just wanted to forget. For whatever reason, Nettleton took his interest in all things Nazi to heights beyond imagination. The apartment they entered was a chaotic wonderland of collected memorabilia, books, and documents.

The room was no more than three hundred square feet with a nicely appointed kitchen area separated from the rest of the space by lower cabinets with a black laminate countertop. A bed was nestled into the corner opposite the kitchen. On the other side, next to the window, was a black lacquered desk. These combined to fill the lower portion of that wall. The wall above the desk and every other inch of wall space in the room was covered with shelves or bookcases. In the center of the room was a rectangular steel table with a cheap plastic laminate top. Every horizontal surface in the apartment was covered with file folders, vinyl records in cardboard boxes, a record player, ancient newspapers and magazines stacked in piles, books and manuals, an assortment of knives, daggers, military hats and helmets, and dozens of prewar cigar boxes full of medals, badges, and colored postcards faded with age. Hanging from the ceiling were banners and flags embroidered with swastikas, golden eagles, lightning bolts, and death heads. Over the bed, encased in a large shadow box, was a white military-style jacket, with a row of gold buttons down the middle and smaller ones on the flaps that folded over the two breast pockets. This item seemed to shine amid the aging beige, browns, and blacks of everything else.

Nettleton, noticing what had caught their attention, explained.

"One of the pretty costumes Hermann Goering designed for himself. Pity someone removed the epaulets before I was able to acquire it. But otherwise in nice condition, don't you think?" Nettleton liked to punctuate his observations with a rhetorical question that ended any potential debate. "You know, there was a joke that went around that he designed an admiral's uniform to wear whenever he took a bath. He was at his physical peak, if you get my gist, when he wore this one; can't you tell? Pleased to meet you, by the way. You must be Fraulein Goetz, and this is?"

"I'm Christoph Mueller."

"Ah, Mr. Mueller." Nettleton extended his hand. "So nice to make your acquaintance. American, I reckon, with a German ancestry. Am I not right?"

"Exactamundo," exclaimed Christoph. "Where'd you get all this stuff?"

"Well, I'd hardly describe this magnificent collection of mine as 'stuff,' but taking into consideration your obvious favorable impression of what surrounds you, I have no negative feelings from your unfortunate choice of words. What you see is the reflection of a lifetime love affair that began when I was in prep school, playing with Airfix aeroplane models and reading *Commando* comic books. As with all true love, it's grown and softened, but never diminished. You, no doubt, have yet to find your true love."

"I guess," said Christoph.

"Don't worry about it, my boy; most people never do. I, on the other hand, am blessed. But enough about me. You've sought me out for information. You follow in the footsteps of many others, don't you know. Beevor, Hastings, and Ryan, and even your countryman Shirer, have all beaten a path to my door. Hopefully I can be of assistance. Please sit down. Can I get you something? I'm afraid I don't drink, alcohol that is, but perhaps a cup of tea?"

"Coffee?"

"Sorry, I'm a Brit."

"I'll pass, thanks."

"Tea would be fine," interjected Sabine, speaking for the first time. "Nice museum."

Ten minutes later, three chairs having been found and grouped in front of Nettleton's desk, they sat sipping tea, including Christoph. Nettleton's rotund form filled an old oak desk chair, which squeaked as he rocked gently back and forth, holding a cup and saucer on an ample, protruding belly. He was in his late forties. His perfectly round head was bald except for a dense ring of hair that circled this globe before dropping down in front of his ears to form impressive muttonchop sideburns. His eyebrows were also thick and bushy, and overhung the top of his glasses in a distracting way. His voice was a bit high-pitched but melodic.

"Standartenführer Joachim Peiper," he said, reading the name on the envelope. "Now this is a very interesting fellow, don't you know?"

"To be honest, I have no idea who he is."

"I must say, that's a terribly sad state of affairs, you being an American and all that. Have you not heard of the Malmedy Massacre?"

"Nope, 'fraid not."

"The film, *Battle of the Bulge* with Henry Fonda, Charles Bronson, Telly Savalas?"

"Nope."

Nettleton rolled his eyes back into his head, turned, and placed the saucer on his desk.

"Okay. History lesson time for the American. I do wonder about the school system in your country.

"In December 1944, as a last-ditch, desperation move, Germany—Hitler's idea—launched as big a counteroffensive as they could put together on the western front, Operation Watch on the Rhine. I won't go into the details except to point out that this offensive targeted the advancing Americans in the Ardennes and was spearheaded by a Panzer division commanded by none other than your Joachim Peiper. Along the way Peiper's troops captured about a hundred Americans who were gathered into a meadow, disarmed, and mowed down where they stood with machine guns, assault rifles actually, mostly Sturmgewehr forty-fours, which were fairly new at the time. This has come to be known as the Malmedy Massacre."

"Jeez, this Peiper's a nice guy."

"Well, it's questionable as to how direct Peiper's involvement was, though he certainly was a hardened veteran who had spent a long time on the Russian front, don't you know. He would certainly have had a 'take no prisoners' approach to this mission. In any case he paid for it, don't you know. After the war he was tried and sentenced to death, which was later commuted to life. Eventually he was one of the last German officers to be released from prison in 1956."

"Where is he now? I still want to get this letter to him."

"He's in Bavaria, but you won't be able to deliver that letter."

"Is he in hiding or something?"

"Dead, my boy, and therein lies another intriguing story. He was murdered."

"Dead?"

"Assassinated."

Christoph's shoulders dropped as he realized the quest he'd so recently embraced seemed suddenly over. Now what? He didn't want to go back, not to the comfortable, boring life of a business school dropout, while the whole world was focused right here in Germany. He'd walked with the crowds protesting in the rain. He'd heard them chanting their way to Alexanderplatz, calling for reform and revolution, glasnost and perestroika! He'd seen the thousands and thousands converge to pack the monstrous

gray square below the watchful, blinking blue eye of the space-age telephone tower. He'd heard the cheers and jeers as poets and former politburo
members pleaded their case through scratchy bullhorns in the rain.

He imagined this was like the mythical sixties, or Russia after World
War 1, and he sensed he was possibly in the middle of a momentous
turning point. He didn't want to go home.

He looked at Sabine. No, he didn't want to go home.

As these thoughts heaved in his mind, it was Sabine who injected
the next question.

"Assassinated? When did that happen?"

"Sometime in the midseventies. I think 1976. I can look it up if you
want. A real shoot-out in France. Peiper was a real soldier. Granted, at
one time he was Himmler's adjutant, but most of the war he was on the
front lines. He was a warrior, don't you know. They say the Communists
came for him in the night. He didn't go down easily. He was found, in-
cinerated in his burned-out home, clutching a rifle, with a handgun and
a shotgun nearby. All had been fired.

"I should say, it's believed the charred and shriveled corpse was
Peiper. Terribly hard to make a positive ID when seventy percent of the
body was gone, don't you know?"

"Would you consider selling that letter to me now that you know the
addressee is, should I say, indisposed? It would be a fabulous addition to
my museum," inquired Nettleton, tossing an ingratiating smile at Sabine.

"No."

The word leaped out of Sabine's mouth as she looked at Christoph.

"I mean, Christoph, it's the only memento of your grandmother. It's
a family heirloom, not some piece of merchandise to be sold off."

"You're right, but that's only the half of it," said Christoph solemnly.
"If I can't give it to Joachim Peiper, I'm keeping it. It's more than just
something my grandmother treasured. You see, it was written by my
grandfather. It's a family heirloom."

Sabine's eyes widened, but Christoph didn't notice the surprise they expressed.

It was Nettleton who spoke first. "Who's von Ritter?"

"His name was Johann von Ritter. He was a lieutenant in the SS." He was looking at Sabine. "But in the last months of the war, it seems he had some kind of a desk job. I'm told he met my grandmother in a hospital on the eastern front that was swallowed by the Russian army. He died there, but my grandmother got away, carrying this letter. It's a real story."

"I'll give you one hundred dollars for that letter," said Nettleton. "That's a ridiculous amount, but considering the circumstances, don't you know?"

"Sorry, Mr. Nettleton."

"Would you consider providing me with a Xerox copy?"

Christoph thought briefly before replying. "I'll tell you what. I want the chance to open and read it before I make any deal. There could be stuff in it that I wouldn't want to share." He looked at Sabine. "We need go back to your place. I'll need you to help translate."

"Fair enough," said Nettleton. He stood and reached over to his desk, picked up a business card, and handed it to Christoph. "Just give me a call either way. Oh, and just in case, do you have a phone number where I can call you, Miss Goetz?"

"You can contact me at the Neue Nationalgalerie, where I work."

■ ■ ■

Five minutes later Christoph and Sabine left the apartment, each for their own reasons, eager to read the treasured letter. They hailed a taxi, and Sabine gave the driver her address. On the way, she explained that she had to return to the office for a couple hours, so he was on his own until she got back. What she really wanted to do was contact Sherlock.

41

After she dropped Christoph off at her apartment, Sabine took the taxi to Sherlock's. She got out five blocks from his building. The instant she turned the corner onto his street she knew something was wrong. An unmistakable police presence greeted her, highlighted by the uniformed officer standing guard at the front entrance. She walked on by, trying to show just the right amount of innocent curiosity, and as she passed she caught a glimpse of a figure in the window she knew to be Sherlock's study.

It wasn't him.

A prickly sensation crawled across her skin. They had Sherlock, whichever "they" it was, and it meant they could well be coming after her, or maybe not. There was one certain fact; she was on her own now. She had to move fast. Christoph's letter had to be opened and its secret revealed.

She decided to avoid a taxi, which could be traced, and took a bus back to her apartment. When she got there, Christoph was gone. On the counter next to the espresso machine was a note.

Gone to CA-DA-Vee to meet Onkel Kurt at the food court.

■ ■ ■

Detective Erich Schneider's day had been long and trying. He'd visited many victims in intensive care in his time, bandaged, sedated, stuck with IVs, and wired to monitors. He was used to it. It's different—it's personal and hits you hard—when it's your mentor and friend. It makes you mad, like watching a guy punch a little kid in the face or hearing a judge let a creep go free on a technicality. He didn't stay long at the hospital. He didn't like the misery that resided there, and he was eager to get the investigation going. All morning and into the afternoon he'd gone door-to-door in Krüger's building and around the neighborhood. No one had seen anything. Before he left he made one last visit to Krüger's apartment. He wandered around the study. He wasn't sure what he was looking for, but like Krüger, he didn't believe in coincidence. There were too many possible connections: Krüger's interest in Lupus, the murdered Stasi, and now this, a mundane mugging, but why? Nothing seemed to be missing. Krüger's wallet was still in his jacket pocket, and his watch hadn't been taken. There must have been something. Did the attacker just panic? Not likely, he stayed long enough to administer a kick to the ribs.

He looked at the clock, still early. He sighed. Soon it would be time to go home, which meant he would no longer have the distraction of his work to save him from himself. For many years the weight of depression had been suffocating him. Some mornings he'd awake and his chest felt like a gigantic press was relentlessly bearing down on him, making the very act of clambering out of bed nearly impossible. Every morning he'd struggle to find his way to the police station, where a miniscule of relevance awaited, and another day could grind by.

He realized he must have been sitting there for a long time. Slowly he started the mundane task of going through all the papers that had accumulated in the basket on his desk, among them the surveillance report from the night before. Before he got to it, the phone rang.

"Schneider here."

"It's Kahn; I'm at KaDeWe, and I thought you might like to know what's going on. Have you read my report from yesterday?"

KaDeWe, thought Schneider. This had better be good.

"Not yet, I just got back. Shoot."

"I picked up Lupus this morning when he left his apartment. He went right back to the same hotel he was at last night. It's in my report. Here's where it starts to get weird. Inside he gets into a confrontation with an old graybeard, who he knocks over before running out of the hotel and through traffic like he'd seen a ghost, and down into the U-Bahn. He's sitting there, kind of dazed, when the same old guy appears. He leaps behind a column to hide. The old guy makes a phone call and starts walking away. Then, guess what? Lupus follows him all the way to KaDeWe, where they settle in at the food court."

"Let me get this straight. Lupus is tailing this guy. Do you think he's looking for revenge?"

"Could be. It was the old guy who came on to Lupus at the hotel. He busted in on a phone call Lupus was making, and I heard him swear at him just before Lupus knocked him down and split."

"Interesting."

"There's one more twist. Another guy just arrived here and joined the graybeard; it's the American from the hotel, Christoph Mueller, contact number two in my report. I was watching Lupus; he was real interested in this guy. I could feel his pulse rate jump from across the room."

Schneider thought he had this figured out.

"I haven't read the report yet. How old's the American?"

"Early to midtwenties."

"Fits the MO. Stay with them; I'm on the way."

Schneider was thinking hard. If they could catch the psycho in the act, it would clinch the deal and they could put him away forever. That would take some delicate surveillance, involve a load of risk, and need a good helping of luck. He could see a hundred ways this might play out. His black mood turned to gray, and a thought struck him; he wished Krüger knew about it.

■ ■ ■

There he was, the bastard. Wolfgang felt like a penniless boy in a candy store. No more than fifty feet away was the object of his obsession and lust, the soul he craved but for the moment couldn't have, not yet. Such a fine strong neck; he could imagine his fingers around it squeezing, his thumbs slowly crushing the windpipe as he watched the bastard's eyes roll. He wanted to get a closer look but didn't dare, not with the old fart there. Who was that guy anyway? He looked familiar, but old people all appeared the same: bald, wrinkled, and stooped. How was he going to do this? Follow when they leave, hope they separate, and then go after the bastard? He'd have to wait and see.

These ramblings continued uncontrollable until abruptly interrupted by the arrival of Sabine. He thought he'd go nuts trying to figure out how this would play out, doubting his ability to manage things. The woman complicated an already screwed-up situation. It was pretty obvious that the bastard would go home with her again, in which case he'd have to follow and bide his time, unless he took them both on at the same time and got her out of the way, but that could be ugly and probably disastrous. It wouldn't be a proper taking.

A light went off in his head, more like a small explosion. It was so simple yet perfect: honesty. Brilliant! Why should he slink around like this, constantly frustrated, when he could come out into the open and be part of the party? He'd have to apologize to the old-timer, but there must be a perfectly acceptable reason for his behavior at the hotel. He'd think of something. He hesitated. His hunter's experience told him that the relationship with the donor must be intimate to make sure of the quality of the experience, and the security of secrecy. If he exposed himself, he'd have to think of something for dealing with the aftermath, some way to cover his tracks. He'd kept his eyes on the bastard while he was thinking this through, and the urge to go there was too strong. He took a deep breath, stood and walked across the room, oblivious to the symphony of conversations from the shoppers and diners and the rattle of plates and tableware that filled the huge open space. He found himself at the table where Kurt Webber, Christoph Mueller, and Sabine Goetz sat.

Christoph was the first to notice the newcomer. When their eyes met, Wolfgang spoke to him.

"Forgive my intrusion; my name is Wolfgang Reisen. I believe we're related."

Three pairs of eyes locked onto the stranger, and no one said a word, each preoccupied with their own thoughts inspired by this bizarre apparition.

In the backpack, hanging on the back of Christoph's chair, was a letter written in 1945.

■ ■ ■

On the trip from headquarters to KaDeWe, Schneider read the surveillance report from the day before, and by the time he stepped out of the car at the Tauentsienstrasse entrance, he knew that the perpetrator of the assault on Krüger was Wolfgang Reisen, but knowing this brought more questions. A motive was hard to come by. Like the case of the dead Stasi agent, if Lupus was the killer, this attack wasn't his MO; something had changed. Lupus couldn't have connected Krüger to any investigation, and even if by some freak chance he had, this wouldn't motivate the attempted killing of a retired policeman. Getting rid of one detective wouldn't make the case record go away. No, it had to be the briefcase, something inside it. Krüger must have found something, and Lupus must have known, but what, photos? Krüger didn't mention anything when they spoke on the phone Sunday morning, just eight hours before the attack. What happened in those goddamn eight missing hours? And why did Krüger instruct him not to inform their East German counterparts about Lupus's visit last Friday night? There was definitely something here his friend and mentor had kept from him, something that underpinned the whole investigation, and, Schneider was certain, this something was the reason Wolfgang Reisen was still a free man.

So what was Lupus up to now? After the assault on Krüger yesterday, he started acting like a stalker again with the strange series of events around the Hotel Bärlin, and now this. Who was this American, and was he connected to Lupus's uncharacteristic behavior, or just a reversion to his normal homicidal pattern? Whatever was going on, he was going to nail the *Arschloch*, and soon.

The department store Kaufhaus Des Westens, or KaDaWe, was the epitome of Western capitalism, and its food court was the jewel in the crown, taking up the entire sixth floor. When Schneider stepped out of the elevator, he was met with a cacophony of sound and a vision of the expansive space filled with diners and service personnel furiously pursuing the rites of economic success. It took him a few moments to locate Lothar Kahn.

"He's to your left," said Kahn, after the two men had greeted each other conspicuously, as though this was a prearranged meeting of old friends and Schneider had returned from the food area with a pastry and coffee. "And the group with the American is behind you. Since I called you, the woman he was with last night has arrived and joined them."

As he sipped his coffee, Schneider located Lupus in the corner of his eye, who at that moment rose from his seat and started to walk toward the two policemen. Schneider caught his breath but remained calm, asked Kahn a question about his wife, and was relieved, then surprised, when Wolfgang passed them and stopped somewhere behind him.

"He's talking to the American," whispered Kahn. "He's standing up; they're shaking hands. Looks like Lupus is going to join them."

"Keep on them. I'm going to call for backup. This may be the best chance yet to put the maniac away forever." Schneider casually took a sip of coffee and looked around to locate a phone.

■ ■ ■

Sabine Goetz could hardly believe what she had just heard. It seemed impossible that Wolfgang Reisen, mass murderer and dangerous challenger for the letter, now stood next to her, nearly touching her. It took a monumental exercise of will to remain in control of her emotions and keep her body language from giving away the shock that had just struck. Her mind raced. Was there a connection between this surprise arrival and the police presence at Krüger's apartment building? How could she protect Christoph and the letter? Somehow she had to get him away.

She glanced over at him. Their eyes met momentarily, and a smile twitched at the corners of his mouth; then he returned his attention to his newest relative. That brief connection produced a warm, moist sensation, something she hadn't felt for a long time. It told Sabine what she wanted to know. He was hers for the taking. All she had to do was ask, and she knew she would.

Now the game was in her comfort zone. She had only to negotiate Christoph away from Reisen, and she had the tools to do it. Tonight they would open the letter, and more.

Reisen was apologizing for his actions earlier at the hotel, confessing that he was stupid and panicked, and was spinning the tale of his uncle and Lena, and how great it was that he found his unknown distant cousin thanks to Dr. Braun at the sanitarium. Christoph seemed delighted, but Sabine sensed a very different vibe coming from the silent Kurt Webber, who, like an angry caged animal, stared furiously at the intruder. She recognized an ally, at least for now, if needed. As if to confirm her thoughts, Webber suddenly leaned forward and spoke for the first time; it came as a growl in German.

"Erst verfolgen Sie mich, dann schlagen Sie mich nieder, ja." (You knock me down and then stalk me here.)

"When I saw you in the U-Bahn, I didn't think you'd be happy to see me. I apologize again; I just wanted to find Christoph."

"How is it you know all this about Lena, and she never heard of you?" responded Webber, still speaking German, his eyes hard and cold, unblinking.

"My father knew Lena Mueller in the war," responded Wolfgang, again in English. "Apparently he learned about her from his colleague, Dr. Braun. My mother and I knew nothing until Father died, and we were going through his papers. I found out about Lena fairly recently, reading his diary."

"Sie waren dort am sanatorium, nicht wahr?" (You were at the sanitarium?)

"No, why do you think that?"

"Ich habe sie gesehen."

"Sorry, must be someone else. I've never been there."

Webber leaped to his feet, startling everyone. "You're a fucking liar. You were there in the middle of the night Lena died. *Ich weiss das.*"

To Sabine, he seemed to straighten and grow taller, while at the same time she noticed Wolfgang recede, his head drooping slightly, yielding to the dominance of the old man. It occurred to her that if he had ears that moved, they'd be folded back like a dog.

"I've never been there. Why should I lie?" It sounded like a whine.

"Bullshit. Ich weiss Ihr Spiel." (I know your game.) "Christoph, we gotta go."

■ ■ ■

"What's going on?" said Schneider. Kahn's eyes told him that something interesting was happening behind his back.

"The old guy's giving Lupus a hard time," said Kahn. "He stood and is pissed off at something. Shit, they're leaving. Wait, the American is still talking to Lupus, and the woman's standing by. The old guy's already headed for the elevator. Okay, now they're going. Lupus is staying; he just sat back down."

Schneider made a quick decision.

"You stay on Lupus; I'm going after the American and his friends." With that he crossed to the elevator just in time to cram in and found himself conveniently squeezed between Webber and Christoph.

42

They accompanied Webber to the Kurfürstendamm station. He was adamant about getting home that night. That was fine with Christoph, who was now getting annoyed by the constant harangues about the letter and the evil it represented.

"It's ridiculous," he said. "I don't care if he's the shadow figure I saw coming out of his hospital room. There's nothing wrong about that. I sure don't think that this otherwise perfectly pleasant stranger, my cousin, had anything to do with the thump in the night."

"There's something in that letter, and if so, he's wants it. You gotta believe me. I've seen bad stuff and devils. He's one."

"Onkel Kurt."

"No, I'm gone. Be careful,"

He disappeared into the subway.

Sabine refused to take his side and surprised him when she scolded him for telling Wolfgang the address of her apartment. She was upset, and way over the top on that score.

"Germans are hard to figure out," said Christoph.

After Webber left they went back to her apartment. They didn't talk, but by the time they got there, Sabine's mood had improved and they'd discussed the letter, speculating on its content.

They were sitting on her white couch in the white room, with a couple pilsners opened. In front of them on the low white table, in contrast, was the yellowing envelope. Sabine had changed into jeans and a blue satin blouse that hung loosely, falling across her breasts to create a compelling sight that competed with the stark letter for Christoph's attention.

"Well, open it," said Sabine.

With the temerity of one approaching a sacred relic, Christoph picked up the letter and held it for a long time, staring at the archaic script as if to see into the past. Sabine tapped him on the arm and held out an ivory letter opener, shaking him out of his reverie. Lovingly, with great care, he inserted the blade and slit open the envelope.

The single sheet of paper crinkled as he unfolded it, as if in pain from its long entombment. One side was covered with the same tightly scrolled handwriting. He handed it to Sabine and asked her to read it to him. She took it from him and read it to herself.

> March 1945
> Loco Imperatoris, Tiergarten, 117.72
>
> Dearest Jochen,
> By the time you get this letter, if indeed you do, you will know that I am dead. I write to you badly wounded in field hospital near the eastern front, expecting the Russians to arrive soon. When they do, I will die.
> Some days ago, I was entrusted with orders from none other than HH (I will not honor him with any of his official

titles) to deliver a small strongbox to a warehouse in Stettin. But he is a rat fleeing a sinking ship, and for the first time in my military life, I disobeyed an order. HH will not find his filthy contraband waiting for him. It has been diverted, and only I know where it is.

I want the truth to be known and the rat to receive his due. You must help. But I fear for your safety, as this is a dangerous course I have taken. My initial thought was to tell you the hiding place in this letter, but I realize that such knowledge could put you, or anyone who has it, in harm's way. Should this letter fall into the wrong hands, what I have done and risked could be for nothing. So I have tried to be clever, I hope not too clever.

I have written already to Hilde, and if she gets the letter, you may expect her to contact you. With these letters, a good campaigner like you may be able to locate the hoard.

I am unhappy to be putting this burden on you but have no better idea.

Please think well of me, and do not grieve. It has been my honor to serve under your command since that day at the Victory Column. Long live the Fatherland.

Hermann Sontowski
23.4.35–11.2.36
Zu früh fur uns
Doch Gottes wille

Your loyal friend and officer
Johann

As she absorbed the words, it became clear that this letter was virtually the same as the one to Hilde, except at the very end. She figured out at once that the apparently random footnotes at the bottom of each letter were connected. They were the inscriptions from a gravestone. Was the strongbox buried at a gravesite?

"My God, it's all here."

"What're you talking about?" asked Christoph.

At that moment Sabine arrived at a crisis point in her life. She was looking at Christoph and seeing into her own heart. She could scramble and lie to cover up the secret she'd just discovered and revealed at the same time, or, she could make the possibly rash decision to draw him into the mystery. If she didn't, it meant farewell to him. She was so over being a spy and living lies. She wanted to be with this guy, to be honest for once. Could she trust these unaccustomed feelings that seemed more than just hormone driven? In that instant she leaped.

She shifted and leaned toward Christoph and planted a brief spontaneous kiss on his cheek.

"Before I read this, I have a confession to make."

"Okay, I'm listening."

"I know about things in this letter, and our meeting last night wasn't coincidental. It was contrived. Don't hate me, please."

Christoph looked at her, then looked away, and said nothing for a while. Sabine waited. When he finally spoke, his voice was calm and wistful.

"Lately it occurs to me what a long, strange trip it's been. And it's only been four days so far. Lay it on me." He looked at Sabine with an expression that said what the heck.

"Life in Berlin," she began, "isn't always what it seems." For the next ten minutes she shared most of what she knew.

"This is insane," said Christoph when she'd finished. "Am I in a movie? Where are the cameras? Buried Nazi treasure? I've got a serial killer cousin who's stalking me? My life is in danger, but I could get rich. Brilliant. Oscar material."

He paused and leaned back with his hands behind his head. "I don't believe it. You're kidding me. Where's the other letter, then?"

Sabine quickly produced the photocopy and laid it on the table beside the other one. There was no question that they were written by the same hand, and even in German, Christoph could tell how similar they were. She read each one and, pointing to the letters, said, "If you read the two passages at the end of each letter together, it's got to be the inscription on a gravestone:

HIER RUHT IN GOTT UNSER LIEBER SOHN
(Here lies with God, Our dear son)
Hermann Sontowski
23.4.35–11.2.36
Zu früh fur uns Doch Gottes wille
(Too early for us, but God's will)

"Okay," said Christoph, "but where's the grave? I bet Peiper knew. I bet Hermann 'what's his name' was someone they both knew, someone in their regiment maybe. What do you think?"

"I think Hermann was just a baby. See the dates?"

"Right, okay, what about the Hermann's father then? There might be an SS officer Sontowski. Nettleton could find out."

"I guess it's one possibility, but think about the context. It's the end of the war, battles going on all around, refugees clogging the roads, and von Ritter has a serious injury. Could he really have sought out the grave of someone they both knew? I don't know where Himmler's HQ was, but this grave had to be within a day's return trip to Stettin, or Szczecin as it's now called. It's in Poland, you know. It would have been pure luck that such a thing was there, and he knew about it. The baby died in 1936; that's nine years difference. No, I think he buried the strongbox at a random grave."

"Well, if that's the case, there must be something else in the letters."

They were sitting side by side on the sofa, excitedly bending forward to examine the two letters laid out on the table. Christoph leaned slightly to his left to look at the letter to Hilde, and their knees touched. Like electronically charged particles in a magnetic field, the touch became a press, which the opposites pretended to ignore even as juices began to flow. Christoph forced himself to concentrate with increased effort on the letters; Sabine simply waited. She was enjoying his American enthusiasm. There was no rush.

Whether it was the impulses surging through the knees or just a matter of time, the clue they were looking for suddenly leaped off the page, and like many good secrets, it was right there in front of them.

"I got it," said Christoph, his eyes shining. "There." He stabbed at the second line of each letter. "I have no idea what '*Loco Imperatoris*, Tiergarten' means, but see, the number afterward is different. It's got to mean something, something that only makes sense when the two numbers are set together. Tiergarten is here in Berlin, right? Is there a cemetery there?"

As he turned to face her, his mind on fire, their bodies met, spontaneously intertwined, and von Ritter's secret was put on ice.

■ ■ ■

Later, as he lay beside a sleeping Sabine, wrapped in the enveloping silence of the night, his hands behind his head, Christoph, awake and deep in thought, replayed the letters over and over, searching for an answer. Sabine had told him there wasn't a cemetery in the Tiergarten, but maybe there was something there that pointed to the hiding place. It had to be in the numbers. The more he thought about it, the more certain he became that the letters contained a hidden message that would decipher these numbers. There was no way he was going to sleep, despite the lengthy romp with Sabine, so he carefully slid out of bed, grabbed his clothes off the floor, and crept out of the bedroom.

Looking at the letters, questions and answers crowded his brain. Why the 37.2°? This would be Celsius, and doing a rough calculation, he knew that was pretty hot but doubted it was the same as the 117.72 found in the Lena letter, meaning that number wasn't the Fahrenheit equivalent. Besides, the Lena letter didn't have the degree symbol. Could it have something to do with a particular location? Maybe it referenced a record temperature somewhere or something like that. If it had to do with temperatures, the 117.72 might indicate the day of the year starting January 1. He did another calculation and came up with the end of April. That didn't seem likely. But it could be an event of significance was going to happen on that date in 1945, or, of course, it could have already taken place in any year for that matter, a needle in a haystack. What did *Loco Imperatoris* mean? Crazy emperor? Whatever the translation, it was a common point of reference associated with the numbers.

He was getting tired, getting nowhere, and about to give up when the thought occurred to him that he wasn't being very systematic about this. He pulled a pad out of his backpack and set up two columns, one for each letter. In each column he wrote down the portions of the letters that were different. When he was done, he studied his handiwork, but he soon fell back, closed his eyes, and was asleep almost instantly, no closer to solving the puzzle crafted by his ancestor.

43

The morning woke up gray, and there was a moist chill in the air that probed with sharp incision the leather jacket Peter Buckner wore. A numbing coldness invaded and clutched his core, constricting his breathing. Each short exhale sent a small cloud of vapors that languished behind as he strode down the street toward Sabine's apartment. The raw weather was just another ingredient in the soup of misery he'd become. He hadn't slept. He'd tried to come up with a plan all night, but persistent devils and fiends of doubt and dread fabricated visions of disaster, making cohesive thinking impossible. His stomach was a knot, his eyes burned, and his mouth was a desert. He felt like shit.

Endless scenarios pummeled his mind, all ending badly. He'd always been the good soldier right from the start when they set him up and sent him out into the cold. He'd built a team and done his job. He'd legally, perhaps under false pretenses at times, gathered, collected, and provided the Firm with a steady flow of information. That's what they'd asked of him, until last Friday. That was when the message came to meet with another agent, not one of his team, no one he'd ever heard of before: the agent Sherlock. That had never happened before. He couldn't shake the feeling that he was being set up, and Sabine was a pawn in the game. Now he wished he'd gone himself that night.

The message he received last night from his handler was even more unsettling. Sabine had gone rogue, and he was instructed to get a letter from her, an old letter, and he was to use any method necessary.

He was fighting another urge, to flee and defect, confess his whole secret life, and trade what he knew for amnesty, and the closer he got to Sabine's, the stronger the feeling. He kept telling himself not to panic or do anything desperate, and he didn't want to find himself in a position to have to use the Walther 9 mm that was burning a hole in his jacket pocket. The handgun hadn't left its hiding place in his clothes closet for years, and he wasn't sure if the time came to use it, he could. He wasn't even sure why he brought it.

He found himself standing in front of the door of Sabine's apartment building, undecided and confused, with no idea what he was going to do. For a long time he just stared unfocused at the row of doorbells. He didn't notice a figure passing behind him, back and forth three times, and when he finally pushed the button to her apartment and the door buzzed open, Wolfgang Reisen accompanied him into the building.

The two men stood at the elevator, respectfully ignoring each other, assuming there was a mundane reason for being there. When the doors opened, Buckner was first in.

"Which floor?" he asked the other.

"Three, thanks."

When the doors opened, Buckner walked out, but the other rider stayed, and the doors slowly closed again. That's a little strange, reckoned Buckner, but his mind was too preoccupied with the task ahead to give it another thought. The American, who was waiting for him in the hallway, greeted him as he came out of the elevator.

"Hi, Peter, good to see you again." Christoph, barefoot, extended a cheerful hand. The two men shook and entered the apartment.

The first thing Buckner saw were papers lying out in the open on the table, and his heart rate jumped a bit. The letter in plain sight? It might be easier than he anticipated. He had to fight the insane urge to grab the objects and run. He knew better. Whatever secret the letter held, it was big enough for someone high up in the Firm to send him with the ultimate authority. He had to think that Sabine, and probably this Yank, knew its importance too. There was no way they'd let him run out of there with it. On the other hand, they weren't very cautious leaving it out for the world to see. Maybe they didn't know what they had. That notion was quickly dispelled when Christoph, seeing Buckner's gaze lingering on the letters, gathered them together a bit hurriedly and slipped them roughly into a backpack leaning in the corner of the couch, leaving the edge of the paper tantalizingly exposed.

"Can I make you a cappuccino?" Christoph deflected.

"An espresso, perhaps," suggested Buckner. "Where's Sabine?"

"She's getting ready for work. I heard her moving about."

Buckner's mind was calculating, but nothing subtle or clever was emerging, and the handgun was weighing down his jacket.

"Take your coat off and make yourself at home, as we say in the States," said Christoph as he filled the espresso machine. There was the answer to Buckner's problem. He tossed the jacket in a way that it partially covered the backpack. It would be easy to slip the letter out of the pack when he picked it up later. A cup of coffee now sounded like a very good idea.

At that moment there was a knock on the door. "I'll get it," Buckner said, thinking the last thing he needed was another visitor.

When he opened the door, he had just enough time to recognize the face of the man who'd come up in the elevator with him before a blurry black shape filled the landscape, and a blinding explosion became his world. He staggered back and his leg hit the low coffee table, sending him cartwheeling into the room. His head smashed into the floor with a sickening, crunching sound, and the lights went out.

■ ■ ■

Sabine was in a happy place, as happy as she'd been in a long time. Their lovemaking had started like a wrestling match, two sweaty contestants vying to be first to climax, before mellowing into a long, lingering process of exploration to be followed by more furious quests. How many times, she could only guess. Not even the rude arrival of Peter Buckner could bring her down this morning. She would send him on his way. She was spiking her hair and recalling the night when the sounds of violence crashed in on her reverie. Something terrible was taking place out there. The world stopped as she strained to listen. She could hear a voice she didn't recognize ordering Christoph to stand still, followed by the sound of something being dragged across the floor.

"Sit," the voice commanded.

She heard something about *Klebeband,* duct tape, being a wonderful invention. She hadn't moved, hardly breathing when she heard the voice ask where the woman was.

"She's gone to work," she heard Christoph say.

"We'll see about that."

Sabine's heart was pounding; she had to hide. The bathroom provided nothing, so she moved quickly into the bedroom where the open closet was her only choice. Silently, she slipped in and moved toward the far end behind the hanging clothes. Too late she realized she could have, should have, slid the door closed, but at least she was able to maneuver so that she was as far from the opening as she could get. She couldn't reach the far corner, which was taken up by her stowed camping gear. It would have to do. She froze and waited, hardly breathing.

Footsteps came into the room and then crossed to the bathroom. She heard the intruder as he turned and approached the closet, and stopped. She felt the unseen presence, which seemed to seep into the closet like the fumes of a deadly poisonous gas, evil and threatening. The clothes rustled. She closed her eyes; then he was gone.

She fought the urge to gasp for air as the footsteps faded back into the living room. She listened.

"So, cousin, we meet again, and I must say, I've waited for this moment with great expectation. I apologize that this is necessarily a one-way conversation, but you understand, I can't have our short time together interrupted, so the impolite tape."

The voice was different than she remembered, now syrupy and full of malice, and she shrunk farther back into the corner, pressing hard against the camping equipment in an involuntary reaction.

"The von Ritters have a long, proud history. We are Prussians, you know, and have fought for Bismarck, von Clausewitz, von Schlieffen, and as far back as von Blücher at Waterloo. You've heard of Waterloo, yes? We're driven by honor and hold purity as the highest value. Purity. You, cousin, are a bastard, a nurse's bastard's bastard. You cannot exist for the von Ritters."

There was a long, heavy silence. Sabine realized her leg was falling asleep, numbed by the blood flow being cut off by the hard edge of the equipment she was pressing against as she cowered in the corner. She shifted slightly. It was then she saw what caused her discomfort: the camping hatchet strapped to the backpack.

"Do you believe in the soul, cousin? Doesn't matter either way, because you'll learn. Too bad it will be the last thing you learn. You see, I'll soon extract and absorb yours."

Sabine heard the sounds of something bumping on the floor, followed by a smack, skin to skin, and a muffled groan.

"So, it seems you're anxious to proceed, and I'm happy and eager to oblige. By the way, did you fuck the woman last night? I hope so, and I hope it was the best fuck of your life. You want to know why? Because it's the last fuck you'll ever get. Save the best for last, they say."

Sabine heard a self-indulgent laugh, and the fear that had clutched her brain began to turn toward anger, but the sense of helplessness still clung firmly.

"I'm quite experienced at this," the voice continued. "Usually I drug the donor, that's you, but we don't have that option today, so this will be a little different for me. The soul must have a smooth release; it gives the journey sacredness. So I like to take my time. It must also be peaceful, and I've learned that a carefully controlled execution, double entendre intended, works best. You have a wonderful, strong-looking neck."

The hatchet. Why hadn't she thought of that sooner? At least she had a chance to do something. Slowly, quietly, she worked the straps loose and freed the weapon. She removed the leather cover from the blade. Here I come, asshole. She crept silently out of the closet and entered the short hallway. From her position she could see into the living room, and what she saw stopped her dead in place. The monster had his back to her. He was standing behind Christoph, who was sitting in one of the dining room chairs, and rubbing his captive's neck.

"And so we begin our journey together," crooned Wolfgang Reisen.

His shoulder tensed, and Christoph twisted violently in the chair as the dance to death commenced. She heard the muffled screams, which shook her into action.

Sabine was a couple meters away when she stepped on a squeaky floorboard, but Wolfgang was now in the throes of rapture, his entire being and all his senses ready for the climax, the moment the bastard's soul would be released to join with his. His world was reduced to this, nothing else, and he didn't hear her. Spurred by the possibility that her presence was given away, she took three quick steps, wound up her arm, and with all her strength and the momentum of her final charge, she swung the hatchet.

She must have closed her eyes because she didn't see the impact, but she felt it, and at the same instant the weapon was torn from her hands. For a moment she thought he'd blocked the blow and wrenched away the hatchet, but when she opened her eyes, she saw Wolfgang teeter backward, his arms hanging limply at his sides and a look of confusion on his face. He swayed and dropped to his knees, as if to pray. He held this position for a moment, and then his eyes rolled up into his head and his body crumbled sideways to the floor. The hatchet remained stuck in his neck, wedged between the C4 and C5 vertebrae, having severed the jugular vein and carotid artery on the way. A dark red stain was spreading away from his head across the pristine white carpet. He twitched once, then laid still.

A gurgling sound snatched her attention away from the bloody train wreck. Christoph sat in the dining chair, his head bent forward, and his arms and legs bound to the frame with duct tape, another band of tape wound around his head. She could see his chest heaving. Still alive! She ran into the kitchen, grabbed a paring knife from a drawer, and set upon the tape, slicing and ripping it off his head. With his mouth free, he gulped huge amounts of air while she worked on the rest of the tape. When this was done, she somehow managed to lift him out of the chair and lay him on the floor. It was only then that she felt a wave of exhaustion rush across her body. She had to sit down.

She negotiated her way to the couch and sat heavily. Trying to gather her thoughts, she noticed for the first time that her clothes were splattered with blood. The fact occurred to her that the fabric was ruined, and the carpet was definitely destroyed. Her dream adventure had turned into a horror show. Three men lay prone on her floor, one of them certainly dead, and for what? Those fucking letters. Born out of the malice and treachery of the greatest murderer of all time, they represented the worst of mankind, encouraging the most sordid urges—fertilizing greed, deceit, hate, and violence for over forty years. Von Ritter, and who knows whom else, fell victim to these false gods; now she, too, was a murderer. She detested those letters. Suddenly, with clarity, she knew what she had to do. Where were the letters?

She remembered them on the table, but now they were gone. She started to get up, and then she saw them, sticking out of the backpack right beside to her. She seized them and stood. Without hesitation, she tore them into shreds, bunched the ragged pieces into a ball, and walked to the bathroom where she tossed it all into the toilet and flushed; gone.

She stood there watching the bowl refill. For the first time she noticed the smell of the coffee Christoph had been making.

At that very moment, Detective Erich Schneider and two other Berlin police officers burst through the door of the apartment.

EPILOGUE

He buckled the seat belt, leaned back, and closed his eyes. Eight days, only eight days ago, he had been just another college graduate wondering what's next, hanging at the beach, playing softball, basketball, and the occasional game of poker with all the other guys, all doing the same thing. It all seemed meaningless, the normal life.

She'd said she wanted to leave Berlin. He'd said he wanted to stay in Berlin. The cops told him he might have to return. He hoped so.

The plane began to push away. He looked out the window and saw her standing in the terminal. He waved but doubted she saw.

Last night the Wall came down. They were there with the thousands celebrating the end, or maybe the beginning. They made love. How could anything be normal?

He closed his eyes again.

He was awakened by the sound of the flight attendants coming through with the drinks. He decided he'd write her a letter. He wanted to be with her again but deep inside suspected that might never happen. This wasn't a Hollywood movie. He pushed the button to turn on the overhead light, pulled his backpack out from under the seat in front of him, and opened it to get the yellow pad that would have to do for stationery. As he took out the pad, in the glare of the airplane light, he noticed a crumpled piece of paper flattened at the bottom of the bag. He took it out and placed it on the tray, smoothing out the wrinkles and creases.

For a long time he just stared at it.

END

ABOUT THE AUTHOR

 American Edwin M. Todd grew up in Scotland in the 1950s and 1960s, when the specter of World War II was still a very real presence. His fascination with that conflict stems from the war games he played and the comics he read as a boy. He earned his law degree from the University of California, Hastings College.

Todd has been a lawyer and owner of a construction company, and he presently serves as the director of the referee department for USA Rugby. In these capacities, he has gained extensive technical writing experience, while his historical thriller *The Nibelungen Hoard* is his first work of fiction.

Married with two children, Todd lives in Boulder, Colorado.

www.ingramcontent.com/pod-product-compliance
Lightning Source LLC
Chambersburg PA
CBHW071256170626
46809CB00001B/239